A MARRIAGE OF CONVENIENCE

A MARRIAGE OF CONVENIENCE

MILLCASTLE
BOOK FIVE

KATE PEARCE

ISBN-13: 978-1-857727-04-2 (paperback)

CHAPTER ONE

GRAFTON HALL, MILLCASTLE. 1842

*J*ust one more step…

Ruby turned into the wind and stumbled forward, the distant lights of the house appearing and disappearing through the trees as she navigated the treacherously icy grounds. The skirts of her gown were soaked and dragging her down, her boots were worn through, and the weight of her burdens felt as insurmountable as the relentless rain. She kept moving, her gaze on the promise of warmth and security. Not love—she couldn't expect that—but at least she'd survive.

Her feet hit the graveled surface of the drive, and she went toward the huge oak-fronted door. With the last of her strength, she lifted the brass knocker and hammered on the door.

A confusion of noise—dogs barking, people shouting, and suddenly, a familiar voice that made her sink to her knees, weak with relief.

"Caroline…" she whispered as the darkness threatened to overcome her. "Help my daughter."

THE NEXT TIME she woke up was to sunlight shining through half-opened curtains. The brightness made her eyes hurt. Her older sister sat beside her bed reading a book.

"Where's Nora?" Ruby whispered.

"She's in the nursery." Caroline hesitated. "Nurse is watching over her. She seems overly warm, as do you."

"I want her with me."

"Then I will fetch her." Caroline stood up. "You both have a fever. I have asked Dr. Nash to come and see you when he returns from Millcastle."

A shudder ran through Ruby. "I can't afford a doctor," she murmured as she shifted restlessly against the sheets. "And they can't do anything anyway."

"Dr. Nash would disagree with you. He considers himself very competent, indeed." Caroline paused to stroke Ruby's lank hair away from her face. "Try and sleep. I'll be back as soon as I can."

Ruby forced herself to stay awake until Caroline returned with Nora and tucked the bairn in beside her. She desperately wanted to rest but was terrified that Nora was barely conscious and very hot.

"Don't let her die," she whispered. "She's all I have left."

"We'll do our very best," Caroline reassured her. There was a murmur of voices and the door opened. "Dr. Nash has just arrived." She turned her head. "Good evening, doctor. This is my sister Ruby and her daughter Nora. They are both feverish."

"Ma'am." Dr. Nash—tall, dark, and unsmiling—nodded as he removed his coat and rolled up his sleeves. "May I attend to the baby first?"

"Don't hurt her." Ruby reluctantly released Nora into his large, capable hands.

"I'm a trained physician, ma'am. My calling in life bids me do no harm," he said, his upper-class accent becoming more

2

pronounced. "How old is Nora?" He set Nora on his knee and listened to her breathing.

"Almost one."

"Have either of you been in contact with anyone who has recently been unwell?"

Ruby tried to smile. "We lived in a crowded tenement, sir. Someone was always sick."

"Any other symptoms? Bloody flux, coughing, retching, stomach spasms, disordered bowels?"

"It's not cholera, if that's what you're asking." Ruby was aware of Caroline's involuntary gasp. "I'd not bring that to my sister's house."

"I don't think it is, either." The doctor turned to Caroline. "Can you hold the child while I examine the mother?"

After washing his hands, he came toward the bed. Ruby was suddenly aware of the stink of her unwashed body and clothing and the coal dust that constantly clung to her skin. He listened to her rasping breath, felt her forehead, and took her pulse with a calm efficiency that was somehow soothing.

"Do you know what afflicts them, Dr. Nash?" Caroline asked in a low tone as she gave Nora back to Ruby.

"Nothing I can put a name to, but that's not unusual when dealing with illnesses in crowded, badly ventilated spaces." Dr. Nash's gaze lingered on Nora. "We need to bring their temperatures down and feed them plain victuals. They should drink plenty of water that's been boiled to prevent infection. I suspect a few days of good food, rest, and your staff's attention will do wonders."

Even as she struggled to concentrate, Ruby was aware of something in the doctor's voice. Was he angry because he'd been asked to treat her? Did he consider the working class beneath him?

"I will care for my sister, *myself*, Doctor Nash," Caroline said.

"And there is no need to take that tone with me. I didn't cause any of this."

Ruby's gaze flew to the doctor's face.

Grimacing, he said, "I apologize, my lady, I meant no disrespect. It simply annoys me that people are forced to live in such conditions." He put his coat back on and took a brown glass bottle out of his bag. "If your sister becomes feverish again, administer a teaspoon of this in water. Don't give it to the child."

"Thank you."

He nodded and came back to the bed to look down at Ruby. "You should be feeling a lot better in a day or two, but please ask for me if you experience any other symptoms."

Ruby nodded.

His expression softened as he said, "Good morning, ma'am."

He left the room and Caroline let out a huff of breath. "He really is the most infuriating man."

"He was kind to me." Ruby gazed at Nora's flushed face.

"No one denies that he is an excellent doctor," Caroline said. "It's just that he can be rather abrasive. He obviously thinks I have failed in my duty toward you. Would you like me to bathe Nora while you take a nap?"

"If you bathe her where I can see you."

"Of course." Caroline rang the bell and a maid appeared like magic.

Ruby had almost forgotten what it was like to have other people caring for your needs. Within minutes a small bath filled with lukewarm water was set on the chest of drawers.

After Caroline gently undressed the baby, she glanced over at Ruby. "There are several items of clothing my children have outgrown that might be suitable for Nora. May I fetch some of them?"

"You may dress her how you please, sister." Ruby was too

tired to argue about stupid things. "I'd like to see her looking well."

Caroline gently lowered the baby into the water and scooped water over her body.

"Goodness! Her hair is fair."

Ruby had a vivid memory of Sidney holding his daughter and exclaiming over the same thing. After he'd gone, keeping Nora clean enough to maintain the brightness of her hair had become less important than surviving.

Guilt flooded Ruby. "You mean she's filthy and that I should be ashamed of myself."

"Ruby..." Caroline wrapped Nora in a soft towel and brought her back to the bed. "I know how hard it is to get clean water when you're living in a tenement. We all lived like that once."

Ruby cuddled her daughter and inhaled the sweet scent of the lemon soap Caroline had used in the bathwater.

"She'll need feeding. I... don't have enough milk."

"Then I'll find someone who does." Caroline swooped in and picked up Nora again. "You need to sleep. I will take Nora up to the nursery, find her some new clothing, and consult with Nurse."

Ruby began to protest but Caroline held up her finger. "Do you trust me, sister?"

"Yes, of course."

"Then allow me to do this for you." Caroline held her gaze. Ruby often forgot that her older sister was formidable in her own way. "I promise I will take care of her and bring her back very promptly."

After Ruby nodded, Caroline smiled and walked away the baby cradled in her arms.

It took less than a minute for Ruby to fall into a deep, and thankfully dreamless, sleep.

～

"Nash? Come and have a drink with me."

Charles paused at the bottom of the stairs and looked inquiringly over at his host, Francis, Viscount Grafton-Wesley. The viscount beckoned impatiently from the doorway of his study.

"I was intending to speak to your esteemed wife," Charles said.

"She's upstairs in the nursery and will join us in a moment." The viscount stepped back and held the door open wide. "Come along."

Charles, who was considered brusque himself, had nothing on the viscount. He meekly did as he was told.

"How is Ruby?" Grafton asked as he poured them both a brandy.

"She's feverish, malnourished, and needs a good bath," Charles said bluntly as he took the offered brandy. "But I don't believe she has anything that can be caught by other members of your household, so you may rest easy."

"I'm not worried about that. I've seen worse; so have you." The viscount offered him a cigar, which he declined.

"I sometimes forget you were also in India." Charles sipped the excellent brandy.

"It was an experience I will never forget. I was lucky to survive." Grafton's expression turned inward. "I've seen cholera and yellow fever rage through whole villages and forts. I've had both."

"Then you will be pleased to hear that your sister-in-law has neither."

"And the child?"

"Very much the same as the mother, but as she is so young, she will need to be carefully watched."

The viscount took a moment to light a cigar. "A damned bad

business all around," he said. "We weren't even aware that Ruby had a child. The last time I saw Ruby was when Ivy went to stay with her after the birth of Rose. She must have been pregnant then, but she didn't mention it."

Charles tactfully didn't bring up that scandal, as Lady Ivy Grovedale had since returned home and was considered an exemplary wife to her husband and child.

"And before you ask, we have no idea if Ruby is married or who the father of her child is. Ruby has always been a law unto herself—much to my wife's consternation." Viscount Grafton fixed him with a hard stare. "I only mention these matters to help with your treatments."

"I did wonder why the sister of a viscountess had been brought so low," Charles acknowledged.

"Ruby chose that life. She left home with a man who agitated at one of the local mills to further the cause of voting rights. Caroline tried to stop her, but I told her to let her leave."

"Why?"

The viscount raised an eyebrow. "Because some people only learn by experience. You know that yourself, as do I."

"The only reason I was able to become a physician was because my godmother left me money, which paid for my training and allowed me to sell out my commission in the army. If she hadn't done so, I would've been trapped, regardless of my inclinations or wishes. If I might be blunt, one might assume from her condition that your sister-in-law was cast out without a penny."

"Then you'd assume wrong. I continued to pay her an allowance. It's not my fault if she chose to use it for purposes other than caring for herself and her daughter."

"Such as?"

"Politics," Grafton said bluntly. "Supporting the cause of universal suffrage."

"And you *allowed* that?"

Grafton raised a dark eyebrow. "Ruby is an intelligent and independent woman. Why would I curtail her freedom to live as she wishes?"

"Because she is part of your family?"

"And I choose to treat her in the same way as I would if she were a man." Grafton blew out a long stream of smoke. "As someone capable of making her own decisions about her own life and finances. I'm surprised that a man such as yourself would consider that unreasonable."

Charles was about to reply when the door opened, and Lady Caroline came in. "Ruby has gone to sleep," she said. "I have taken Nora up to the nursery where she is currently being fed."

"I'm glad to hear it." Grafton looked at his wife and poured her a brandy. "Nash here thinks terribly badly of us for letting Ruby get into such a state."

"So I noticed." Lady Caroline gave Charles a severe look. "I hope you were able to articulate our position to him in rather more respectful terms than I was tempted to use when he looked down his nose at me."

"I apologize if I gave offense." Charles inclined his head. "It was something of a surprise."

"To see my sister dressed like a coalminer's wife?" Caroline sighed. "I must confess that she looked far more prosperous last time Francis saw her. I suspect something has gone wrong."

"Well, obviously, my love, or she wouldn't have found her way back here," Grafton said. "She would be far too proud to ask for help unless she was desperate."

"I suspect Nora's father abandoned them," Caroline said. "And, if she had no one to bring in a wage, she wouldn't be able to pay rent." She shuddered. "Having been in a similar situation I know how frightening it can be."

Charles studied Caroline Grafton's face. She didn't look like a woman who had suffered any hardship, but there was something in her voice that made him believe differently.

She glanced over at him. "After my first husband died, I had to provide for my mother and two sisters. We worked at the dressmakers in Millcastle and rented two rooms in Three Coins."

"From me," Grafton added. "Which is how we met." He exchanged a remarkably intimate smile with his wife. "Poor Ruby has not had the same luck."

"But she is in a much better place now." Unused to seeing such blatant lust in a marriage, Charles set down his glass and rose to his feet. "I have a meeting with Mr. Hepworth in town this evening, but I'll be back to check on my patients."

"I suspect Ruby will sleep through until the morning," Caroline said. "And we can easily care for Nora in the nursery until her mother awakens."

"What does Hepworth want?" Grafton asked.

"He's offered to set me up in a medical practice in town."

"Is that something that appeals to you?"

"Yes. I'm tired of London. The workload at the hospital was overwhelming." There were other reasons why it was necessary for him to get out of the city, but they were none of the Graftons' concern.

"He'll want something in return," Francis warned Charles as he walked him into the hall.

"I'm well aware of that. He needs a physician for his navvies and their families. I'm more than willing to assist him, which will leave me time to gather my own private patient list in town."

"I'd be happy to assist you financially if I could also call on your services for my own family and staff," Grafton said.

Charles raised an eyebrow. "Are you quite certain your wife would agree to that? She was not impressed with me today."

"Ruby's unexpected appearance and current condition were bound to raise questions in anyone's mind. Caroline is far too intelligent to take offense over something so minor when she's already seen you do so much good." Grafton patted him on the shoulder. "Speak to Hepworth and let me know what you decide."

Before Charles could leave, the butler called out to him. "Dr. Nash? A letter has been delivered for you."

"Thank you." Charles grimaced as he recognized the handwriting of his father's secretary. He stuffed the missive in his pocket.

The butler coughed gently. "The man who brought it is awaiting an immediate reply, sir."

"Can you keep him well fed and content until I return from town? I have an appointment I cannot afford to miss."

"Yes, of course, Dr. Nash." The butler bowed. "We'll look after him in the kitchen."

"Thank you."

Charles walked out of the side door and took the path toward the stables at the rear of the house. His steps slowed and with a muttered curse, he took out the letter, broke the seal imprinted with his father's signet ring, and began to read.

"Damnation."

Dread stirred in his gut. The news about his retreat from London had traveled farther than he'd anticipated, and the scoundrels had dared to contact his father and demand financial reparations directly. He'd been summoned home, and this time there was no excuse in the world that would get him out of the hole he'd dug for himself.

He looked up, his gaze unfocused as he folded the letter with shaking hands and replaced it in his pocket.

There was something he could salvage—a steady income and a clean start in Millcastle with people who still respected him and his work with his patients. He took a deep, steadying breath and set off for the stables. It was important that he continued to make a good impression on Mr. Hepworth, who wasn't the kind of man to tolerate failure, especially on his own financial projects.

Charles could set up a medical practice and work in Millcastle far away from the temptations of the city and make a good life for himself—if his father let him, and if he didn't end up in a debtor's prison with no hope of ever being set free.

Charles did what he usually did and pushed all the unpleasantness to one side. Millcastle needed physicians and he was very well qualified. That was all Mr. Hepworth needed to know.

CHAPTER TWO

"Where is she?" Ruby was aware that shouting at the maid was neither fair, nor likely to accomplish anything, but somehow, she couldn't stop herself.

"I'll find her ladyship!" The young girl fled from Ruby's bedroom, her expression terrified.

Ruby sat back against the pillows, already exhausted from her outburst. She'd woken up alone in her bed and panicked when she couldn't find Nora. Had Sidney appeared at night and taken her?

Caroline came in and rushed over to the bed. "Whatever is the matter? You've made Bridget cry."

"Where is Nora?"

"She's sleeping comfortably in the nursery. Where else would she be?"

"Here with me? You promised—"

"I asked you to trust me to take care of her, and that's what I've done," Caroline said firmly. "When she wakes up, and after she's been fed, I'll bring her to you."

"I don't even know what day it is," Ruby said as she glanced out of the window. She knew she owed her sister an apology but didn't seem to have the ability to offer one.

"That's because we left you to sleep. You've been oblivious for almost two full days." Caroline started opening drawers in the cupboard. "I've left some of my clothes here for you. We're of a similar size. If you want to get up and walk to the nursery, I'll help you dress."

Ruby's stomach growled, and Caroline smiled. "Or you can have something to eat and join me when you're ready?"

The lure of hot food fought with Ruby's desire to see her baby.

"Can someone bring me something to eat in the nursery?"

"Of course." Caroline placed a pair of pantaloons, a shift, some stockings, and a corset at the end of Ruby's bed along with the gown. "Come along, then."

With her sister's competent assistance, Ruby was soon dressed in a dark blue gown and on her way upstairs.

"Will you apologize to the maid for me?" she asked as they went into the nursery.

"You can do it yourself." Caroline pointed toward the fireplace where a very young and anxious face looked back at them. "Bridget is one of the nursery maids."

Ruby went forward and stopped in front of the girl. "I shouldn't have shouted at you. I apologize."

"That's all right, miss." Bridget bobbed a curtsey. "You probably woke up in a bit of a fright because of the baby."

"I did, but that was no excuse for my behavior."

Caroline came to stand beside them. "Is Nora still sleeping?"

"Nurse just took her to the wetnurse to feed, my lady. She'll be back in a tick." Bridget had a hint of an Irish brogue. "Would you like me to fetch Miss Louisa for you?"

"Yes, please. And after you've done that, can you go down to the kitchen and ask Cook for a tray of food for my sister?"

Caroline turned to Ruby, her smile soft. "My daughter is not much older than your Nora. I do hope they can be friends."

"I doubt that. Louisa is the daughter of a viscount, and Nora is a bastard."

"They are still cousins." Caroline held Ruby's gaze. "Surely that is the important thing?"

"Not to society, and probably not to your husband."

Caroline chuckled. "You of all people know that Francis has no time for such nonsense. He married *me* for goodness' sake—the woman who was his mistress and managed his books."

Ruby wasn't sure why she had to be so disagreeable to the people who were providing her with shelter. The bitterness that had entered her veins after Sidney's betrayal affected everything and kept seeping out.

When Bridget departed to fetch Louisa, Ruby touched Caroline's arm.

"I'm sorry."

"You've obviously had a difficult time." Caroline set her hand over Ruby's. "Perhaps when you feel better, you will tell me what happened?"

"And why I ended up begging on your doorstop?"

"You hardly did that. You are my sister. You are always welcome here."

Ruby nodded even though she was aware that on her previous visit to celebrate Ivy's wedding she had done nothing to endear herself to anyone. In truth, she'd gone out of her way to be dismissive and insulting to her sister's guests. She'd been filled with a sense of righteous indignation about the inequalities of the world and had been more than willing to share her radical opinions with the gentry and the factory owners, whether they wanted to hear her or not.

Since Nora's birth and Sidney's departure, all her certainties had disappeared...

"Here she is, my lady." Bridget returned with Louisa in her arms. "Bright and bonny from her nap."

Caroline took baby Louisa in her arms and lightly kissed the top of her head. "Good afternoon, my darling."

"Mama." The baby patted her face and beamed.

Ruby leaned in closer to get a better view of the child. She had her father's dark hair and fixed Ruby with a piercing blue stare.

"She looks just like Francis," Ruby said.

"I know." Caroline sighed. "She even has his beak of a nose. I suspect she'll be quite formidable when she comes of age. Neither of my children look like me, whereas your Nora is a mirror image of you."

"Apart from her hair." Ruby pictured Nora's little face. "I can't see it myself."

"Perhaps it's because I remember you and Ivy when you were young and can see it more clearly." Caroline went to sit by the fire and placed the baby on her lap. "What is Nora's birthdate?"

Ruby took the seat opposite her sister, glad of both the warmth of the fire and the chance to sit down. Her legs were shaking. "She'll be a year old on September the first."

"And Louisa will be one and a half in a week." Caroline smiled down at her daughter who was standing on her lap clutching onto her mother's sleeve. "They are only a few months apart in age."

The door opened and Bridget returned with a covered tray she placed next to Ruby.

"Cook says to eat up, and if you want more, she'll be happy to provide it for you."

"Thank you."

Ruby's stomach growled as she contemplated the bowl of chicken soup, bread, and cheese. She couldn't remember the last time she'd had fresh bread, having been reduced to buying the stale ends and leftovers from the baker at the corner of her street. He allegedly put chalk and ash in his dough.

"Don't eat too fast," Caroline said quietly.

"I haven't forgotten the lessons we learned when we had very little, sister," Ruby said. "They've stood me in good stead over the past few years."

She sipped the soup and almost groaned at the richness of the broth. The tender chunks of chicken were even better. She forced herself to slow down and savor each bite as Caroline played and sang with her daughter. She still had a sense that she was living in a dream—that at any moment someone would click their fingers and she'd be transported back to her bedroom in Leeds where there was no fire, nothing to eat, and a baby who cried constantly with hunger...

"Ruby?"

She looked over at Caroline who was frowning. "What?"

"Are you feeling well? You seem very... faraway."

"The soup is delicious."

"I'll tell Cook." Caroline smiled. "Perhaps if you continue to eat well, you can feed Nora again yourself."

Even the thought of trying to do that made Ruby anxious, so she concentrated on eating. Her head came up as she heard Nora chuckling. She watched Bridget come through the door carrying Nora.

"Here's your little one, ma'am." Bridget handed Nora over. "Wet nurse says she's doing very well now."

"So I can see." Ruby smiled at her daughter, aware of the differences a few good meals had made. "Please thank her for me."

"I will, ma'am." Bridget turned to Caroline. "I'll just go down to the kitchen and fetch the young master's milk and biscuits, my lady."

"Please do. He'll be back from his ride with his father at any moment. You haven't met Joseph yet, have you, Ruby? He's somewhat of a whirlwind."

As Joseph announced his presence by shouting as he came up the stairs, Ruby immediately knew what Caroline meant. She stiffened in her chair as Francis followed his son into the nursery.

"Be quiet, young man. You'll frighten your sister." Francis looked over at Ruby, his expression as inscrutable as ever. "Good afternoon. You look much better."

"Hard to look worse." Ruby made herself meet his gaze. "Thank you for allowing me to stay with you."

"If I hadn't, Caroline would have taken my children and followed you down the lane."

Despite his pleasant tone, Ruby was reminded once again that only his fierce loyalty to Caroline made Francis tolerate her family.

"I had a message from your mother, Caroline," Francis continued. "She and Ivy are coming to visit Ruby at three o'clock on Friday."

Caroline frowned. "Who told them she was here?"

Francis shrugged. "I have no idea, but as half our staff have relatives who work at Grovedale Hall, I suspect the news traveled fast."

Ruby fought a grimace. The last thing she wanted was for the rest of her family to descend on her. They were all sympathetic to her plight right now, but soon questions would be asked about how she'd allowed herself to be brought so low. Her mother would declare she'd told Ruby not to leave Grafton Hall and, whether they said anything to Ruby's face or not, everyone would silently judge her.

And perhaps she deserved their condemnation, but she'd done what she'd believed was right, and she refused to be ashamed of that.

"You don't have to see them if you don't want to," Francis said idly as he reached out to hold his daughter. Ruby reminded herself that he missed very little. "You can retire to your bed. Caroline and I will guard your door from any unwanted intrusions."

Ruby shot him a look, and he raised an eyebrow. "Your mother in full flow is somewhat overwhelming, and Ivy does have an unfortunate tendency to speak her truth with great disregard as to the effect of her words."

Ruby sighed and sat up straight. "It might be better to get it over with."

"I admire your optimism that *maman* would ever let anything be over." Caroline smiled as Louisa patted Francis's face. "She's still annoyed that Alice married Mr. Hepworth."

"Why would she be annoyed about that?" Ruby asked, glad for the distraction.

"Because Alice was supposed to live quietly at Grovedale Hall for the rest of her life and support Ivy."

"Then Alice made a wise decision to choose her own path," Ruby said. "I met Mr. Hepworth at the wedding. He is something of a character."

"He is indeed, and he does love Alice with all his heart." Caroline looked over at her husband. "And he helped make Francis even richer by bringing the railway to Millcastle."

Ruby opened her mouth to pour scorn on such a decision and remembered that her brother-in-law and sister had given her shelter when no one else would.

"The railway does offer the working man a great opportunity to travel beyond his usual existence," Ruby said instead. "It has certainly helped spread the word about universal suffrage."

"Indeed." Francis winced as Louisa pulled his hair and Joseph tugged on his coat sleeve. "I think my son is getting jealous of his sister having all my attention." He handed Louisa back to her mother and took Joseph's hand. "Come and sit at the table and have your milk."

His ease and obvious familiarity with his children were quite unexpected. Ruby had assumed he'd be a cold and distant father like most of the aristocracy—seeing his progeny only when necessary.

Nora gave a tiny snore and Ruby eased the blanket away from her face.

"Does she need a nap?" Caroline asked as she beckoned to Bridget. "She looks very peaceful."

"Yes," Ruby said softly.

"Shall I put her down to sleep for you ma'am?" Bridget asked.

"I'd prefer to do that myself if you can show me her crib."

Ruby stood up, aware that she was extremely tired herself. Letting Nora remain in the nursery and not by her side was a way of showing Caroline how much she trusted her. If her mother and sister were truly coming to visit at the end of the week, she'd need to gather all her resources before she could face them.

"THEN, if you're agreeable to my terms, Dr. Nash, I'll get my secretary to draw up a contract between us."

Mr. Hepworth looked inquiringly at Charles, his pen in his hand. He was a broad, harsh-faced man who made no pretense of being a gentleman and ruled his rapidly expanding commercial empire with an iron fist. He happily displayed his wealth and made no concessions to the nobility or those he considered corrupt. He was also one of the most honest and straightforward men Charles had ever met, and they'd taken to each other immediately.

"Totton will take you to see the building I own near the new railway station. It has room for your consulting rooms on the ground floor with two further levels above for your personal use." Hepworth dipped his pen in the inkwell and scribbled something on the paper in front of him. His office was a symphony of dark mahogany, tall glass bookcases, and the smell of new leather. "Here's a draft on my bank for your use."

"You don't need to do that." Charles frowned.

"Aye, I do." Hepworth's light blue gaze fastened on Charles. "I didn't make this offer without doing some checking up on you, Dr. Nash. You might have a fancy accent and an aristocratic family, but you've no funds of your own and a rather spotty past."

"What exactly did you find out about me?" Charles asked carefully.

"Enough to know that I'll be watching the books." Hepworth winked as he held out the bank draft Charles wished he could refuse. "I'm willing to overlook youthful mistakes and offer anyone a second chance. But don't try and fool me, Nash, or I'll kick you out on your arse."

Charles took the draft, blinking after the unexpected ripping away of his carefully constructed façade.

"Do you really investigate all your business partners so thoroughly, or was there something about me that stuck out?"

Hepworth sat back and contemplated Charles, his gaze shrewd. "I always do my due diligence, but I had to wonder why a gentleman such as yourself was willing to work with my navvies when no one else would."

"I see."

"I'm not the kind of man to spread gossip about my partners, so your secrets are safe with me." Hepworth paused. "And I haven't forgotten how hard you fought to save my wife and baby daughter."

"How are Mrs. Hepworth and Amelia?" Charles asked, grateful for the change in subject.

"Doing very well, thank you."

Hepworth smiled for the first time. Having been at the difficult birth, Charles was aware how much value Hepworth placed on his wife Alice and how devastated he would've been if she'd died. The baby had been breech, and the labor had exhausted Alice Hepworth to the point where Charles had feared he'd have to sacrifice one or the other.

"My wife is quite recovered now."

"I will make sure to call on her in the near future and see how she does," Charles promised.

"She'd appreciate that." Hepworth hesitated. "She does worry about the bairn."

"Is there anything in particular she should be worrying about?"

"Not that I've noticed, and I have some experience in this matter." Hepworth looked down at his hands. "I've grieved for children of my own before."

"Then perhaps I should come sooner and make sure Mrs. Hepworth's worries are set to one side."

"Aye, you can come to lunch with me at the end of the week and see what you make of the state of things. I'll be going home early to celebrate Dan's birthday. You can tell me what you think of the new premises then." He stood and held out his hand. "Now, I'll wish you good day, doctor. You'll find Totton in his office down the hall."

Charles accepted the strong handshake and went out, the draft from Hepworth's bank clasped in his fingers. He paused outside Totton's door to secure it safely in his pocket. He'd set up a new bank account in town to avoid his creditors in London and save his money. At least he now had the funds to travel and see his father, but that could wait until he'd established himself in Millcastle.

He knocked sharply on the secretary's door and went in. "Good morning, Mr. Totton. I understand that you are going to show me the new premises near the railway."

"Good morning, Dr. Nash." Mr. Totton was already rising to his feet. "I have the keys. Shall we proceed to the newly refurbished accommodation?"

CHAPTER THREE

*R*uby awaited her family in the drawing room. She wore Caroline's castoffs—a dress, underthings, and stockings—and her hair was pulled back into a severe bun at the nape of her neck. Still, she was not prepared for the inevitable confrontation ahead.

"*Maman.*" Ruby smiled as her mother came rushing toward her, rose to her feet, and accepted her embrace.

Her mother drew back to study Ruby's face. "You are too thin. What on earth have you been doing to yourself?"

"Trying to survive." Ruby eased out of her mother's arms and sat down. "You know how that goes."

"True. I have had my share of trials and tribulations," her mother acknowledged. "But none of them have been of my own choosing."

Caroline cleared her throat. "I've ordered some tea. It should be here shortly."

"Thank you." Her mother sat as well, smoothing the skirts of her silk gown. "Ivy will be here in a moment. She wanted to speak to Francis."

"He's just arrived back from London," Caroline said. "He might not be in a very receptive mood."

"Is he ever? I think Ivy wants him to invest in her husband's proposed publishing venture." Mrs. Delisle took off her gloves and set them on the side table.

"I hadn't heard about that." Caroline frowned.

"Then thank the lord that you don't live with them, because I have heard nothing else for the past week." Her mother sighed. "If Alice had done her duty and stayed with Ivy instead of marrying that railway navvy, I wouldn't have to put up with it."

"At one point we all thought Alice was going to marry Ian, *maman*," Caroline reminded her. "It's hardly likely she'd wish to live with the woman who took her place."

"Francis should have told Alice to do her duty to her family. She should've showed more gratitude, considering her tenuous social position."

"Regardless of the circumstances of her birth, Francis considers Alice his true sister," Caroline snapped back. "And as she is very happy with her extremely rich and successful husband, I suspect he would consider he made the correct decision to support her choices."

"About what?" Ivy came into the room. "What did I miss?"

"Nothing in particular." Caroline smiled as she went to embrace her younger sister. "*Maman* just mentioned that Ian is considering setting up a publishing company,"

Ivy came over to hug Ruby, her expression full of sweetness. "I am so glad you have returned to us. I have missed you *so* much."

Ruby hugged her sister back. They'd been inseparable for years—Ruby the fierce protector and Ivy the shrinking violet— but things had changed. Despite adversity, Ivy had grown into a strong woman, leaving Ruby floundering in the mire behind her.

Ivy moved her chair as close to Ruby's as possible and reached over to take her hand. "How is Nora?"

"She is doing very well." Ruby glanced over at Caroline who nodded.

Her mother sniffed. "And where exactly *is* your husband, Ruby?"

"I'm not sure whom you are referring to, *maman*, because I do not have one," Ruby said steadily.

"Then if you aren't married, your child is a bastard."

"My child is loved and wanted." Ruby held her mother's gaze. "And you are her grandmother, whether you choose to acknowledge that relationship or not."

Mrs. Delisle tossed her head. "I am not one to speak ill of my own family in public, but I will tell you privately that I do not approve of such irresponsible behavior. Your reputation is ruined."

"I am well aware of that," Ruby said. "But as I have no intention of reentering society or marrying it doesn't matter to me."

"What about your sisters and me?"

"Caroline and Ivy are already married, and their reputations, along with yours, are unlikely to be sullied by mine."

"If you have no husband, how are you going to support yourself and your child?" her mother demanded. "Do you intend to live off your relatives for the rest of your life?"

Her mother had squandered her own inheritance and lived off her daughters. Ruby felt an old spark come to life, urging her to remind her mother of this fact, but she tamped it down. She was too exhausted to start another fight.

Ivy squeezed her hand. "Ruby will always have a home with me, and I know Caroline feels the same."

"Absolutely." Caroline looked up as the butler and parlor maid came in bringing the tea tray and a collection of cakes. "Thank you." She started pouring the tea and Ivy got up to pass the cups around. "Make sure Ruby has some cake."

"She should." Ivy winked at Ruby as she set the cup down. "Caroline's cook is the best in the county."

"Thank you." Ruby accepted both the tea and the pile of cakes on her plate. She found most of the food too rich and struggled to enjoy it.

After making sure everyone was settled, Caroline turned to Ivy. "What is this publishing lark all about?"

"Oh! Ian thinks he should stay at home for a year or so and compile his notebooks, diaries, and botanical drawings into a series of published books." Ivy ate a cake. "I suspect part of his reasoning is to keep an eye on me so that I don't abandon him and our child again, but it is something he is genuinely interested in pursuing."

"He should stay home," Mrs. Delisle said. "He's too old to be gallivanting around the world while his child is so young, and he needs an heir."

Ruby noticed Ivy's shudder. Her sister had fallen into a great melancholy after the birth of her first child and at one point had left her at home and run away to Leeds, which had caused a host of complications in Ruby's life before Francis had arrived to take Ivy home. She wished she had the energy to defend Ivy against her mother but that part of her, the defiant flicker of rage that had propelled her into leaving Millcastle in the first place, had been extinguished long before Sidney left her.

Luckily, Caroline was made of sterner stuff and was quite happy to engage with her mother and set her straight.

"Ivy and Ian have years ahead of them to have more children, *maman,* and with all due respect, it is none of your business."

"I do live there," her mother objected. "I *am* a part of the household."

"And a very valued part, I'm sure," Caroline replied.

"Yes, indeed," Ivy added. "I don't know how we would get on without you."

For a moment, Ruby wondered whether all was well with

Ivy's marriage if she still needed her mother to live with her. Was *maman* her companion or her watchdog? If she could find the energy, she'd ask Caroline about it later.

She abruptly stood up. "I need to feed Nora."

Her mother looked scandalized. "I thought Caroline said she'd brought in a wet nurse so that you could recover your strength and not worry about such things."

Ruby looked over at Caroline. "Will you excuse me, please?"

"Of course," Caroline said, even though she knew full well that Ruby still couldn't feed Nora. "I will be going out in an hour or so to visit Alice, if you wish to accompany me?"

"I suspect I'll be asleep." Ruby tried to smile. "But thank you for the invitation."

"Why are you visiting Alice?" Mrs. Delisle demanded.

"Why would I not?" Caroline raised an eyebrow. "I am extremely fond of her."

"She coveted Ivy's husband!"

"*Maman.*" Ivy sighed. "Alice had every right to assume Ian was going to propose to her because he fully intended to. You know that better than anyone."

Ruby headed to the door as a headache crept up the back of her neck. She couldn't deal with her mother at the best of times, and this wasn't one of them. The argument continued as she quietly closed the door behind her. She went up the stairs, her energy disappearing through the leaden soles of her feet, making each step an effort.

The curtains in her room were open, but she didn't bother to close them. At least she'd done her duty and met her mother again, which was enough for now. She took off her borrowed shoes, climbed into bed, and fell asleep the moment her head touched the pillow.

∾

AN HOUR LATER, she was wide awake, her body simply not used to the luxury of being able to sleep whenever she felt like it. She went up to the nursery, but Nora had just been put down for her nap and was sleeping peacefully in her cradle with a nurserymaid sitting beside her in case she needed anything.

At a loss for something to do and unwilling to return to her bedchamber and the darkness of her own thoughts, Ruby went down into the hall where she discovered Caroline just putting on her bonnet.

"Ruby!"

"Do you think Alice would object to my presence if I accompanied you?" Ruby asked.

"Not at all. She is part of our family, and I trust her implicitly." Caroline helped Ruby find her new cloak and bonnet. "And it will do you good to get some fresh air. You haven't been out in almost a week."

Ruby allowed the footman to help her into the carriage. She marveled again at how some women were treated as helpless ornaments, while other toiled in factories for lower wages than the men. Factory owners thought women were more docile and less likely to rebel because of their need to provide for their children.

The luxury that surrounded her now felt as unreal as her other life, and she wondered if she'd ever be able to reconcile the two. Shaking off her sense of unreality, she focused her gaze on the scenery, all too aware of the smoking chimneys behind them in Millcastle and the ugly scar of the railway dissecting the hills surrounding the valley.

To her surprise, Alice's house was a square, stone-built Georgian building with a sweeping drive and extensive gardens flowing down toward the local river.

"I assumed Mr. Hepworth would require something far larger and more modern," Ruby said as the carriage stopped at the front door. "This is charming."

"Despite what you might think, Mr. Hepworth is completely under his wife's thumb," Caroline said. "Alice loved this house, so he bought it for her. He also gave her carte blanche to furnish and decorate it, which for a man who knows exactly how many nails are needed to build a station platform, was quite a concession."

"Lucky Alice." Ruby stepped out of the carriage into the weak sunshine and appreciated the silence settling around them.

"I do believe she had a lucky escape from Ian. Ivy's intervention was good for all of them."

"Even Ivy?" Ruby looked at her sister. "Is she truly happy?"

"I think she has the capacity to be happy," Caroline said carefully. "But it might take time for her and Ian to trust each other completely again."

"Understandable when she ran away from him."

"Some women struggle after giving birth. If you'd been here—"

Ruby interrupted her sister. "You don't have to explain. I saw how she was when she arrived in Leeds and threw herself on my mercy. I am not criticizing her."

Caroline touched her sleeve. "Alice had a very difficult birth, and she and her daughter still seem quite fragile."

Ruby raised her chin. "Thank you for the warning. I'll try not to say anything insensitive."

Caroline rolled her eyes as she knocked on the door. "I can't decide if I'm glad to see you being prickly again or offended that you'd think I didn't know you'd be kind."

"You don't know me very well anymore, sister. And, in truth, as I don't know myself, I appreciate your warning."

The door was opened by a parlor maid who bobbed a curtsy and invited them into the spacious hall. "Sorry, my lady. It's the butler's afternoon off and Mrs. Hepworth was just up in the nursery." She smiled as she took their cloaks and gloves. "She's in the drawing room now, and I was just about to fetch her some tea."

"Thank you." Caroline was always so gracious one might think she'd been born a viscountess. "There's no need to announce us. We'll go and find her while you get on."

"Thank you, my lady."

Ruby followed her sister into a sunlit drawing room decorated in subtle cream and blue. The room was dominated by a large portrait hanging over the mantel of Mr. Hepworth scowling ferociously. She was already regretting her decision to accompany Caroline, a feeling that didn't abate when she realized their hostess was already entertaining another guest.

Dr. Nash rose to his feet and bowed to them both.

"Viscountess Grafton-Wesley. Ma'am. I didn't realize you intended to visit Mrs. Hepworth this afternoon. I was with Mr. Hepworth, and he brought me here for lunch and then had to leave rather suddenly. I can go if you prefer to enjoy your visit in peace?"

"It is of no matter," Caroline said easily. "In fact, we can take you back to Grafton Hall when we leave, if you wish."

"I would appreciate that." Dr. Nash nodded his thanks.

Ruby went over to greet Alice. "You probably don't remember me, Mrs. Hepworth, but I was at Ivy and Ian's wedding,"

"I remember you very well." Alice, who was as blond and dainty as spun glass, smiled warmly at Ruby. "You were one of the few guests my future husband approved of."

"He was something of an anomaly at that wedding," Ruby acknowledged. "A self-made man and proud of it."

Alice gestured for them all to sit down. "He is proud of his background. And why shouldn't he be? Not many men can build railways and bring them in on time and at a profit."

"Hear, hear." Dr. Nash's aristocratic drawl was always surprising considering the company he kept. For the first time

Ruby wondered what had brought him to Millcastle and whether he intended to stay.

Was he one of those younger sons of the aristocracy who had no chance of inheriting a title and frittered his life away in society? She studied him covertly. Perhaps that was unfair. He had trained in a respectable profession.

Although he was currently residing at the hall, she'd barely seen him. He spent his days either attending Mr. Hepworth in Millcastle or dealing with his patients. He came over to sit beside her as Caroline and Alice discussed the weather.

"You are looking much better, ma'am."

"Thank you." Ruby risked a cautious smile. "Nora is also thriving."

"I know. I visit her in the nursery every morning and speak to her nurse."

"I was unaware of that." Ruby wasn't sure how she felt about Dr. Nash checking on her child. "I can assure you that I would ask for your assistance if I thought she needed it."

His sudden grin caught her unawares. "There's no need to glare at me, Mrs.…." He frowned. "I'm not sure I know your last name."

"It's Miss Delisle." Ruby held his gaze. "And I would appreciate it if you spoke to me about my child rather than to her nurse."

"Noted, Miss Delisle." He paused. "Although I must say in my own defense that I've been reluctant to wake you up that early in the morning merely to hear what a very competent nursery nurse can tell me to my face."

"As you can see, I am quite recovered now. Perhaps you could speak to me at breakfast if you have any further concerns?"

"If you are up and about at six then I shall certainly do so." He inclined his head. "I understand that your appetite has improved considerably."

"You've been keeping an eye on me as well, have you?"

He raised his eyebrows. "I'm a doctor, Miss Delisle, and you are a patient under my care."

"Then I willingly release you from that duty," Ruby said. "I am completely recovered."

He studied her for a long moment. "As you wish."

"Thank you." Ruby looked past him toward the door where the parlor maid was bringing in the tea. She raised her voice so that her hostess could hear her. "I do hope to meet your new daughter, Mrs. Hepworth. Caroline tells me she is of a similar age to my Nora."

"I'd be delighted to take you up to the nursery after we've finished our tea, and please call me Alice. We are practically family." She looked at Dr. Nash. "Will you take Ruby's tea to her, please?"

Dr. Nash rose to his feet and brought the delicate cup of tea back to Ruby.

"Thank you."

"You are most welcome." He returned for his own cup and somehow managed to juggle two plates along with his tea, one of which he set in front of Ruby.

"I didn't ask for any further refreshments," Ruby said.

"You need your strength."

"I thought we just agreed that my medical concerns were no longer any of your business?"

"Force of habit?" He ignored his cake but drank his tea in two gulps before rising to his feet. "If you'll excuse me for a moment, Mrs. Hepworth, I'll take a turn around the garden." He looked at Caroline. "I'll make sure to be back by the time you are ready to depart."

The three ladies watched him stroll out of one of the French windows, his hand already reaching into his coat pocket for his cigar case. Ruby realized that Alice and Caroline were staring at her.

"I wasn't aware that you and Dr. Nash didn't get along." Caroline was the first to speak.

"Neither was I," Alice said. "Or I wouldn't have encouraged him to stay while you were visiting me."

"I'm not sure what you are talking about," Ruby said. "We were simply having a frank discussion about the limits of a physician's care."

"Oh, is that all?" Caroline asked. "Because it looked as if you were arguing, and as I've never heard Dr. Nash raise his voice to anyone, it was something of a surprise."

"I asked him not to continue to treat me as his patient, and that if he wished to discuss Nora's care, he should speak to me directly and not to her nurse."

Caroline grimaced. "That was my fault. You desperately needed your rest. When Dr. Nash asked me what he should do about Nora, I took it upon myself to suggest he speak to me or the nurse if you were not present."

"Oh." Ruby paused. "He didn't mention that part."

In truth, he'd accepted he was at fault and not blamed anyone except himself. For some reason, that didn't make Ruby feel any better about their encounter. While Caroline told Alice what Francis had been doing in London, Ruby busied herself drinking her tea and ate the slice of angel cake Dr. Nash had set beside her.

Eventually, after she'd eaten both her cake and Dr. Nash's, Ruby rose to her feet to accompany her sister and Alice up to the nursery. She was vaguely aware that Mr. Hepworth had other children but there was no sign of them.

"Is Dan at school?" Caroline asked as they reached the nursery door.

"He's out with his tutor in Millcastle learning how the cloth trade works at the piece hall, and then he's having tea with his father to celebrate his birthday." Alice smiled. "He has no interest in going away to boarding school and would prefer to work his way up in the world like his father. Elijah thinks it will be the making of him."

"Good for Dan," Caroline said. "I have still not asked Francis whether he believes Joseph should be sent to Harrow when he is seven."

"It seems cruel to send them away when they are so young," Alice said. "I am glad Dan will stay home with me and Amelia."

"Crueler to put them to work in a mill," Ruby said before she could stop herself.

"We are aware of that, Ruby," Caroline said gently. "And we're both actively campaigning to force parliament to pass legislation to improve child labor laws."

"I'd be glad to help with that," Ruby said. "It is a cause close to my heart."

"Then when you are feeling better, I'll introduce you to our local committee. Your opinion would be most welcome."

Caroline went into the nursery and Ruby followed her. Did she really want to get involved with politics again? The last few frantic years had almost broken her, but she still had a clear sense of the injustices of life, and having lived through some of the worst of them, she did have valuable experience to contribute. Whether the well-meaning ladies of Millcastle would listen to her was another thing entirely…

"This is my daughter, Amelia." Alice came toward Ruby, holding a little girl. "She is quite shy."

Amelia was fair-haired like her parents and had cornflower-blue eyes that peeked shyly at Ruby over her mother's shoulder.

"Hello, Amelia," Ruby spoke softly. "What a very pretty dress you are wearing."

The little girl immediately turned her head into her mother's neck and held on even tighter.

Alice smiled. "She was the same with Dr. Nash until he coaxed her out of her shyness by being extremely silly."

"I can't imagine him lowering himself to be silly," Ruby said.

"You'd be surprised what he'll do for his patients." Caroline sat by the fire and Ruby and Alice joined her. "He is an exemplary physician."

Alice nodded as she settled Amelia on her lap. "He saved our lives. At one point during the birth, Elijah thought he would have to choose which one of us to save, but Dr. Nash made sure that he didn't have to make such an awful decision."

"I'm glad about that," Caroline said.

"Dr. Nash said he just happened to come to lunch today because he was working with Elijah close by," Alice said. "But I am fairly certain my husband asked him to come and see how we are doing. He is a terrible worrier."

Ruby couldn't imagine Mr. Hepworth worrying about anything but had to take his wife's word for it. Perhaps beneath his blustering exterior he was a soft-hearted man.

"And *are* you both well?" Caroline asked.

"I have recovered completely," Alice said. "Amelia seems..." She sighed. "She isn't talking at all yet, and her appetite is very uncertain."

Ruby glanced at the little girl who was sitting on her mother's lap, her gaze on the light streaming through the window.

"Not all children progress at the same rate," Ruby reminded her hostess. "My Nora doesn't speak much, either."

Ruby blamed herself for that. Just getting through each day and providing warmth, food, and somewhere to sleep had exhausted her so much that she'd had little time to play with her child. And Nora seemed to have been born knowing she needed to be quiet, because a constantly screaming baby in a tenement might provoke someone to violence.

"They are of a similar age," Caroline agreed. "Perhaps they might enjoy each other's company and learn together?"

Alice smiled at Ruby. "I think that is a delightful idea, don't you?"

"Yes, indeed. Nora would probably enjoy that."

For some reason, Ruby felt more comfortable in the Hepworth home than Francis's mansion. The idea of having Alice as a friend appealed to her. She had her sisters and mother in her life, but sometimes she felt as if she didn't fit in anymore. They'd all decided who she was and what she deserved years ago, and nothing she said would change that. She felt guilty even thinking such a thing when everyone had been so kind to her, but it was the truth.

Caroline went over to the window and looked down into the garden.

"I can see a trail of smoke but no sign of Dr. Nash."

"Perhaps he has left?" Alice suggested.

"Not if he wishes to accompany us back to the hall," Caroline said. "The clouds are gathering again. I do hope he hasn't decided to walk."

Alice handed her daughter over to the nurse. "Perhaps we should go and find our errant guest so that you can all be on your way."

Ruby stood and followed her sister and Alice down the stairs to the hall where Dr. Nash awaited them. He looked pensive in his dark coat, his medical bag in his hand, and smelled faintly of smoke.

"I do hope you are still willing to give me a seat in your carriage, my lady." His voice rose toward them as they descended. "Otherwise, I am destined for a soaking."

"You are most welcome to join us," Caroline said as she reached his side.

"Then I will ask for your carriage to be brought round." Alice headed for the kitchen.

Dr. Nash's gaze fell on Ruby. "When I passed through the drawing room, I noticed you'd eaten all the cake."

"Perhaps it was my sister." Ruby met his gaze. "Or one of the maids."

A small smile tugged at the side of his mouth, making him

look far more attractive. "I'm sure a true gentleman would agree with you and not mention that you have a dab of white icing on your cheek."

Her fingers flew to her face, and he offered her his handkerchief. "Just to the right of your nose, if that helps."

"Thank you." Ruby scrubbed at the spot and risked a glance at her companion. "It was very good cake."

CHAPTER FOUR

*C*harles hated Nash Hall and everything it stood for, but he'd had no choice but to return to the place of his birth before his father sent someone to fetch him like a naughty schoolboy. He reminded himself that he was an independent man and that his father had no real power over him, but it didn't help much.

"Thank you, Benson." Charles handed his hat and cloak to the butler and followed him across the large marble hall and down a dark corridor to his father's study.

The butler knocked on the door and then stood aside for Charles to enter. "Mr. Charles, my lord."

His father sat behind his desk, his spectacles on his thin nose, his gaze on the accounts book in front of him.

"Good afternoon, sir."

Charles waited for a reply, his gaze drifting around the vast room, from the books adorning the shelves he was certain his father never read, to the dour family portraits and hunting scenes his father favored. Nothing had changed except he was no longer a small, scared boy desperately trying to win his father's approval.

His father's old tactic of making him wait to be acknowledged didn't work anymore, either.

For a while, the faint scratching of his father's pen against the paper and the tick of the mantelpiece clock were the only sounds in the vast room. Charles consulted his pocket watch and looked up to find his father's gaze fixed on him.

"You've taken long enough to get here."

Charles inclined his head. "I have an obligation to my patients, sir. I can't just up and leave."

"That's not what I've heard."

Charles had no reply but refused to look away or apologize. "Is there something specific you wished to discuss me with me, sir? I need to get back to work as soon as possible."

"In Millcastle?"

"That is where I have my medical practice." He wasn't surprised his father knew all about his recent change of address and had known exactly where to find him.

His father nodded. "Working for a self-made man, I hear."

"I thought you'd be pleased I'd found gainful employment."

"Not with a cit. A man of your rank should be working for the interests of his family."

"I'm quite certain you are fully capable of fulfilling all those requirements for many years to come without any help from me."

"I will agree that you are of no use to me in most matters, but there is one thing I need from you."

"And what is that?" Charles met his father's gaze. "Unfortunately, despite my profession, I am unable to perform miracles and resurrect your true heir."

"You will marry and produce an heir to continue my name and line."

"Oh, I don't know about that." Charles smiled. "Who on earth would want to marry me, and why would I want to perpetuate a line that considers me a failure?"

His father raised an eyebrow. "I have already found you a willing bride. You will be married by the end of the year."

"I beg to differ."

"You will do as you are told or suffer the consequences."

Charles shrugged. "You've already cut off my allowance and presumably written me out of your will. I know you can't take away the title, but that is meaningless to me anyway. So, what else can you do?"

His father opened a drawer in his desk and took out a stack of papers.

"It might interest you to know that I bought your London debts."

For a second, Charles fought to breathe before regaining the ability to speak.

"Thank you?"

"I don't want your gratitude. I want you to do what you are told."

"When have I ever done that?" Charles asked lightly. "In truth, you buying back my debts makes my life much easier."

"Ah, but the cost of doing so needs to be absorbed by the estate, which might necessitate other... economies."

"A few less racing horses in your stables won't cause you much pain, sir," Charles said.

His father looked directly at him. "I was thinking more about your mother's needs."

Coldness crashed over him and his fingers curled into fists as his father continued speaking.

"It would be more economical to find somewhere she can be confined more easily. In her less lucid moments, she does tend to wander, and one would not wish harm to befall her."

"No one here would cause her harm."

"One cannot guarantee that."

"What exactly are you suggesting?" Charles forced himself to ask the question.

"You're a physician, perhaps you might have recommendations for the kind of help she requires? I'm not suggesting we place her in a common asylum, but there must be more private establishments that would be able to restrain her... excesses?"

Charles leaned forward and placed his hands on his father's desk. "If you harm her, I'll bloody kill you."

"There's no need to be so melodramatic. You sound like your mother. Remember it's your debts that have brought about this unfortunate situation. Your marriage will help to secure your mother's future here." His father sat back, smiling. "Perhaps you might think about that. I require your agreement by the end of the month, or I shall pursue other options."

"This is contemptible, even for you."

"I am merely securing my line, son. All you have to do is marry and produce an heir, and I will destroy your notes of promise and make sure your mother's existence remains as pleasant and untroubled as I can make it."

Charles headed for the door before he said or did something that would make matters worse. Not that they could get much worse. He didn't care about the debts. His love for his mother would always come first, and his father knew it, which made his current position untenable. There was also no point in calling his father's bluff, as he always followed through on any promise he made.

"Mr. Charles? May I help you, sir?"

Charles only realized he was standing in the hall staring at the front door when the butler spoke to him.

"I'd like to see my mother, Benson. Do you know if it is a convenient time?"

The butler glanced at the clock. "Mrs. Jones just sent her lunch up, sir."

"Then she'll probably be awake and willing to see me." Charles found a smile as he headed for the stairs. "How are your family? All well I hope?"

"Yes, indeed, sir, and thank you for asking. My daughter's about to give birth to my first grandchild."

"Make sure to tell your midwife or doctor to wash their hands with soap before they lay a finger on her," Charles advised.

The butler nodded. "Is that the latest science from London?"

"It is. I won't bore you with the details, but it makes for a far healthier outcome for both mother and child."

"Then I'll be sure to mention it." The butler hesitated. "You will be staying the night, won't you, sir? It's started raining quite heavily. I would be wary of attempting to cross the ford in the dark when the river is already high."

"I'll stay the night, but I'll be off again at dawn."

"I'll make sure to inform the stables and kitchens, sir."

"Thank you."

The butler bowed and Charles continued up the stairs until he was outside his mother's suite of rooms. He knocked on the door, and her full-time companion, Miss Martha Evans, opened the door a crack.

"Dr. Nash! What a pleasant surprise."

She was a middle-aged woman who claimed some distant kinship with the family. She'd come to live at the hall and quickly become his mother's mainstay, steering her through the tempestuous swing of her moods with a calm good sense and kindness that Charles could only admire. What would happen to Miss Evans if his mother was taken away? Would she lose her occupation and her home as well? Charles wouldn't put it past his father to deal him a double blow.

"Miss Evans." He smiled at her. "How is she today?"

"Very much present and aware." Miss Evans lowered her voice. "She is looking forward to seeing you."

Miss Evan opened the door wider and turned toward the large, four-poster bed. "Look who has just arrived, my lady."

"Charles!"

His mother was sitting up in bed, a lace cap covered her fair hair. She had a lunch tray beside her and two small dogs curled at her feet.

"Mother." Charles strode across to the bed and bent to kiss her cheek. "You look very fetching in that cap."

"It is pretty, is it not? Martha made it for me. She is very clever."

Charles sat down on the chair next to the bed and carefully observed his mother's face. She looked as beautiful as ever, the only signs of her struggles evident in the hard lines around her mouth and on her brow and the overbrightness of her blue eyes. She had gotten a lot worse after the death of Charles's older brother, Benjamin, and had never quite recovered her nerves or equilibrium.

"Are you here for long, Charlie?" She nibbled at a piece of bread and butter and took a sip of hot chocolate.

"Alas, not for long. I have patients to see."

She sighed. "Is your father being horrible to you?"

"I think in his own way he is still grieving for Benjamin." Charles tried to be tactful. Setting his mother against his implacable father never ended well for her.

His mother snorted. "Paul is incapable of feeling; we both know that." Her lips thinned. "He barely bothers to come and see me anymore."

"One would think that was something to celebrate," Charles said.

Her grin was wicked enough to make him believe that the rest of it—the days when she was unable to get out of bed, or she cried, or raved, or roamed without purpose didn't occur—but he knew better. Such hope was treacherous and wishing she would simply get better was unhelpful. He couldn't imagine what would happen to her if she was held in a place where she wasn't loved or understood.

"Shall we go for a walk, Charlie?"

He glanced over at the window. "It's a charming idea, but it is pouring with rain."

"Is it? Then we can walk in the long gallery and make fun of all the family portraits your father prizes so highly."

Before he replied, Charles glanced over at Miss Evans. After she nodded slightly, he said, "I think that is an excellent idea." He smiled at them both. "I'll wait for you to get dressed."

IT WAS ONLY when he was on the mail coach heading back to Millcastle that he allowed himself to think about his father's threats. Unfortunately, his father knew his weaknesses and had set his trap well. How could Charles allow his mother to end up in a home for "distressed ladies"? He knew what such places were like—had visited the occupants in his professional capacity when he'd practiced in London—and none of them, even the most expensive, were happy places.

In his opinion, the moment someone was held against their will, even in the most luxurious of prisons, their life became subject to the whims of others who might not always have their best interests at heart and might even abuse that power for financial gain. He'd seen perfectly sane women incarcerated by their loving families simply for refusing to marry as directed, or for having an education or a belief of their own.

His delicate mother would wither and die in such a place. He couldn't be the architect of such a disaster, which meant his father had won... again. Everything inside him rebelled at such a capitulation. It had taken years to get away from his family and to learn how to channel his rage into more constructive outlets, but even there, he hadn't quite succeeded, which had led to his current predicament.

From his conversations with his mother and Miss Evans, he surmised that neither of them knew about his father's plans, which was some comfort.

His last act before leaving his father's house was to ask for two month's grace to consider his options and that, if he did agree, he had to meet his proposed bride before the wedding. His father, knowing he held all the cards, had graciously accepted his terms and sent him on his way with a knowing smile.

Charles sighed and leaned his head against the back of the seat. The woman sitting next to him snored away, her shoulder tucked firmly against his, stopping them both from being deposited on the floor as the coach dodged the potholes on the ancient road. Her booted feet were propped up against a wicker basket containing a chicken leaving little room for his long legs.

As a headache threatened, he closed his eyes and tried not to think about anything. He knew such behavior had led to his present woes but reasoned that a good sleep would clear the cobwebs and hopefully present him with some solutions on the morrow.

He had a profession he loved, a steady income, people who respected him, and a place to live. He wondered how his mother and Miss Evans would feel if he brought them to live with him and keep house? He had a terrible suspicion that any change in his mother's circumstances might cause harm, but surely being with him rather than with strangers would be an improvement? His last thought as he succumbed to the lure of sleep was that if he could find a way to thwart his father, he would do it.

RUBY WAS WARMING her hands at the nursery fire when the door opened and Dr. Nash came in, carrying what appeared to be his luggage. He looked like a man who'd spent the night in close proximity to others and smelled of the farmyard. His usually immaculate linen was rumpled, his boots were covered in mud, and a suggestion of stubble covered his chin.

He set down his belongings, removed his hat, and let out a ragged breath.

"Good evening, Miss Delisle. I came to check on your daughter."

Ruby frowned. "Haven't you been away?" Caroline had mentioned the doctor had been called away on family business at dinner earlier.

His eyebrows rose. "What does that have to do with anything?"

"One might have thought you'd be longing for your bed."

"I am, but the welfare of my patients always comes first." He glanced down at his sodden boots and grimaced. "I had to walk from town because the mail coach was so late. The ditch and road were partially flooded."

"Then I am happy to inform you that Nora is sleeping well, her cough has almost gone, and her temperature is normal."

"Thank you, but if you don't mind, I'll just take a peek at her myself." He washed his hands and moved past her toward Nora's door. "You may accompany me if you wish."

"I would do that regardless of your wishes," Ruby whispered as she followed him into the dimly lit room where her daughter slept like a little angel. "The nurse has just gone to the kitchen to fetch more coal for the fire. I am awaiting her return before I leave."

Dr. Nash felt Nora's forehead and then took her pulse before carefully tucking her in.

"Well?" Ruby asked.

"She seems perfectly fine." He came toward her and held the door open for her to leave ahead of him.

"Unlike most sick children, she has the benefit of a full-time staff to monitor her needs," Ruby said.

After shutting the door, they stopped in the nursery's central area where the children ate their meals and played under the watchful eye of the nursery staff.

"One would think that would be considered a blessing, Miss Delisle."

Ruby grimaced. "It is. It's just that sometimes all this—" She gestured at the room, the well-stocked toy shelves, soft couches, and thick rugs. "—feels unreal."

His gaze followed hers around the room. "We both know that the majority of people would bite off their own hand to achieve such abundance."

"And I am very grateful to my sister for everything she has done for me and Nora, but I also worry—" She abruptly stopped speaking and looked up at Dr. Nash. "I do apologize. You must think I have run mad."

"Hardly. I know madness when I see it." He hesitated. "You can say anything you want. I will keep your secrets."

She considered him for a long moment. "I think I am afraid."

"Of losing these comforts again?"

"That is part of it, but it's more that... I fear that I might lose myself if I stay here on my sister's charity, even if she never begrudges me a thing." She sank onto one of the chairs and stared down at her twisted fingers.

He nodded slowly. "Being beholden is never easy, even if the persons intentions are pure."

"I think they want me to become the old Ruby—the one they loved. They expect me to settle down and resume my place as if nothing happened." She slowly raised her gaze to meet his. "But I'm not that girl anymore. I have a child. I lived with a man I loved and experienced so many things."

"Then what *do* you want?"

"Some measure of financial independence? Some sense of self and pride in my own achievements?"

He smiled. "You could work in one of the local mills. I'm sure they'd be delighted to have you."

She raised her chin. "It wouldn't be the first time I've worked in a mill, Dr. Nash."

"I don't doubt it." He inclined his head an inch. "I'm merely asking the questions, Miss Delisle. I'm not trying to undermine you."

She sighed. "And yet this whole conversation is ridiculous. I have everything a woman could want, and I'm still complaining."

"I... have some sympathy for you." He paused. "I too chose a different path, one that my family did not approve of, because I hated the idea that I had to become the person they expected me to be. I can't say that decision has made my life easier, but I like the person I am far more than the old me."

Ruby attempted a smile. "Thank you for saying that. I still feel ungrateful. If I expressed such an opinion to my mother and sisters, they'd be dreadfully hurt."

"Then it's a good thing you spoke to me." Dr. Nash bent to pick up his bags. "My advice to you, Miss Delisle, is to work out exactly how you want your life to proceed and find a way to achieve your aims."

Ruby stood and curtsied. "Why thank you, Dr. Nash. When you put it like that it sounds so simple."

She surprised a smile out of him as he turned to the door.

"I'm glad to be of service, Miss Delisle."

She hurried after him and touched his shoulder. "Truly, I appreciate that you took the time to listen to me."

He looked down at her, his frowning gaze lingering on her mouth and for a second. A tremor of excitement went through her before he lifted his head.

"It was nothing. I wish you good night."

"Indeed." Ruby stepped away from him. "Thank you, again."

He left the room, leaving Ruby staring after him. She had no idea why she'd suddenly decided to confide in a man she barely knew and whom she suspected had little tolerance for the imagined woes of the privileged. But he said he understood her, and she believed him.

The nursery maid came through the servant's door with a bucket full of coal and smiled at Ruby. "Thank you for waiting, ma'am." Bridget set the bucket beside the fire and made a tsking sound. "I'll just wash my hands and put on a clean apron. I'm covered in coal dust."

"Then I'll leave you to get on," Ruby said.

"All the children are sleeping through the night now, which means I have very little to do." Bridget smiled as she untied the bow on her apron. "I'll be able to get some knitting done."

"I'm glad to hear it." Ruby went toward the door.

"She'll be as blithe and bonny as Miss Louisa before you know it, miss."

"I'm sure she will. Goodnight, Bridget."

"Goodnight, miss."

She was dispatched with a cheery wave and went toward her bedroom deep in thought. Even though Dr. Nash could be somewhat abrasive, his advice about deciding how she wanted to manage her life going forward was accurate. She tried to think about her ideal situation but was already aware that her options were limited. Poor women worked in the factories or at home. Ladies were protected by their families until they married a suitable man. She didn't fit into either category.

She slowly undressed and put on her nightgown. Were there careers open to women apart from the obvious one of marriage? She didn't have the ability to pretend she was a widow, and she had a child born out of wedlock. Lady's companions and governesses had to have spotless reputations.

52

Most gentleman would consider her ineligible, despite her connection with Francis...

She sighed and got into bed, grateful for the warmth of the freshly banked fire and the thickness of the covers surrounding her. Perhaps like most gentlemen, Dr. Nash believed it was easy to make decisions and act upon them. As a woman, she didn't see a way to achieve her desires, and that wasn't helpful at all.

CHAPTER FIVE

"*S*he isn't an acceptable bride." Charles faced his father in his study. "We have nothing in common, she is obviously terrified of me, and has been coerced into accepting this alliance by her overbearing mother."

His father shrugged. "Miss Barton will do as she is told. That is all I require of you as well."

"She's barely seventeen! I'm twice her age."

"And she'll have years to breed me an heir." His father frowned. "Why are you being so difficult? You know the consequences of a refusal to do my will."

Charles walked away from his father to look out of the window. His mother hadn't taken part in the grand dinner organized for Miss Barton and her parents. She was in one of her more exhausted moods and didn't have the energy to leave her room. Charles knew from experience that nothing would tempt her out of bed. Expecting her to rush to his defense over the matter of an arranged marriage would involve complex explanations that hinged on her own fate. He would never put her through that.

"There has to be someone else."

His father sighed. "You are being unreasonable. There are very few families willing to allow their precious daughters to ally with you."

"I would've thought your family name would be enough, sir."

"Your reputation as a wastrel is well known."

Charles swung back to face his father. "A reputation I shed after I went to India and came back to train in a real and meaningful profession."

"Not entirely. Your debts speak for themselves."

"I've been paying them down ever since I started to earn an income."

His father went to his desk and sat down. "I think a three-month courtship and a wedding in the autumn would be sufficient, yes? You can return next week and propose. I've had your mother's engagement ring cleaned and reset."

"Or you'll do what? Throw my mother into a madhouse?" Charles asked. "Do you think society will allow you to do that without condemnation? I can assure you I won't remain quiet and will do everything in my power to help her leave you."

His father smiled. "If you attempt any such thing, I'll move her to a new location, and you will be the last person on earth to know where she is." He sat back. "You have lost this round, Charles. Admit it, marry the girl, and all will be forgotten and forgiven."

Charles turned on his heel and left, slamming the door hard behind him. He marched into the entrance hall where Miss Evans was just descending the stairs. She still wore the plain brown silk gown she'd donned for dinner. She took one look at his face and came over to him.

"Is everything all right?"

He took hold of her elbow and led her into the rarely used morning room just off the hall. He closed the door and leaned against it.

"I have something to tell you in confidence."

"Does it concern your mother?" Miss Evans asked. "Because I have become aware of various 'narratives' in the servants hall that have caused me some unease."

"My father is thinking of having her confined in a private home for distressed gentlewomen."

Miss Evans briefly pressed her fingers to her lips and then met his gaze with a calmness he could only admire. "Ah, that makes sense of the whisperings I have heard. Why now? She has been remarkably stable for months."

"He intends to use her confinement as a threat against me if I do not marry as directed."

"Hence the appearance of Miss Barton and her unpleasant mother." She nodded. "I did wonder about the purpose of this dinner party."

"I am attempting to find a solution and having an ally such as yourself would prove very useful."

"I am more than willing to help, sir. I am very fond of your mother."

"And she of you," Charles said. "I would appreciate it if you could write to me if anything… untoward happens while I am not here to stop it."

"I will do my best, Dr. Nash." She hesitated. "I would be more than willing to accompany her if she needs to leave in a hurry at your direction."

"I hope it will not come to that." He stepped away from the door. "You have my new address in Millcastle?"

"Yes, indeed."

"Then we will do our best to salvage this appalling situation."

She headed for the stairs beside him while the servants continued to return the dining room to its usual pristine state. He bade her goodnight on the first landing and retired to his bed, almost too angry to think, but grateful at least to have one ally in the house.

He didn't bother to ring for the servant his father provided for him on his visits and undressed himself. If he didn't come up with a solution, in a week's time he would find himself engaged to Miss Barton and married before the end of the year.

∾

ALICE AND RUBY alighted from the carriage in front of sturdy brick building on the corner of a new road leading down to the station. It was three stories high with a slate roof, sashed windows, and a side entrance leading to a cobbled stable yard and some outbuildings.

"I sent a message to Dr. Nash that we would be visiting him today. I do hope he is at home." Alice knocked on the door. "I wonder if he has employed any staff to manage his house?"

As a shirt-sleeved Dr. Nash opened the door to them himself, Ruby guessed not.

"What is it now? Haven't I told you to use the rear door into my consulting rooms?" He looked his usual arrogant self, his expression not entirely welcoming as he barked the question. He recoiled the moment he recognized them. "Mrs. Hepworth, Miss Delisle. I do apologize." He gestured for them to enter. "Please come in."

The house smelled pleasantly of fresh paint, plaster, and new floorboards. Ruby glanced into the two spacious rooms at the front and noted Dr. Nash had almost no furniture.

"I'll have to entertain you in the kitchen, as the rest of the house isn't yet habitable." Dr. Nash kept talking as he walked along the central corridor. "Please come through."

Alice looked around as she untied the ribbons of her bonnet. "We do have some furniture we no longer use in the attics, Dr. Nash. You are more than welcome to whatever you need, and I'll have it delivered."

Dr. Nash set the kettle to boil on the stove and put on a coat that had been draped over a chair. "That's very kind, but you've done more than enough for me already."

"Where are the cups?" Ruby asked.

"In the cupboard beside the sink." Dr. Nash was busy spooning tea into the pot. "I think I have at least three."

There were exactly four cups, four plates, four bowls, and very little else.

"Have you not found someone to manage your house for you yet?" Alice asked as she found the covered milk jug, sniffed it, and hastily set it down again.

"I haven't had time to look." Dr. Nash turned to look at them. "And I must admit that I have no idea how to go about hiring staff in the first place."

"I can—"

Dr. Nash spoke over Alice. "As I've said you've done enough. I'm certain I have the intelligence to work it out for myself. It can't be that hard."

"You'd be surprised." Ruby set the cups on the table as Dr. Nash filled the teapot with the boiling water. "And if you require someone to help you with your medical practice, they'll have to be properly trained."

Dr. Nash raised his eyebrows. "I don't suppose you want a job, Miss Delisle? I suspect you'd make an admirable and formidable secretary."

"Don't be silly, Doctor." Alice laughed. "Ruby doesn't need to work. She has her daughter to bring up and many important family obligations."

Ruby tried to smile as Dr. Nash poured the tea and offered them milk, which they both declined. Her main family obligation consisted of dealing with a parent who constantly lamented her shortcomings as an unmarried mother with no financial expectations and prophesized the worst for her. Caroline and Ivy tried to provide errands and tasks to keep her occupied, but in truth, she was bored.

Her family had saved her life and that of her daughter, and at some level she was ungrateful, which was appalling.

Alice was speaking again. "If you don't wish to accept my offer of help, perhaps you might speak with Mr. Totton? He is extremely good at managing staff and properties."

"That is an excellent suggestion, ma'am." Dr. Nash sat down, sipped his tea, and shuddered. "The milk is off."

He got to his feet, poured the contents of his cup down the sink, and refilled it from the pot. A beam of sunlight penetrated the dirty windows and shone onto his head, revealing hints of brown in his black hair. Ruby noticed his shirt needed darning and that two of the buttons at his cuff were in danger of falling off.

"I should thank you for the tea as well, ma'am." Dr. Nash cupped his large hands around his mug. "The hamper you sent me from Leeds had all the necessities a man could ever need."

"You are most welcome, Dr. Nash. My husband wants you to settle in Millcastle." Alice set down her cup and looked at Ruby. "Would you mind waiting here while I run a quick errand across the street? It is not that I don't require your company, but the person I'm visiting is rather shy and currently bedridden."

"Then I assume it's not your husband," Dr. Nash said, his gaze fixed on Ruby as if he was seeing her for the first time. "I'll take good care of Miss Delisle, ma'am, don't you worry."

"Thank you." Alice picked up her bonnet. "Miss Pimms lives very close by. I won't be a moment."

Her exit left a sudden silence Ruby had no intention of filling with idle chat. In truth, she was enjoying sitting at the scarred pine table with Dr. Nash, who had no expectations of her whatsoever.

He sipped his tea and then set his mug down on the table with a decisive thump.

"Miss Delisle, I'm not sure how to approach this subject, but I am quite desperate."

Ruby blinked at him. "I beg your pardon?"

He raised his dark gaze to meet hers. "I am in need of a wife."

"It would certainly solve your current domestic issues," Ruby agreed as she looked around the sparse kitchen. "Do you want me to draw you up a list of eligible young ladies?"

"I believe I've already found the person who would fulfill my requirements."

"Then propose to her. You're a doctor, you have a settled income, a respectable profession, and from the sound of your accent, a family somewhere who will eventually leave you money."

"As you wish." He took a quick breath. "Miss Delisle, will you do me the honor of becoming my wife?"

Ruby nodded encouragingly. "That's exactly how you should do it."

"Then you accept?" He sat back. "I thought it would be much harder than this. I have a whole list of arguments lined up to convince you to become my wife."

Ruby's mouth fell open. "You are jesting."

"No, I'm very serious. If I don't find myself a wife within the next month, my father will force me to marry a seventeen-year-old."

"He cannot force you," Ruby objected. "You are a grown man."

His mouth set in a hard, uncompromising line. "Let's just say that he can, because he is a complete bastard who knows exactly how to compel my obedience."

Ruby folded her arms over her chest. "This is ridiculous."

"I agree, but I am still asking you to marry me."

She stared at his resolute expression. "Perhaps you *should* go through your list of arguments."

His brows drew together. "I fully intended to when you confused me by appearing to agree with me and accepted my proposal!"

Ruby waved his objections aside. "Please, carry on."

"As I said, my father wishes me to marry a girl I've only met once, and I don't wish to do that. There are personal reasons why I cannot simply ignore his machinations. I've been racking my brains to come up with a solution to my problems. When Mrs. Hepworth mentioned your capabilities, it occurred to me that we might work to help each other."

"How so?"

"We marry, which will get my father off my back."

"And what do I gain from this unholy alliance?"

He shrugged. "Freedom to have your own home, respectability, a father for your child, and the opportunity to be my helpmate?"

Ruby studied him. "Why would you think those things were important to me?"

His eyebrows shot up. "Because I am more aware than most of the restrictions society imposes on women such as yourself."

"An unmarried woman with a child."

"Correct."

"But how would marriage set me free?"

"I have a high opinion of your intelligence, Miss Delisle, so I think you already know the answer to that. I am more than willing to discuss terms." He turned toward the door. "I hear Mrs. Hepworth returning. Will you think about what I've said and let me know if you are agreeable?"

Ruby barely had time to nod before Alice came into the kitchen full of apologies. They prepared to leave, and as they went through the narrow hallway, Ruby tugged on Dr. Nash's coat sleeve. "Will you be at dinner tonight?"

"I intend to be there unless my work calls me away, why?"

"Because I might wish to discuss this matter further."

"I'm glad to hear it." He looked down at her, his expression serious, his voice pitched low. "I don't have much time to dither on this matter."

"Then I will do my best to give you an answer as swiftly as possible."

Ruby stepped up into the carriage, and Alice, who was already seated, looked at her closely.

"You appear to be in somewhat of a daze, Ruby. What on earth did Dr. Nash say to you while I was gone?"

"He asked me to marry him."

"My goodness!" Alice sat up straight. "And what did you say?"

"I asked him for time to think about it."

"A reasonable request when his proposal was apparently unexpected." Alice paused. "Some might say he would be a good match. Both Caroline and I thought he was attracted to you."

"I know almost nothing about him."

Alice smiled. "I knew very little about my husband-to-be, but I was willing to take a chance. For some reason I trusted him implicitly."

"Mr. Hepworth is a man of his word."

"As is Dr. Nash. Elijah thinks very highly of him."

"But is that enough? I don't know anything about his past, his family, or why he turned up in Millcastle in the first place. And all he knows about me is that I am an unmarried mother and a disgrace to my family."

"You are not a disgrace," Alice said swiftly. "You were abandoned by a wicked man."

There was a lot Ruby wanted to say about Alice's condemnation of Sidney, but what was the point?

"Dr. Nash would give you respectability and some measure of independence," Alice said carefully. "Having grown up in a socially precarious position, myself, I feel I have the right to say that to you even if it is rather blunt."

"I appreciate your advice." Ruby nodded. "Currently, I am dependent on my sisters and mother for my upkeep, housing, *and* the shreds of my reputation. But would marrying Dr. Nash improve my lot or make it worse?"

Alice sat back. "If I was in your position, I would listen to what Dr. Nash has to say and make up my own mind."

Ruby nodded, her thoughts swirling in her head with a thousand questions and possibilities. To say that Dr. Nash had taken her by surprise was an understatement. She'd believed there was only one path for her life, and he'd presented her with an entirely unexpected alternative.

But was he trustworthy? Ruby gazed unseeingly out of the window as the carriage left Millcastle and turned out onto the county road that led to Grafton Hall. She had staked her future and reputation on Sidney's professions of honesty, which had led to her current state of uncertainty and dependency on others. But could she form a pact with Dr. Nash that could benefit them both? As Alice had suggested, talking the whole preposterous proposal through with Dr. Nash seemed the only way forward.

CHARLES BARELY NOTICED what he ate for dinner or what he contributed to the conversation. Finally, he and Francis were left alone at the table after the ladies withdrew. He'd been far too aware of Ruby Delisle sitting quietly beside her sister and her inability to meet his gaze. Had she already decided he was not worth the effort? He almost couldn't blame her. His desperate plea for help had surprised even him and seemed more absurd the longer he thought about it.

After a short while, his host stopped talking, lit a cigar, and offered him one.

"Your mind is obviously occupied with loftier thoughts then my mutterings about the current state of the country, Nash."

"I do apologize." Charles refused the cigar. "I had no intention of—"

Francis waved his apology away. "If you have more important matters to attend to, please go ahead. I am the last man on earth to take offense."

"I appreciate your consideration." Charles rose to his feet. "Thank you. I have some patient notes to write up before I forget what transpired."

"Then get to it, man." Francis nodded through a cloud of smoke. "Don't forget to make your excuses to the ladies before you disappear. Caroline was complaining that she barely sees you these days."

"I will certainly do that." Charles headed for the door. "Goodnight, my lord."

"Francis will do perfectly well."

"Thank you, I'll try to remember that."

Would his host withdraw that familiarity when he realized Charles was attempting to persuade his sister-in-law to marry him? With Grafton's notoriously unpredictable temperament, one could never be sure.

Charles headed for the drawing room where he found Miss Delisle seated by herself by the fire. She wore a high-necked, plum-colored gown and had a paisley shawl around her shoulders. Her hair was in braids and coiled high on her head.

She looked up when he came in and offered him a slight smile. "Caroline is in the nursery. She'll be down when she's finished settling the children."

"I didn't want to speak to her." Charles held her gaze. "I wondered if you'd had any more thoughts about our earlier conversation."

She rose to her feet. "Shall we find somewhere more private to talk? There is a morning room at the end of the passageway that almost no one uses."

"As you wish."

He followed her down the badly lit corridor toward the older part of the house—he had to bend his head to avoid the low-beamed doorways—and into a small, limewashed chamber. He took a moment to light some of the candles from the embers of the banked fire and set them on the oak chest beside the door.

She turned to face him, her expression calm but determined. "If your father wants you marry this particular girl then surely marrying me won't solve your problems."

"I don't think it matters whom I marry," Charles said carefully. "He just wants the family line to continue beyond me."

"Why?"

"Because I am a disappointment to him. He wishes to erase me, take control of my son, and raise him properly." He considered what to say next. "He believes my mother spoiled and ruined me."

"He sounds appalling."

"He is." Charles shrugged. "Although, if you asked him, he'd say that he was merely doing his duty to his family."

"Are you quite sure you can't simply defy him and not marry at all?"

"Quite sure."

He had no intention of telling her about his mother or his debts if he could help it. Some things were too personal to share even with a potential wife. And, if she agreed to marry him, and his father left things alone, there would be nothing to tell.

She took a short turn around the room and came back to him, her arms folded across her chest.

"I know very little about you."

He leaned back against the door. "I might say the same about you."

"You know I have a child born out of wedlock and that I had to throw myself on the mercy of my sister to survive."

He inclined his head. "Yes, but none of that makes me see you in a bad light."

"I have an illegitimate *child*."

"And I'm a doctor. You're not the first unmarried and abandoned mother I've encountered." Her brows drew together, and he hastened to continue. "If I were to be blunt, I'd say my father would consider your... proven fertility a bonus."

She stared at him, and he reluctantly kept going.

"If you wish to know more about me, I grew up in Yorkshire, went to Harrow and Eton, and then into the army where I served in India. I met Viscount Grafton-Wesley at some point, and we remained friends. When I returned to England, a legacy from my godmother allowed me to resign my commission and pay for my medical training in Edinburgh." He paused. "My father wasn't happy about my decision, and we became estranged."

"Do you have a mother or any siblings?"

"I had an older brother who died about two years ago. My mother is still alive, although not in the best of health."

"Does she have no say about whom you marry?"

"None at all. My father makes such decisions. Asking for her support when she has never been able to stand against him would be pointless and detrimental to her continued good health."

Ruby nodded. "My mother has never been a reliable source of comfort to any of us, but more through her own selfishness than anything else."

"I understand that Mrs. Delisle expects you to live with her at your sister Ivy's and manage her household and children." He couldn't help but notice her slight shudder, which gave him the courage to continue. "If you wish for a life that is independent of your mother and sisters' goodwill, I can provide it. You can choose to be my wife in name only and benefit from a home of your own, a husband who will respect you, and who will treat your child like his daughter."

"What if I don't love you?"

He shrugged. "I'm not pretending to be in love with you. I am proposing a practical arrangement to suit us both based on respect and a desire to work together for our mutual benefit."

She looked up at him. "I have no money to bring into the marriage."

"My profession should ensure us a decent standard of living, and I have a monthly income from my grandmother's estate to allow for the small luxuries of life. I will, of course, give you a housekeeping allowance and pin money for your own use." He met her gaze. "I'm not the kind of man who expects a woman to account for every penny."

She walked away from him again and stood looking out of the window.

"What happens if we find out we loathe each other?"

"Then we lead separate lives as do most married couples I know."

She looked over her shoulder at him, her expression grave. "You would not interfere with how I brought my daughter up?"

"Only if you tried to train her for the circus or sell her off to a chimney sweep." He paused. "Is it possible that her father might return and want her back?"

"It is extremely unlikely."

"He is still alive, I take it?"

"I haven't heard otherwise, but as I am no longer in Leeds, I probably wouldn't know." She took a deep breath and finally turned to face him. "I can't think of any other questions to ask, and yet I'm sure there must be a thousand of them."

"I wish I had the time to answer them all, but if I am to thwart my father's plans, I need to get a special license so that our marriage can take place before the end of the month."

"What if I refuse?"

He straightened and walked toward her. "Why would you? I am offering you the closest to an independent life that a woman without her own inherited money can achieve."

Her sudden smile surprised him. "Your honesty is quite refreshing. At least we wouldn't be starting our life together with lies."

He took her hand. "Then you agree to be my wife?"

She met his gaze and slowly nodded. "Yes, I will."

He kissed her forehead, a sense of relief surging through his veins. He'd always been a gambler, and he had a sense that he was about to win the biggest game of his life.

"Then let's go and share our good news with your sister and Grafton. I suspect I will need his support against my father."

CHAPTER SIX

"I still don't understand why you need to be married so quickly," Caroline said as she watched the seamstress repair the hem of Ruby's hastily altered wedding dress.

"There is no reason for us to wait," Ruby said, her gaze on her profile in the mirror. The dress was one of Caroline's ball gowns and had the most enormous stuffed sleeves Ruby had ever worn. "Dr. Nash's house is large enough to accommodate us, and everyone agrees that he needs help to run his life, which I can provide."

"But you hardly know him."

"We've been acquainted for three months. I know enough to believe he will make me a good husband."

Caroline still looked doubtful. "Has he told his family of his plans?"

"He intends to write to his father once we are married. He has enlisted Francis to write a letter about my good character and family connections, which he hopes will reassure his father as to the suitability of the match."

"Dr. Nash has no need to be ashamed of marrying you, sister. I am more concerned as to his motives."

"He needs a wife and a helpmate," Ruby said. "And I need a home and something to do, which means we understand each other."

"What about love?"

The seamstress stood up and smiled at Ruby. "You look lovely, miss. Can you step down onto the floor and turn around for me?"

"Yes, of course." Ruby enjoyed the rustle of the blush-rose satin as she slowly turned a full circle. "Thank you, Mrs. Smith. You have achieved the impossible in a very short space of time."

"It's my pleasure, miss." She reached over to check the neckline of the dress and then stepped back. "You will make a beautiful bride."

Mrs. Smith gathered her things and exited the room, leaving the two sisters alone for the first time in what seemed like days. Ivy and their mother were expected at any moment. and the ceremony would be performed at midday in the local parish church. The guest list remained small, as neither Dr. Nash nor Ruby wanted to draw attention to themselves or had many acquaintances to invite. Her husband-to-be had returned with the special license late on the previous night, and she hadn't yet seen him.

Caroline came over and took her hand. "Are you certain this is what you want? You know that Francis and I—"

Ruby squeezed her sister's fingers. "I know you would happily house and feed me for the rest of my days, and I am immensely grateful for that. I want something of my own, and I believe Dr. Nash can give it to me."

"If you are sure..."

Ruby met Caroline's troubled gaze. "I am."

"Then I will support you in every way I can starting with offering you the contents of our attics to furnish your house," Caroline spoke briskly. "The sooner that place is habitable, the sooner you can move in, and start your new life."

"Thank you for everything, sister." Ruby kissed Caroline's cheek.

"I have done nothing that anyone wouldn't do for someone they love." Her sister turned away but not before Ruby noticed the tear on her cheek. Caroline was an immensely strong person and had been like a mother to her younger sisters. "Well, we should get on, or *maman* will be here to criticize our every decision and bewail your fate."

"Your maid is coming to do my hair, and then I'll be ready," Ruby reassured her. "Why don't you go and make sure the children are all right?"

"I shall do that, and I'll make sure Francis keeps *maman* and Ivy downstairs." Caroline headed for the door as the maid knocked and came in. "We will await you in the hall."

Charles checked the time on his pocket watch and glanced down the aisle of the old parish church. The building was nestled in the shadows of the newly built railway station and hotel and had almost no natural light coming through its windows.

"Don't worry, lad. She'll turn up if she's got any sense, and from what I've heard, she's got plenty of that." Elijah Hepworth, who was acting as his best man, nudged his elbow. "Alice thinks very highly of her."

"Miss Delisle is everything a man could want in a helpmate," Charles murmured, his gaze falling on the front pew on the groom's side of the church, where the rest of the Hepworth family was sitting. "I am extremely lucky."

"That's not what I've heard." Hepworth winked at him. "Keep your nerve, Doctor. There's not long to wait now."

Charles turned to the front of the church again and gazed at the stained-glass window of some martyr dying horribly. He kept expecting his father to appear and stop everything. He'd sent a letter to Miss Evans to warn her of his plans and one to his father explaining nothing except that he was now a married man and that he would bring his new bride up to Yorkshire to meet the family when he had time. He'd enclosed the letter from Francis, extolling Ruby's connections and lineage, and hoped it would be enough to tamp down his father's ire at being thwarted.

Would being faced with a *fait accompli* make his father back down on his threats? Charles still wasn't certain, but anything was better than being forced into marrying an unwilling seventeen-year-old. Ruby Delisle was a sensible woman who was entering into marriage for her own reasons and that was good enough for him.

There was a slight cough from the rear of the church, and the vicar came up the aisle followed by members of Ruby's family. Mrs. Delisle, Caroline, and Ivy and her husband, Ian, took their seats. Both sisters smiled encouragingly at him. He already knew from Ruby that they had their doubts about the marriage. He couldn't blame them but was determined to prove the whole family wrong. Francis had been surprisingly understanding about the news. Charles suspected he had a far greater knowledge of his torrid past than he'd let on and knew it was a good solution for his sister-in-law and Charles's problems. He also had no doubt that if Francis felt he was failing Ruby, his vengeance would be swift.

"Good day, gentlemen." The vicar stepped in front of him and Hepworth.

There was a pause as they waited for the bride and Francis, her escort, to come up the aisle. Charles didn't risk a glance until Ruby was right beside him and then couldn't see her face because of her bonnet. She wore a rose silk gown with an embroidered hem, large, puffed sleeves, and a border of lace around the bodice. The relief that she'd decided to appear was enough to make him giddy.

She spoke her vows in a steady voice, as did he, and when he placed the hastily purchased ring on her finger, she met his gaze with a clarity he could only admire.

As the vicar concluded the final blessing, Charles leaned in and gently kissed her mouth. "Thank you."

"I might say the same to you." The side of her mouth quirked up. "I am now a respectably married woman."

"And I a married man with a respectable profession." He took her hand in his. "I promise I will do my best for you."

"And I you."

She squeezed his fingers and then they turned together to face the congregation. He noted several of his patients and Hepworth's staff occupied the pews, which was an unexpected surprise. Everyone looked very happy for them.

"Shall we go?" Ruby asked. Her composure continued to amaze him. "Caroline has organized a splendid wedding breakfast for us up at the hall."

Charles smiled down at her. "That is very good of her."

The bells rang as they left the church and proceeded down the path to the carriage that had been decorated with white bows on the door handles. It was a working day and there were no gawkers, as the mills had shut their doors earlier and the next shift wouldn't start for hours.

Charles helped Ruby into the carriage and sat opposite her— the width of her skirts took up her whole side. Their guests gathered to wave them off and then quickly dispersed to their own conveyances to make the journey to Grafton Hall for the wedding breakfast.

Charles expected to feel a measure of relief now that his plan had worked, but he wouldn't feel safe until he'd heard from his father, who had an uncanny knack for ruining his life.

"Are you all right?" Miss Delisle asked.

Mrs. Nash, now, he reminded himself. His *wife*. He found a smile for her. "I suspect I'm slightly overtired after my rush to get the special license from the bishop."

"It has been something of a whirlwind," she agreed. "I do not regret my decision."

"Neither do I." He held her gaze. "I will admit that I am anxious to find out how my father will view this matter."

"I suspect you already know that he won't like to be disobeyed."

"Indeed." He contemplated her calm expression. "He'll be furious. I'm more concerned about how he'll deal with me when I *have* fulfilled his request to marry—even if it is to the wrong woman."

"As you pointed out before our marriage, you have your profession, a house to live in, and a private income, none of which your father can take away from you. What more could he want for you?"

"Control?" Charles suggested.

Her slow smile left him staring at her mouth. "I doubt he has ever been able to control you, Dr. Nash."

"Charles," he reminded her. "We are legally married in the sight of God."

"Charles, then," she replied, her gaze turning to the window. "How long do you think it will be before we can move into the house? Caroline is very anxious to get rid of her old furniture."

"I'll take you there tomorrow, and you can decide what needs to be done and when we can realistically take full possession." Charles tried to match her calm conversational tone. "I don't think it will be that long. The structure is sound."

"I'm sure Mr. Hepworth made certain it was," she agreed. "If you wish me to help you with your patients, we might need a maid to come in."

He raised his eyebrows. "We'll need a full kitchen staff and a nurse for Nora."

"Hardly. I am quite capable of caring for our needs."

"I'm sure you are, but it isn't necessary," he countered. "I didn't marry you to acquire free staff."

"No, you married me to thwart your father's wishes." She held his gaze. "Will I ever have the privilege of meeting him and your mother?"

"That depends on how he takes the news." There was a certain relief in being able to talk naturally about his strained relationship with his father. "I have suggested we visit him when time allows."

She nodded. "I assume you haven't mentioned Nora."

"That is none of his business." He looked ahead as the carriage slowed for the turn into the long drive leading to Grafton Hall and proceeded up to the house. "We are almost here. Good Lord. The staff are lined up on the front step."

"Then we will smile and thank them for their kindness," Ruby said as she retied the ribbons of her bonnet. "According to the nursery maids, they are thrilled that we fell in love while both staying at the hall."

Charles grimaced. "I am not sure I have the ability to pretend that well."

He surprised a chuckle out of her. "You must at least try. We wouldn't want word to get back to your father that the bridegroom was scowling."

"I can muster a smile." As the carriage drew to a stop in front of the house, he got out and held up his hand to Ruby. "Come along, my dear."

"Thank you." She winked and took his hand. "Chin up."

MUCH LATER, after Ruby had been up to the nursery to supervise Nora's bedtime, she went into her dressing room to find one of the footmen setting Dr. Nash's medicinal bag on the chest of drawers. The wedding breakfast and the rest of the day had passed in a blur as she did her best to be as happy a bride as everyone expected. Everyone seemed delighted for both her and Dr. Nash, which was something of a surprise.

She stopped and stared foolishly at the footman.

"Good evening, ma'am. Her ladyship thought this was the better of the two bedrooms and asked me to move Dr. Nash's belongings in. I'll be finished in just a moment."

"Thank you." Ruby noted that half the drawers now held Dr. Nash's underthings.

She walked back through to the bedroom and contemplated the large four poster bed. She hadn't thought much about the reality of being married to Dr. Nash and the natural assumption that they would share a bed. During their short engagement he'd occasionally kissed her cheek and held her ungloved hand, but that was the extent of their intimacy. Not that he was an unattractive man—she'd seen the way his female patients looked at him—but she hadn't slept with anyone except Sidney.

"Good Lord."

She turned to find her new husband coming through the outer door, his startled expression mirroring her own. He strolled over to stand beside her.

"Don't worry. It's a very large bed."

She swallowed hard. "Indeed, it is. Your... valet is arranging your belongings in my—in our—dressing room."

"I don't have a valet or need one. Francis lent me one of his footmen for the duration of my stay." He looked over her head as the man emerged from the dressing room. "Ah, thank you, Peterson."

"You are welcome, Dr. Nash. I wish you both good night."

"Thank you." Charles nodded. "I won't require your services anymore this evening."

After the door closed, Ruby looked up at him. "Are you expecting me to undress you?"

He frowned. "I'm quite capable of doing that for myself. Peterson helps me shave and makes sure my clothes are laundered." He paused. "I appreciate that this might be… awkward, but I think it best if we share a bed."

"In case your father hears, otherwise," Ruby said. "I understand the necessity. It's just that I haven't slept in the same bed as a man for almost a year."

"You can rest assured that I won't demand my conjugal rights." He held her gaze. "I'm not a complete bastard."

"I appreciate that," Ruby said.

"Good." He awkwardly patted her cheek. "I think I'll take a turn around the gardens before I come up. I'll try not to disturb you when I return."

"As you wish."

He hesitated. "Do you need any assistance getting out of that ridiculous dress?"

"It would be helpful if you could unlace the back so that I don't have to call the maid." Ruby turned around. "I don't normally wear clothes I can't manage for myself, but this is one of Caroline's ball gowns. She wanted me to look nice on my wedding day."

She felt the brush of his fingertips at the nape of her neck and shivered.

"You looked very nice," Charles murmured as he leaned closer, his warm breath on her skin. He dropped a kiss on her shoulder. "It's lucky that I've assisted many women out of their clothing, because these fastenings are absurdly small."

"They are designed for a lady who has a dresser to help her," Ruby reminded him. "I usually stick with much simpler styles." She sighed as he released the back of her gown.

Dr. Nash frowned. "Those sleeves alone must weight five pounds apiece. Fashion is quite ridiculous."

"I agree." Ruby let the silk gown fall to the floor and stepped out of it with a relieved sigh. "Immensely impractical, too."

He smiled as she bent to gather up the gown. "You appear to have the makings of a perfect physician's wife, my dear."

"I'm glad to hear it." She paused. "I do want to help you with your work."

The weeks she'd spent with Caroline had reinforced her belief that she needed purpose in her life. The thought of filling her time with meaningless committees, morning calls, and endless embroidery made her want to scream.

He grimaced. "You'll have no choice. My position in town means that there are knocks on my door all hours of the day and night."

Ruby set the gown over the back of a chair. "Well, we can't have that. You need your rest."

He blew her a kiss as he turned toward the door. "As I said, the perfect wife. I'll be back in a while."

Her smile died as he closed the door behind him, and a yawn shook through her. It had been a challenging day, and she longed for the oblivion of sleep. Yet how could she rest easy when Dr. Nash would return, undress, and climb in beside her? She remembered the small bed she'd shared with Sidney, how closely they'd slept together, sharing warmth, laughter, and love. Until he'd left her...

With a shake of her head, she threw off the past and sat at her dressing table to unpin her hair. There was no point in regretting her decisions. As her mother had so accurately pointed out earlier at the wedding breakfast, she'd made her bed and now had to lie on it. She had no doubt Dr. Nash would keep his word about not consummating their marriage, but that still allowed her room to lie awake and then the doubts would creep in about her decision to marry him in the first place.

Should she have at least attempted to contact Sidney and tell him her plans? And what would that have achieved anyway? Knowing him, he would simply wish her all the best and carry on with his personal crusade against the government, regardless. Nora needed a reliable father and Dr. Nash for all his eccentricities would surely be that. She'd made the best choices available to her and that was that.

She brushed out her hair, braided it down her back, put on her nightgown, and climbed into bed. The clock on the mantelpiece ticked solidly away and the fire only crackled to life when the coal flared red. Ruby stared up at the canopy and willed herself to stay awake, but it was impossible. With a soft sigh, she turned onto her side and fell instantly asleep.

"I DIDN'T EXPECT to find you down here on your wedding night."

Charles looked up from his contemplation of the fire to find his host standing in front of him, two glasses of brandy in his hands. He'd taken refuge in Francis's study and hadn't expected his friend to appear.

"I am attempting to be considerate of my new wife."

Francis handed him a glass and sat opposite him. "As a gentleman should." He paused. "I am aware that this marriage is one of convenience rather than love."

"Cheers." Charles raised his glass.

Francis returned the gesture and took a sip of brandy before he resumed speaking.

"You know that Ruby had a difficult time when she was in Leeds?"

"Yes, of course."

"I doubt she's told you all of it but suffice to say she was living a very precarious life with a bunch of zealots who were far more interested in the rights of man than in protecting their own women and children."

"I know she was abandoned by the father of her child and had to seek sanctuary here."

His host contemplated his glass of brandy. "I might have said a few choice words to Ruby's lover when I went to collect Ivy from Leeds. I've often wondered if that played a part in his decision to abandon her."

"What exactly did you say?" Charles asked.

Francis shrugged. "I offered to pay him to leave the Delisle family alone."

"Does Ruby know about this?"

"I certainly haven't mentioned it to her or to Caroline." Francis finally looked up. "And I expect the same discretion from you."

"Did he take your money?"

"No, he was offended and claimed to be an honorable man." Francis paused. "In truth, I think he believes that with all his heart. But when I suggested a donation to his cause was hardly the same as a bribe, he became more amenable and said he would think about it."

"Did he collect on that donation?"

"Not yet, but I wouldn't be surprised if he does so in the future."

"Then you can hardly blame yourself for his decision to leave Ruby six months ago."

"I'm not so sure about that." Francis sat back. "Knowing that he could call on me for financial aid might have influenced his thinking. I was already paying him a monthly stipend to ensure that Ruby at least had her basic needs met."

"He might have been planning to leave anyway, and you'll never hear from him again."

"Would you care to place a bet on that?" Francis's smile wasn't reassuring. "I am inclined to think that he'll eventually bury his pride and ask."

Charles set down his glass and held out his hand. "I'll wager he won't."

"A guinea for the winner?" Francis asked. When Charles nodded, he shook his hand. "May the best man win. Now may I suggest you return to your bride? I don't want my staff gossiping that the marriage is already a disaster before it has even begun."

Charles went up the back stairs and entered through the dressing room where a single lit candle sat on the chest of drawers. He undressed with some care, making sure his best coat was brushed and put away and that his nightshirt had been freshly laundered. At some level he was aware that he was procrastinating but the last thing he wanted was to frighten his new bride.

Leaving the candle where it was, he opened the door into the bedroom to make sure of his bearings and then blew out the flame. The only light in the bedroom came from the banked coal fire and the bed was in shadow. A faint snoring sound from his wife's side of the bed made him pause and then smile. She was fast asleep. All he had to do was stay away from her for the rest of the night and all would be well.

As he rolled onto his side and stared resolutely into the darkness, he wondered just for a moment how it might feel to turn toward her and be welcomed into her arms... But she didn't want that nonsense from him. She'd already been betrayed by one man's lust. The last thing she needed was him behaving like a fool.

CHAPTER SEVEN

"*T*here." Ruby straightened the tablecloth and stood back to admire her efforts.

"It looks very nice." Alice, who had been of immense help with the furnishing of the house, smiled at her. "Much better than when Dr. Nash was a bachelor."

"It could hardly have looked worse." Ruby turned in a slow circle and admired the dresser full of her best china, the pine kitchen table, and her pride and joy—the newly installed closed coal stove. "Although to be fair, Charles was residing at the hall for the most part."

"Is he happy with your efforts?" Alice inquired as Ruby set the kettle to boil on the stove.

"I'm not sure he's noticed," Ruby admitted. "He's been too busy attending the navvy camps."

"There have been far too many injuries and illnesses up there of late." Alice frowned. "I've tried to ask Elijah about it, but he says the current project is more dangerous to tunnel through than he anticipated. There are bound to be issues that arise."

"I didn't mean to criticize your husband," Ruby said quickly. "I'm sure Charles is needed."

In truth, the last thing Charles needed was for her to criticize the man who employed and housed him, especially when she was about to move in with her child. It was two months since their hasty wedding, and her desire to be settled in her own home was overwhelming. After some disagreements about staffing, they had settled on a live-in nurse for Nora, a cook who came in daily, and a maid of all work.

"Don't worry. I won't take offense, and I certainly won't share your opinion with Elijah." Alice smiled at her. "I find it exasperating when Elijah is never home to discuss matters with me, as well." Alice stood up. "Will you show me what else you've achieved since my last visit? I'd love to see Nora's nursery. We can have our tea when we've finished."

"Yes, of course." Ruby hurried to the door. Alice really was a dear. "We have a very nice parlor and dining room at the front. There's a study for Charles on the right of the house, while the extension at the back is mainly given up to medical matters." She opened the doors off the central corridor that led to the front door to allow Alice to peep inside. "The scullery is behind the kitchen and beside what is now Charles's consulting room, giving us both access to water. The patients can come to see him through the stable yard at side of the house without bothering me."

"It's all worked out very well," Alice said as they mounted the stairs.

"There are three bedrooms on this floor and three more on the top floor which we will use as a nursery, a bedroom for the nurse, and a guest bedroom." Ruby ushered Alice into the large, sunny room she would share with Charles which faced the rear of the house and the small garden.

"Have you managed to find a cook and a nursery maid yet?"

"Yes, but only because Caroline offered me Bridget and Mrs. Jenkins, her cook's assistant."

Alice smiled. "How lovely. Nora will hardly notice she's moved if Bridget accompanies her here."

They climbed the slightly steeper stairs up to the top of the house. There was a wooden gate at the top Ruby opened and shut behind them. She'd had the rooms painted in light colors and tried to make sure that the nursery was a warm and welcoming place.

"It's very pleasant," Alice said, her hand resting on one of the comfortable armchairs that faced the fireplace and newly swept chimney. "Nora will be very happy here."

"I hope we will all be happy."

"Have you heard from Dr. Nash's family yet?"

"Not yet." Ruby moved restlessly around the room, setting things in place that didn't need it. Several weeks had passed since their wedding, which was ample time for the letters Charles had written to be delivered.

"They can't do anything to prevent a marriage that has already taken place," Alice reminded her. "And there is no reason why they won't come to like you when you meet."

"Apart from me having a child that is not my husband's?" Ruby asked. "I'm fairly certain that won't be met with approval."

"Even so, they'll have to get used to it," Alice said bracingly. "If you prove to be an exemplary wife, then they will have nothing to criticize."

"I admire your optimism." Ruby turned to leave. "Shall we go down and make that tea? I don't want the kettle to boil dry. It's been a very productive morning. I do believe we'll be ready to move in at the end of the week."

"THIS IS ALL VERY PLEASANT." Charles glanced across the dining room table at his wife as they ate their first meal in their new home. "You have worked wonders."

Ruby smiled at him through the candlelight. "I'm glad you approve. I did worry if I'd done things you wouldn't like."

"Not at all. If it had been left to me, the place would still be empty." He ate another morsel of chicken. "The food is excellent."

"Mrs. Jenkins lives in Millcastle and much prefers working here. She doesn't have to stay at the hall anymore and can tend to her own family's needs far better."

"Jenkins… Does her husband work for Mr. Hepworth?"

"I believe he does," Ruby said. "You have an excellent memory."

"Which is useful in my chosen profession." He set down his fork. "I intend to officially open my consulting rooms next week."

"Then I would suggest you post your hours of operation to prevent people wandering into my kitchen looking for you."

He raised his eyebrows. "Do they really do that?"

"Yes, sometimes carrying a crying child or dripping blood on Mrs. Jenkins's just-cleaned floors."

"We can't have that," Charles said. "I'll make sure to point them in the right direction."

"I've already asked Mr. Porter to make you some signs. All he needs from you is the correct wordage."

He smiled at her. "You really are a treasure, my dear."

"Thank you." She returned his smile.

"Has Nora settled in the nursery?"

She looked up at the ceiling. "I can't hear her crying, and Bridget said she slept well during her naps in her new crib."

"That is excellent news."

"I suspect she might miss her cousin, but Caroline has promised to bring Louisa to visit."

"And your sister is definitely a woman of her word." He paused. "You are dealing with all this in a remarkably calm manner."

She raised her eyebrows. "Would you prefer me to be in hysterics?"

"Not at all."

"I'm simply doing my best to provide a good home for you."

"I suppose I'm just..." He waved his hand around to encompass the whole room. "Attempting to come to terms with the changes in my life."

"Changes you instigated by asking me to marry you?"

"I'm well aware that this is all my own doing, Ruby."

"You almost sound as if you are regretting it."

Aware that she had stopped smiling, he considered what to say next. "If I appear worried it's because I'm still wondering what my father will do."

"Which is hardly something I can influence."

"You're right." He met her gaze with something of a challenge. "How silly of me to mention it."

She rose to her feet. "Shall I clear the table? Mrs. Jenkins prepared a steamed pudding and custard."

He caught her hand as she went past him.

"Did I say something wrong?" She attempted to ease her fingers free, but he held on. "Ruby..."

She looked down at him. "You don't need to tell me anything, Charles. I'm well aware that our marriage wasn't founded on a desire for intimacy."

He grimaced. "Perhaps we are both still learning and inclined to take offence when none is meant? That is perfectly understandable considering the unorthodox beginnings of our relationship and our naturally suspicious natures." He squeezed her hand. "After we've had our pudding, I'll help you clear up, and we can take a cup of tea together in the sitting room."

A smile tugged at her lips. "You are quite remarkable, Dr. Nash."

"How so?"

"Your ability to accept the realities of life and face them full-on."

He shrugged. "I don't know any other way of living, my dear."

She eased free of his grasp. "I hope you don't mind, but I am rather tired. I'll visit the nursery and then go to bed. I can do the dishes in the morning."

Charles stood up. "There's no need for you to do anything in the kitchen. I'm quite capable. You can go straight to bed."

"Thank you."

He bent to brush a kiss over her lips. She did look a little flushed, but her eyes were bright.

"You've been working very hard on the house. You deserve a good night's sleep."

"It's been a pleasure to..." She hesitated. "Create something for our family—for myself."

He watched her leave and then muttered a curse as he started to clear the table. The kitchen was pristine, apart from the jam pudding and custard awaiting him on the stove. He helped himself to a large bowlful and stood eating it, his gaze turned toward the window that faced the street. He wasn't sure why he'd mentioned he hadn't heard from his father. He tried very hard not to talk about his family to anyone.

He set the plates and his bowl in the sink and washed them up using the kettle of hot water on the stove. The house settled around him, and apart from the occasional whistle from a train or a passing carriage the town was quiet. There was enough water left in the kettle to make himself some tea, but he decided against it.

Some impulse drove him up the stairs and into his bedroom. His wife glanced over in surprise from her seat at the dressing table. She was brushing her hair and was already dressed for bed. The candlelight caught the red and gold undertones in her fair hair and made him want to—

"Is something wrong?"

"No, I..." He paused to consider exactly what he wanted to say. "I wanted to explain."

She set the brush down and turned to look at him. "You've already apologized."

"Yes, but I believe you deserve a full explanation, too."

He wasn't sure if he'd imagined her faint sigh, as her face bore no trace of annoyance.

"I think I envy you," he confessed.

She raised her eyebrows. "For what?"

"Your composure in what is a difficult situation for both of us."

"I suppose I have learned that there is no point in getting anxious about things beyond my control."

He sank down onto the side of the bed. "I know all about feeling as though I don't control my choices. I've spent most of my life being forced into 'doing the right thing.'"

"We are perhaps alike in that." She offered him a conciliatory smile. "Your father will make his own decisions and choose his own path."

"But his decisions affect us."

"They affect *you*." She held his gaze. "In ways that I do not understand because I suspect they go far beyond the unfortunate circumstances of our marriage."

Her ability to see through his stratagems temporarily robbed him of speech. After a moment, he said, "That is remarkably unfair."

"If you say so." She turned away and picked up her brush again.

"I think I prefer it when you argue with me," he muttered as he took off his coat and almost strangled himself in his haste to remove his neckcloth.

"You certainly seem intent on creating disharmony this evening."

"That's better."

She set the brush down with something of slam. "I do not *wish* to argue with you."

"Then come to bed." He unbuttoned his trousers and pulled off his shirt.

"That was already my intention. I didn't expect you to be joining me so soon."

He sat down to remove his shoes and stockings. "It's my bed, too."

"I am well aware of that." She began to braid her hair.

"We can't always be avoiding each other in our own house."

She stood up and marched over to the bed. "I am not avoiding you. This is my first night sleeping in this house, and I am perhaps a little apprehensive."

He pulled back the covers. "Because the bed is so much smaller than the one at Grafton Hall? Might we accidentally touch each other?"

"There is no need to be sarcastic, Dr. Nash."

"We are married."

"I am also aware of that." She positively glared at him as she got into bed. He found himself transfixed by the sharp beauty of her face. "I can assure you that I will do my utmost to keep my cold feet away from you!"

"I'd appreciate that." He found his nightshirt and put it on before blowing out the candle and joining her in bed. "If you could consider not snoring as well, I'd—"

His words were cut off as she thumped him with her pillow, and he fell back against the sheets laughing. After a moment, she gave a little gurgle of laughter and joined him. He put his arm around her shoulders and held her tight.

Eventually, she lightly punched his chest. "You are ridiculous."

"I can't argue with that."

She went silent for a while, and he thought she'd gone to sleep. He nuzzled her hair and breathed in the scent of lemons.

"I'm not very adept at arguing."

"I hadn't noticed," Charles murmured, his eyes half closed as he enjoyed her nearness.

"Sidney would run rings around me," she said. "I'd end up agreeing with him despite myself, or he'd walk away and leave me steaming for days."

"I'd rather we had things out between us," Charles said. "We're married, and we intend to stay together, which means we have to reach a compromise on whatever we disagree on."

"I like that idea." She paused. "I'm not sure how it will work in practical terms."

"It worked this evening," Charles pointed out. "We ended up laughing together."

"Sidney would've left the bed if I'd done that."

"How very noble of him."

She propped herself up on one elbow and looked down at him, her hair pooling on his chest. "There's no need to be sarcastic," she admonished him again.

"Was he a good lover?"

"What a thing to ask!"

He shrugged. "We both know men can take what they want from a woman without bothering to make the experience pleasant."

"He took nothing I wasn't willing to give."

"Good for Sidney."

"There you go again." She hesitated. "I always enjoyed that part of our relationship."

"He must have been very considerate indeed, then."

"Women can… enjoy such things, Dr. Nash. We don't all simply endure."

"I'm a doctor. I'm well aware of a woman's ability to experience pleasure, ma'am."

She gazed down at him, her skepticism apparent on her face. "Really."

He smiled. "I know all the salient parts to… excite."

A faint tremor ran through her, and he tensed, his body coming to life as she considered him. "I could demonstrate if you don't believe me."

"This might surprise you, Charles, but I am fully capable of experimenting myself."

"I'm glad to hear it." He set his hand over the curve of her hip and gently caressed it. "If you permit, I might add to your knowledge of such matters."

He waited to see if she'd ease away from his touch, but she remained where she was. "I'm also very cognizant of ways to prevent conception," he added.

She jerked away as if he'd hit her. "I think I hear Nora crying. Please excuse me."

She left the bed, wrapping a shawl around her shoulders, and disappeared through the door. Charles cursed quietly and closed his eyes. His unfortunate tendency to be too blunt had struck again, and now he'd alienated his wife. The fact he meant everything he said made no difference. He'd scared her off, and he only had himself to blame.

CHAPTER EIGHT

The formal opening of Dr. Nash's medical practice meant that his days became busy, and he was rarely in Ruby's sight. She was glad of that—firstly, because she had a lot to do herself, and secondly, because their recent intimate conversation had unsettled her deeply, and she had yet to decide how to respond.

She knew she should be repulsed by his open offer to bed her, but she wasn't. She hadn't lied when she told him she'd always enjoyed the intimate side of her relationship with Sidney. In truth, she suspected her infatuation with the physical had been a significant factor in her decision to follow him to Leeds and leave her family behind. As a more mature woman, and a mother, she couldn't afford to be so stupid again.

And she was legally married to Charles Nash. He had obligations toward her, and if he didn't fulfill them, her brother-in-law would never let him forget it. Francis might be an aristocrat by birth, but he reminded Ruby of the ruthless working men she'd met during the protests and strikes in Leeds. She doubted Francis would allow a few scruples about fair play and honor to interfere with his revenge.

She set the bonnet she was sewing for Nora on the kitchen table and checked the stove was still burning brightly. As Charles rarely left his rooms before seeing every patient, she'd begun to alter the time of day they ate to accommodate him. He'd told her not to fuss, but she was determined to hold up her side of their bargain and be a good wife. In truth, she took pride in it. For all his faults, Charles was appreciative of her efforts and always thanked her, something Sidney had often failed to do.

She *liked* him... for his brutal honesty, his passion for the things he cared about, for his impatience when things didn't meet his high standards. She'd admired Sidney, but often felt she could never live up to his ideals. Whereas with Charles, she could be herself, good and bad. He wasn't the kind of man who held a grudge and even admitted he was wrong sometimes— something rare among the gentlemen of her acquaintance.

Bridget came down the stairs with Nora in her arms. "I'm taking the little one out for her walk, ma'am. Do you wish to accompany us?"

"No, thank you." Ruby smiled at her daughter who looked the picture of health. "I've got some darning and mending to attend to."

"I'll give you a hand when I get back," Bridget promised. "Has the butcher's boy come by?"

"Yes, he brought some excellent beef for a stew."

Bridget wrinkled her nose. "I suppose you'll make dumplings, as it's cook's day off?"

"Yes, Dr. Nash loves them."

"Then I wonder if you'd be willing to try my mam's recipe?"

"Are mine very bad?"

"They are rather heavy in the stomach, ma'am. If you don't mind me saying."

"I'm not the best of cooks," Ruby admitted. "I seem to have lost the knack for it."

Bridget beamed at her. "I'll find you the recipe and show you how it's done when we get back."

"Thank you." Ruby held the backdoor open as Bridget wrestled with the perambulator they'd inherited from Alice. "Don't go too near the construction sites. Dr. Nash says it's not good for your lungs."

"I'm going to the park. Nora likes the duck pond."

Thanks to Mr. Hepworth and a few of the mill owners, Millcastle now boasted a town park with iron railings, well-tended flower beds, and budding new trees. Privately, Ruby wondered how long the park would thrive in the factory smoke and soot, but she applauded the effort. It was exactly the sort of thing Sidney would've approved of.

Ruby waved Bridget off and returned to the kitchen as the house settled into silence around her. The clock Alice had given them as a wedding present ticked steadily away on the high mantelpiece over the range, offering its own share of stability and sanctuary. She'd pawned everything she'd had in Leeds and had left there with nothing except Nora, her most prized possession.

Ruby gave herself a little shake. How lucky was she now with a roof over her head, a thriving child, and a purpose in life once more? She would never take such things for granted again. She picked up one of her husband's socks and stuck her finger through a hole at the toe. Charles tended to go through a lot of socks, because his work at the navvy camps took him miles into the countryside, and he often had to walk.

She threaded her needle with black wool. It would be no hardship allowing herself to touch Charles Nash... He was a handsome man. Did she really want to live out the rest of her life without being bedded again?

"Ouch!"

"What have you done?"

She looked up to see Charles coming through the door.

He paused at the sight of her. "I thought you'd gone out."

"Or else you wouldn't have come in here?" Ruby asked as she studied the bright red bead of blood on her thumb. "Bridget took Nora out for a walk."

"Ah, that's the commotion I heard." He paused. "We really must get some kind of storage built into the yard for the pram."

"It's fine to keep it in the hall," Ruby countered.

"You're bleeding." He came over and knelt at her side, his hands gentle as he examined her finger.

"It's nothing."

"I've seen people die from less." He drew her to her feet. "Come and wash it at the sink."

Ruby sighed but let him take her where he willed. He pumped some water into the bowl and eased her hand down into it. The coldness made her catch her breath.

"Does it hurt?" He was so close that his breath stirred the hairs at the back of her neck. "Stay right there. I'll fetch something to clean it out properly."

Ruby waited until he returned with an ominous looking brown bottle. He uncorked the stopper and tipped some into the water. This time she did screech.

"That means it's working." He held out a washcloth. "Dry your hand and let me take another look at it."

"I'm not sure I want you to," Ruby grumbled as he bent over her hand.

"Come now, Mrs. Nash, be brave. I won't even charge you."

"One would hope not," Ruby said. "Seeing as I was injured while attempting to darn your sock."

He lightly kissed her knuckles. "I appreciate that."

Her thumb was throbbing slightly. She wasn't sure if it was from the wound or the treatment.

He produced a strip of linen from his pocket and wrapped it tightly around her thumb before securing it with a complicated knot.

"I suggest you keep it like this while you're working today," he said as he reclaimed his bottle and headed for the door. "It should be fine by bedtime."

"Thank you." Ruby had to shout after him as he was moving at some speed.

Maybe she wasn't the only person struck dumb by their nighttime confidences. She couldn't deny that his physical closeness made her yearn for things she thought she'd renounced forever, but did he feel the same? Of course he did; he was a man. But the thought of another pregnancy made her shudder.

His door shut with a bang, and she knew she wouldn't see him until dinnertime. If he'd intended to get himself something to eat, she'd foiled his plan. Ruby went over to the pantry, extracted a loaf of bread, some butter, and the sliced ham from the cold store, and set about making sandwiches.

By the time Bridget returned, she'd brewed a pot of tea and opened a jar of Alice's pickles. She set out three plates and a bowl for Nora, who had recently been introduced to gruel and porridge.

"Thank you, ma'am!" Bridget said as she settled Nora into the highchair at the end of the table. "You didn't need to do that."

"I was making Dr. Nash something for his midday meal and thought I might as well finish up the ham." Ruby pointed at the tray. "Could you possibly take that through to the doctor while I start feeding Nora?"

"Least I can do when you've made me lunch." Bridget winked at her. "And some of those nice pickles, too!"

LATER THAT EVENING, after Nora and Bridget had retired to the top floor, Charles sat opposite Ruby in the parlor, his boots stretched close to the warmth of the hearth, his stomach full of beef stew and vastly improved dumplings. If he hadn't been stupid enough to offer to bed his wife and scare her out of the damn thing, he would've been heartily content. He glanced over at Ruby. She was reading a book, her brow slightly creased as she turned a page, her face serene in the lamplight.

"Did Nora enjoy her outing?"

Ruby briefly looked up. "I believe so. Bridget took her to the new park."

He waited but she didn't elaborate. "Is your thumb feeling any better?"

"It is, thank you."

"Excellent." He stared into the fire, his fingers drumming on the arms of his chair. "Did I mention that I intend to find another physician at some point so that I don't have to be on call all night?"

"Can you afford to do so?"

"Not yet." She nodded and he continued. "As you are the person doing the accounts, ma'am, you would know that better than anyone."

She set her book to one side and looked at him. "You need more patients who can pay you immediately."

He shrugged. "That's not always possible."

"I'm well aware of that. It took me months to pay back the doctor who attended me during Nora's birth."

"You had a doctor in attendance?"

She raised her eyebrows, and he hastened to qualify his remark. "Most women use midwives or have family members present at births."

"I had no one," Ruby said. "Sidney decided to get the doctor when he returned home and found me laboring alone. It didn't occur to him to ask how much it would cost or how we would pay for it."

Charles grimaced.

"It was not a pleasant experience," Ruby said. "In truth, I cannot imagine going through it again."

"I believe a lot of women feel like that," Charles said cautiously. "And it's quite understandable. I've little time for men who think their wives need to be constantly pregnant to keep them occupied."

She took a quick breath and looked down at her hands which were twisted together in her lap. "It is part of the reason why I am reluctant to recommence the activities that lead to pregnancy."

"Ah." Charles nodded. "I see."

He paused to gather his thoughts, aware that it was not the time to blurt out the first thing that came into his head or to joyfully grab his wife's hand and head upstairs.

"As a physician, I am well aware of... practices that might help avoid conception."

"I thought that was illegal."

He shrugged. "As far as I am concerned, what happens between a man and his wife is between them, and nothing to do with a court of law."

"Can you not be prosecuted for offering such advice?"

"I believe so." He smiled. "I regret to say that it won't stop me from doing it. I've seen the misery multiple pregnancies cause." He waited until she lifted her head and looked at him before saying, "If I am understanding you correctly, Mrs. Nash, would you be willing to consider such... advice?"

She held his gaze. "I might be."

"I'm glad to hear it." He hesitated. "As a physician, I have to note that no method of anti-conception except the complete removal of the womb is guaranteed to work."

"Or castration."

Charles shuddered. "Actually—"

She held up her hand. "I'd rather not hear the details, thank you." She rose to her feet. "I think I might go to bed."

He stood as well, and she came over to kiss his cheek. He wrapped his arm around her waist and she went still.

"Do you wish to start tonight?" he asked.

"I thought you needed time to research your options."

"We don't have to do everything at once," he murmured. He kissed her until she sighed and kissed him back, her body leaning into his like it belonged there. "I've always enjoyed experimenting."

She eased out of his arms and turned toward the door. "Goodnight, Dr. Nash."

He waited until her footsteps faded on the stairs and took his cup out to the kitchen. It was foggy outside, the gloom illuminated by a single recently installed streetlamp. Mr. Hepworth had assured Charles that the rest of the street would soon be filled with respectable people and their new houses. At the moment, it was a building site, and it attracted all sorts of undesirables trying to steal anything not nailed in place.

He took his time checking the locks on all the doors and made sure his medical supplies were safely hidden away. During his time as a physician, he'd come across patients who craved the drugs he offered like gamblers craved a new wager. It was most disconcerting. He'd heard tales of respectable women stealing bottles of laudanum and morphine and drinking the contents in one swallow. In such a volatile area as Millcastle, it paid to be cautious. The navvies Mr. Hepworth employed to build his railways were infamously light fingered and prone to violence. He'd patched up the wounds from more than one fight between rival gangs or townsfolk.

He returned to the parlor and made sure the fire was out before banking up the stove and heading up to bed. He paused on the landing, his gentlemanly instinct to knock warring with his conviction that a man shouldn't have to beg for entrance into his own bedroom. He wanted her and he wanted to make things right.

He stepped inside and immediately stopped. Ruby had left a candle burning at the side of the bed and sat up against her pillows. She had taken down her hair and left it loose on her shoulders.

"Oh, you're awake."

She fixed him with a challenging stare. "Would you prefer it if I blew out the candle and pretended I was asleep?"

"No." He fumbled with his neckcloth's knot. "Absolutely not."

He made no effort to fold his clothes and only remembered to put on his nightshirt when Ruby looked at him somewhat apprehensively.

"Are you afraid?" he asked as he climbed into bed beside her.

"Of you? Not particularly." She paused. "But am I alarmed at what I'm contemplating *doing* with you? God, yes."

He leaned in and cupped her cheek. "I promise you I'll do everything in my power to prevent contraception."

She still looked skeptical, and he didn't blame her. Men had held this power over women since time began. He'd seen plenty of men use it to keep women in their place. Mill owners preferred to employ women because they could be paid lower wages. Mothers would put up with the worst conditions simply to feed their children, and their children were employable, too.

"As I said, we're not in any rush," Charles said. "It's not as if I'm in need of an heir..." He stopped, aware that his father might disagree about that. He still hadn't heard back from the old man, and he'd been married for three months.

He kissed Ruby's mouth. "If you'd prefer it, we can extinguish the candle."

"No, thank you."

He smiled into her eyes. "That's my girl." He stroked his index finger down from her chin to her throat and felt her shiver in response. "I believe it's time to make your proper acquaintance. I've barely touched you below the neck."

She made a huffing sound. "Apart from when I arrived at Caroline's house, and you examined me."

"That doesn't count." He kissed his way down her neck. "I prefer my women to be well when I caress them, and I certainly wouldn't want a reputation for molesting my patients."

"You were always very professional," Ruby reassured him. "Positively disinterested."

He paused, his fingers lingering on her shoulder. "You have my full permission to touch me back."

"I fully intend to."

They smiled at each other, and he allowed his hand to drift lower and cup her breast, his thumb finding her already hard nipple. He watched her face as he circled it, and she caught her breath.

"May I see more?"

She nodded and he unbuttoned her starched night dress until he could pull it over her head. His gaze went to her small breasts and taut nipples, and with an appreciative murmur, he bent his head and licked her. She startled, one hand coming into his hair to hold him closer. He took the invitation with a growl and sucked her nipple into his mouth, his hand on her other breast, his fingernail grazing her tender flesh as she gasped his name.

He forgot everything except the taste, texture, and scent of her, his mouth busy, his fingers echoing every motion until her hand tightened painfully in his hair. He slid his palm down to her hip, pushing the bedclothes to one side in his haste to claim new territory.

"Ruby, I want—"

He didn't need to finish the sentence, as she grabbed his hand and put it between her legs where she was already wet for him. Even as his cock throbbed against the constraints of his nightshirt, he reminded himself to slow down and not frighten her. He took several deep breaths and gently disentangled her fingers from his hair.

"Lie back for me."

She did as he asked, her gaze never leaving his face, her body flushed a rosy pink from his attentions. He eased between her thighs and set one of her feet on his shoulder.

She frowned. "What are you doing?"

She stifled a shriek as he bent his head, roughly tongued her already swollen clit, and sucked it into his mouth. He couldn't quite believe it when she stiffened and climaxed against his lips without him even penetrating her. God, he wanted to be inside her so badly, but his fingers and tongue would have to suffice for now.

"Charles…"

He sat back a little so that he could see her face while he pressed two fingers inside her. She gasped and grabbed hold of his wrist.

"Too much?" His fingers slipped in and out in a regular rhythm aided by the press of his thumb on her clit. "Do you wish me to stop?"

"I…"

She came again, and he added a third finger and bent to lick her taut bud as he increased his pace. She went rigid again, and he marveled at her sensuality as he felt another clenching of her passage around his fingers. He slid his free hand under his night shirt and roughly stroked his cock, which was dripping wet with the need to come, and timed his action to coincide with her final climax.

With a groan, he collapsed onto the bed beside her and took several quick breaths. He'd never touched a more responsive woman in his life. By some miracle, she was not only his wife, but apparently willing to allow his attentions.

She suddenly sat up and blew out the candle.

"Are you all right?" Charles asked.

In response, she cuddled against his side. He put his arm around her to draw her even closer. He inhaled the lemony scent of her hair and the warmth from her skin. He took another deep breath and simply enjoyed the sensations coursing through his body. He'd almost fallen asleep when she stirred against him.

"Sidney never did… that," Ruby whispered.

"Any of it?" Charles opened his eyes. "One has to wonder how you got pregnant, then."

"He was quite competent at that part," Ruby said.

Charles considered how to ask the obvious question in an acceptable manner. "Are you saying he didn't believe in… a first course or a pre-dinner cocktail?"

"You mean, did he just get straight on with his dinner?"

"Yes, exactly."

He only realized she was laughing when the bed started shaking.

"What on earth?"

She came up on one elbow and looked down at him, her hair pooling on his chest. "I meant he never put his mouth *there*."

"Then poor old Sidney missed out on one of those most satisfying experiences a man can have," Charles countered. "And his loss is my gain."

She was still laughing softly as she settled onto her side again. "I never know quite what to expect of you, Dr. Nash."

"Good." He kissed the top of her head. "Now go to sleep. It's Sunday tomorrow, and we promised to visit your sister at Grafton Hall after we attend church."

CHAPTER NINE

*A*fter retrieving the post from the front door, Ruby entered the kitchen and almost shrieked when an unknown woman rose from the kitchen table.

"Sorry to bother you, ma'am, but I can't find the doctor."

On closer inspection, the woman was more of a child wearing her mother's best hat and tatty jewelry, but Ruby didn't relax. In Millcastle, children were just as likely to be thieves as adults.

"Dr. Nash's consulting room is at the back of the house," Ruby explained, not for the first time. "Perhaps you might see if he is there?"

The girl bit her rouged lip. "He's not."

"There is a notice on the backdoor clearly stating this house is a private residence."

"He lives here, though, don't he?"

"Yes, but he's not here, and even if he was, he'd be telling you to leave."

The girl started crying, and Ruby suppressed a sigh and held out her handkerchief. "There's no need for that. Just go and wait in the courtyard. He'll probably be back in a tick."

"I can't wait." The girl's glance flew to the clock on the mantelpiece. "I have to get back or I'll be missed."

"Do you have an address where Dr. Nash can visit you?" Ruby found a pencil and a scrap of paper and looked inquiringly at the girl. "I can give him a message if it's urgent."

"He won't come to our place."

"He might surprise you," Ruby said gently. "Where are your family living now?"

"Never had a family, ma'am. Got brought here on a cart when I was five with fifty other orphans and was set to work in the mill."

Ruby sat down. "I assume you're no longer at the mill?"

"I hated it in there and the boys… they wouldn't stop bothering me. I decided if I had to put up with that, I'd rather be paid for it."

Ruby nodded. She'd suspected as much. It wasn't the first time she'd met a young woman who'd been taken in by the factory system to work their life away for pennies. And where could a girl go after that? She either married, became a prostitute, or ended up in the workhouse, because no decent family would hire a nobody to work in their home.

"If you give me your name and address, I'm sure Dr. Nash would be willing to visit you," Ruby said. "If you tell me what it is, I can write it for you."

"I can read and write." The girl snatched the paper and pen from Ruby and scribbled something down. "I still don't think he'll want to touch us lot with a bargepole so I'll come back when I can."

Ruby took back the piece of paper and read the message. "It's been nice to meet you, Tess."

Tess stood up. "Are you his missus?"

"Yes."

"They said he was posh," Tess added as she turned toward the door. "But so are you."

Ruby followed her to the door, aware that the two currant buns she'd left on the table for Charles's tea had disappeared. There didn't seem to be anything else missing, which was a relief. She made sure to lock the backdoor after Tess left and reminded herself not to forget in the future. If she'd left her purse out on the dresser, she might have lost more than a plate of food. She propped the piece of paper up against the tea pot to remind herself to give it to Charles. The address was in one of the poorest parts of Millcastle. Ruby suspected it was a house of ill-repute, not that it would bother her husband. He was willing to treat anyone—something she admired greatly.

It only occurred to her later when she needed her handkerchief to wipe Nora's nose that the girl had taken off with that as well...

WHEN CHARLES eventually returned home it was past Nora's bedtime, and he wasn't in the best of moods. Ruby served him his overcooked dinner and sat opposite while he told her about his latest foray in the navvy camp where a drunken brawl had ended in two broken limbs, the loss of an eye, and a lopped-off finger.

"I told Hepworth he needs to stop them selling spirits at the camp, but he laughed and said he makes a tidy profit off it. I asked if it was worth the loss of four of his workforce, and he had no answer for that." Dr. Nash drank his tea. "Sometimes I wonder why I bother."

"Because Mr. Hepworth at least pays your bills on time," Ruby reminded him. "And how he chooses to run his business is not your concern."

"I'm surprised at you, ma'am. I would've thought you all for workers' rights against their employers."

"That was Sidney's cause, not mine."

He raised an eyebrow. "I'm still surprised."

"I've been poor, Dr. Nash. I know what I prefer." She poured him another cup of tea and slid the piece of paper over to him. "I had a visitor today."

He read the name and address and looked up at her. "I assume she wants me to visit her?"

"She had to get back. She didn't think you'd come to her place of residence, but I assured her that you would."

"It's probably a whorehouse," he said bluntly.

"I guessed as much." Ruby hesitated. "She was very young."

"Of course, she was." Charles grimaced. "Just how the clients like them. I'd best wait until morning. They won't thank me for interfering with their livelihood, and it might be embarrassing if I bump into someone I know."

Ruby reached across the table and took his hand. "You are a good man, Dr. Nash."

"I prefer to see myself as a sinner who is trying to repent."

"How did you sin?"

He sat back releasing her hand. "In too many ways to bore you with, my dear."

"Haven't we all sinned?" she asked, slightly hurt by his refusal to share his confidences with her. "I know I was willing to do anything to make sure Nora survived."

"Anything?"

"Are you asking if I would've prostituted myself to buy her food? Of course, I would've done so." Ruby met his skeptical stare head on. "My sister took employment as Francis's book-keeper so that we could continue to pay our rent."

"That's hardly the same, is it? She took an offer of employment." He paused. "Ah, but this was Francis. I assume that wasn't all he expected of her. What a complete bastard."

"She owed him money. It was the only way to pay off the debt and ensure that the rest of us didn't end up in the workhouse." Ruby grimaced. "She tried to hide it from us, but it was patently obvious what had really happened."

"That's why I'm willing to treat anyone who asks for my help," Charles said slowly. "I am fully aware that life can deal a person a series of blows that might overwhelm the strongest of characters, let alone the weakest."

It went far too quiet for his liking, and when he looked up, Ruby was smiling at him, her expression tender.

"You *are* a good man, Dr. Nash."

"Hardly." He cleared his throat and looked around the kitchen. "Is there no pudding?"

"Our afternoon visitor helped herself to both of the currant buns I had saved for you. And the plate."

Charles looked pained. "The plate?"

"She'll be able to sell it for a few coins."

"Why did you let her come in here?"

"I didn't. She must have let herself in the back when I was speaking to the postman on the front step."

His scowl was immediate. "I told you to lock the back door to stop any incursion into the house."

"I know you did, and I'm sorry." She met his furious gaze. "I'd just sent Bridget and Nora off for their walk and forgot to lock the door behind them."

"It could've been someone with violence on his mind."

"As I said, I'm sorry," Ruby repeated evenly. "It certainly gave me a shock."

"Good." He set down his cup with some force.

Ruby set her jaw. "Would you like to see the rest of the post, or shall I take it through to your study for the morning?"

"I'll have it now, please. I don't want to give you any more reasons for leaving the backdoor unlocked."

She went over to the dresser and retrieved the stack of letters. "You have some from London and one that is franked."

He took the letters and sorted them out, his fingers lingering over the London ones before finally settling on the old-fashioned folded square with the seal and scrawled signature in the corner.

"This is from my father." He used his knife to slit the wax seal and opened the letter. "It's written by his secretary. He didn't even bother to sign it."

"And what does it say?" Ruby asked.

"That we are to present ourselves for his inspection at Nash Hall in two weeks' time." He set the letter down on the table. "Typical. I've told him on several occasions that I can't just walk away from my job, but he refuses to believe me."

"From the little you have told me about him, I assume no one has ever disobeyed an order from him in his life," Ruby said. "He's probably quite unaware how having a paid occupation works."

"Don't make excuses for him."

"I'm not. He simply sounds like a typical aristocrat—used to giving orders and having them instantly obeyed."

He looked at her for a long moment. "Just like Francis."

She shrugged. "He certainly does have his autocratic tendencies, but he's also ruthless."

"And you think my father is not?" Charles shoved a hand through his hair and sighed. "I'm too tired to deal with this tonight, and I'll have to talk to Hepworth about taking some leave." He stood and held out his hand. "Come to bed."

"You go up and I'll join you when I have secured the house," Ruby said. "It won't take me but a moment."

He nodded, came over to kiss her cheek, and went up the stairs, taking care to be quiet and not wake the occupants of the nursery floor. After Ruby checked the backdoor was locked and banked up the stove, she gathered up the post and set it back on the dresser. She'd noticed that anything with a London address made him tense and wondered why. If there was a reason he'd suddenly left London and decided to set up his practice in Millcastle, he hadn't shared it with her.

But he didn't share much about his previous life with her, even though he knew what had happened to her quite well. She had a sense he was hiding things, but did she want to know what they were? They'd married each other for pragmatic reasons, not love. If keeping such secrets were important to him then she wouldn't pry. She had enough secrets of her own.

THE NEXT DAY, Charles sorted through his letters and set aside the ones showing his accounts had been paid in full. He'd started paying off his debts years ago, but the high rates of interest meant he'd barely scratched the capital. He'd kept doing it out of some desperate need to restore his reputation as an honest man, even if it was just for himself.

In one sweep of his pen, his father had paid everything off, but the thought gave Charles no pleasure. In truth, it had been easier paying professional lenders than being beholden to his father, who intended to use the loans to blackmail his own son into obedience.

He placed the letters in the locked drawer of his desk and contemplated the other letter. It was of a more pleasurable nature from an old acquaintance at medical school. Malcolm Fraser was planning a visit to the midlands with an eye to setting up his own practice in one of the thriving industrial towns. If Charles had anything to do with it, he'd make sure Malcolm had Millcastle on his list.

He wrote back, aware of the quietness around him. His patients tended to be a loud and misbehaved lot, and by the time he'd finished his letter, the noise in the courtyard had grown to a rumble topped by the high-pitched cry of a child.

His reputation as a physician willing to see anyone had spread quickly amongst the lower orders. He was already wondering how to manage the number of patients who turned up to see him every day—they would quickly overwhelm his home visits to his more upper-class patients. The working class rarely had enough money to pay him his full fee and offered him the smallest coins, promissory notes, and bartered items. Ruby thought he should be more insistent about payment, but it went against his beliefs. She argued that he had the luxury of a private income to insure him against risk and that if he continued to be so lenient, he would be seen as a greenhorn ripe for easy pickings.

She was probably right. He went to open the door, and as he looked out over the jostling crowd who'd already begun shouting at him, he sighed. She'd also said he needed someone to keep the patients in order and she wasn't wrong about that, either.

He raised his voice. "You know the drill. Babies and children first. I'll get to the rest of you, if you form an orderly line and stop heckling me."

A young woman with a baby pushed her way through the muttering crowd. Still glaring at the other patients, Charles stepped aside to allow her to go past him into the surgery.

"He won't stop crying, Doctor, and he's got a fever."

Charles closed the door behind her and concentrated on his job.

HIS FIFTH PATIENT was a young woman who'd obviously been hit hard on the face. He motioned for her to sit down and handed her a wet cloth to staunch the blood trickling down her neck.

"Who hit you?" he asked without preamble. "Your husband?"

"Don't have one of those."

He assessed her clothing and what he could see of her face. "Your client?"

"Wrong again. It was the brothel owner. She didn't want me coming here to see you, and I told her what to do with herself." She shrugged. "I didn't come about me face. I came the other day, but you weren't here."

"Are you Tess?"

"That's me."

"Don't ever go into my house and alarm my wife!" Charles frowned at her. "Or steal my buns."

"I didn't know they were yours, doctor."

Charles didn't even bother to mention the plate or Ruby's handkerchief, because he knew they would've been sold on by now.

"What can I do for you?"

She pointed at her stomach. "I might have got my own bun in the oven."

"Have you stopped your monthly bleeding?"

She looked at him. "I never got that regular, so I don't know whether it's just that, or if something else is going on. That's why I've come to see you."

"Are your breasts tender? Do you have any nausea in the mornings?"

"My, you are a rude one, aren't you?" Tess raised her eyebrows.

"I find it saves time," Charles said. "Can you answer my questions?"

"Working in a whorehouse means my breasts are often tender and some of the clients make me want to puke, alright."

"When did you last bleed?"

She considered him as she counted on her fingers. He reckoned she was no older than fourteen or fifteen years old.

"Five months ago?"

"Is that usual?"

"I don't know, doctor. You're supposed to be the one telling me."

"If you are pregnant, what do you intend to do?" Charles asked.

She went still. "Mrs. Hobbs says I've got to get rid of it."

"I don't do that kind of work."

"I can pay." She took a gold sovereign out of her pocket.

"It's not that." Charles sat back. "It's too dangerous, and it's illegal."

Tess stood up. "Mrs. Hobbs says it's got to *go*. Don't you understand?"

"I'm sorry I can't help you,"

She shook her fist in his face, her body rigid with anger. "I thought you was a good 'un."

"I am." He held her furious gaze. "Please listen to me very carefully. Anyone who says they can help you with this matter is lying. Chances are you'll die from an infection or in a pool of your own blood on their kitchen table."

"You're a horrible man!"

She spun on her heel and left the room, slamming the door behind her. Charles cursed under his breath and went to write up his notes. If anything did happen to Tess, he wanted to make sure that the authorities knew she'd left *his* premises alive and well.

Ruby arrived with a welcome cup of tea for him in her hand.

"Whatever was that about? Your last patient stormed out into the yard and told all those who were waiting that you were a fake and a charlatan."

Charles groaned. "That was your Tess. I refused to end her pregnancy."

"Oh." Ruby set the cup on his desk. "I do hope she doesn't seek help from others."

"I fear she will." Charles took a sip of tea. "She has the means to pay for assistance."

"Mr. Hepworth stopped by on his way to the railway station to say he's happy for you to take a few days off for your trip to Yorkshire." Ruby paused. "Well, not exactly happy, but resigned."

"I feel much the same," Charles admitted. "Thank you for the tea. I'd better get on."

Ruby hesitated as she turned to the door. "Did you think to mention Dr. and Mrs. Brennan to Tess?"

"What about them?" Charles knew Dr. Brennan on a professional level because they dealt with a similar section of society.

Ruby lowered her voice. "I believe they offer some kind of sanctuary to women in need."

"Need of what?"

She shrugged. "Refuge from abusive spouses, brothel madams, unwanted pregnancies…"

"They'll get into trouble if they're doing that," Charles said flatly.

"Surely they're trying to do some good?"

"I'm not doubting their intentions. Please don't get involved with them, Ruby."

She drew herself up. "Is that an order?"

"Yes. Nothing good will come from associating ourselves with people who are flagrantly disregarding the law."

"I thought you were a healer."

He scowled at her. "You know I bloody well am!"

"Except for women forced into the worst of circumstances."

"That's not what I said, or what I meant."

She headed for the door, much in the same manner as Tess had, and he grimaced. "Can we talk about this later? I have—"

She shut the door behind her before he finished speaking, and he found himself cursing again.

There was a loud knock on the door. "Come on. Dr. Nash, get a move on! It's bloody freezing out here!"

CHAPTER TEN

*C*aroline had insisted on lending Ruby her second-best carriage to take them up to Yorkshire. Charles had grumbled, suggesting the mail coach was cheap and perfectly adequate. Caroline had insisted her sister needed to travel in comfort and, as she was looking after Nora and Bridget, Charles had reluctantly agreed.

In order to have the time to make their trip, Charles had worked long hours at the navvy camps and at his home practice. Ruby had barely seen him, let alone had time to continue their somewhat fractious discussion about who she was *allowed* to associate with.

She contemplated his profile as he sat opposite her. In truth, he looked worn out and kept drifting off to sleep as the well-sprung carriage made its way toward the Great North Road. She had no idea what awaited her at Nash Hall and wasn't sure how to ask without being rebuffed again. Caroline had arranged several stops on the journey to change the horses, but they didn't need to stay overnight at an inn. So if Ruby did want information from Charles, she'd have to approach the subject in the privacy of the carriage.

"You're staring at me."

She blinked as he opened his eyes. "Am I not permitted to gaze at my own husband?"

He straightened and smothered a yawn with his hand. "You're looking remarkably serious."

"I haven't left Nora before."

"I don't imagine Caroline will allow anything to go wrong while Nora is in her care."

"I'm sure she won't, but still…"

He surprised her by reaching across and taking her gloved hand. "I'm sorry about all this."

"It's hardly your fault, is it?"

"That's very supportive of you, my dear, but many would say I'm the one who created this problem. My father is very well respected in society. His word carries weight."

There was a warning behind his words she didn't fully understand.

"Powerful men are never easy to deal with," Ruby said. "Look at Francis."

"My father exercises his power in a less direct manner but he is just as ruthless."

Ruby met her husband's gaze. "How should I deal with him, then? Do you wish me to be sweetly compliant and humble, or—"

"Hardly that." his swift smile was immediate. "I cannot quite see you in that role. I'd rather you were just yourself."

"But how much of myself? I am considered to have a sharp tongue by some."

"I want him to accept our marriage as a settled fact. I can't completely alienate him."

"Why not?"

He took his time in replying. "Because as I mentioned, he is an extremely powerful man with a long reach."

"As far as Millcastle?"

"Further than that. Perhaps you should meet him first and draw your own conclusions as to how we should proceed."

"As you wish."

Ruby was far from satisfied as to what awaited her, but at least he'd put her on her guard. For all she knew, Charles's father could be the nicest gentleman in Yorkshire and her husband the black sheep of a respectable family. From all accounts, Sidney's parents had despaired of their wayward son and tried everything to make him return home, but to no avail. Hearing only one side of a story wasn't ideal, and Charles was right that she should reserve judgment until she met the rest of his family.

She wanted to be on his side.

"You're staring at me again." Charles glanced out of the window as the carriage slowed. "Perhaps you'll feel better after your dinner."

Nash Hall was nestled in a hollow surrounded by a dark forest and gentle hills. The sun was setting over the trees as they finally came up the long, winding drive and stopped in front of the entrance, which had a large, arched oak door and well-worn steps.

"Welcome to Nash Hall," Charles murmured as he came around to open the carriage door for her to descend.

Ruby looked up at the grey stone façade with its tower and crenellations and went still.

"Is it very old?"

"Not as old as it claims to be. It was never a functioning castle, but one of my ancestors decided to pretend that it was." He gestured at the uneven ground in front of the house. "At one point I believe there was even a moat and a portcullis."

Even though she was tired, Ruby had to smile at that. Charles knocked on the front door and stood back.

"My father keeps the minimum of staff and the kitchens are far from the door, so it might take a while." He smiled reassuringly at her. "I do hope you aren't too cold."

"I'm quite well." She looked hopefully at the door. "I wouldn't mind a cup of tea, though."

After another long pause, Charles consulted his watch and went back to speak to the coachman, who nodded and set off around the side of the house.

Charles came back to Ruby. "I've sent him off to the stables where I assured him he would receive a far warmer welcome than we have." He took her hand. "Come on, we'll walk around to the kitchen entrance."

Ruby was glad Charles knew the way, because the tall shadows thrown by the house made the pathways difficult to see.

"I'm glad there is no longer a moat," she murmured as she tripped over the edge of a flower border and was only saved by the strength of his support. "Or else I'd surely be in it by now."

They emerged into a square, cobbled courtyard fitted with gas lamps. The back of the mews was on one side with the carriage house adjacent. The third wing looked like a laundry or dairy and was at a right angle to the stone-clad main house.

"Here we are." Charles unlatched the back door and drew her inside. "At least we're out of the wind."

Like most country houses, the servants' areas were fairly bleak and the temperature frigid to save money. The kitchen itself was an exception, with the warmth of a huge open fire and hearth heating the vast space. There were at least eight people working in the kitchen, and whatever they were preparing smelled delicious.

"Mr. Charles!" An older man in livery who had been sitting

beside the fire in the best spot got to his feet in some haste and set his newspaper aside. "I didn't hear the bell!"

"I'm not surprised with all this clatter." Charles smiled at the man who Ruby assumed was the butler. "We left our baggage in the carriage, Benson. Perhaps you can arrange for someone to take it up to our room?"

"Of course, sir. Joseph! Go and fetch their bags!"

"Yes, Mr. Benson." One of the younger men who'd been setting out dusty wine bottles—obviously just brought up from the cellar—rushed out of the room.

"I'll take you through to your father, sir." The butler nodded at Ruby. "Ma'am."

"Thank you."

Ruby noted how easily Charles dealt with the servants and wondered what the butler would think if he could see his master's son with his sleeves rolled up washing the dinner plates and pots in the sink at their modest home. No wonder Charles had assumed she'd want a full staff. He'd obviously grown up surrounded by them.

They passed through the green baize door into a different world of soft carpets, gilded lamps, and walls filled with paintings. The exterior of the house might be stark, but there was no lack of money to maintain the interior. Not for the first time, Ruby wondered exactly what kind of family she had married into.

The butler paused at a door at the end of yet another corridor and knocked before opening it. "My lord, Mr. Charles has arrived."

"Thank you."

The butler stepped aside and they entered the book-lined study. A warm fire burned in the stone fireplace and four dogs slept on the rug in front of it. An older man, who had the same beak of a nose as Charles, sat behind a vast mahogany desk. He looked up as they approached but didn't rise to his feet. His gaze was as wintry as the outside of his house.

"Charles."

"Father. This is Ruby, my wife."

"So, I see." His disinterested gaze ran over her rather as if she was a disobedient parlor maid about to be let go without a reference. "I'd like to say it's a pleasure, ma'am, but we both know that would be a lie."

Charles said, "Regardless of your feelings on this matter, Father, I expect you to treat my wife with respect."

"Respect is earned." His father's voice was cold, devoid of any emotion.

"Then I am delighted to tell you that she has earned mine. I couldn't wish for a better helpmate in life."

Ruby smiled at him and then at his father. "I'm sure you don't need me to tell you what a remarkable man you son is, sir. His medical knowledge and his compassion are highly valued in Millcastle."

"Indeed."

She noticed he still hadn't met her gaze.

"I will see you at dinner in an hour's time, Charles. Your mother will be attending, so you can introduce your bride to her then." He picked up his pen and appeared to lose interest in them.

Charles took her hand and they left the room. When she judged they were well out of earshot she stopped walking. "Why did the butler call your father 'my lord'?"

Charles sighed. "He's an earl."

"Doesn't that mean…?"

"Yes." He started walking again. "Come along. It's easy to get lost in this place and I've no idea which room the butler has put us in."

∾

CHARLES LOOKED out of the window as Ruby had a long discussion with the maid about pressing their clothing and their breakfast habits. They'd been put in what had once been his bedroom—now redecorated in muted floral wallpaper and devoid of anything he'd cared about or used. The view was still excellent and the ivy growing up the outside of the house would probably still be strong enough to bear his weight if he wanted to escape.

Not that he could escape…a painful but necessary lesson he'd been learning for the past few years. He had responsibilities now—a wife, a daughter, a good reputation, and people who depended on him for their medical care.

"Thank you, Iris." Ruby finished speaking to the maid, who left with a smile and a curtsy.

Charles turned around. "Well done. You handled her perfectly."

"I am well aware that my every utterance and action will be discussed to death in the servants' hall. They're all probably expecting me to be a disaster."

"I'd love to disagree with you, but I suspect you're right." He turned fully to look at her. "What did you think of the old man?"

"Your father?" She considered him. "A hard man to please."

"Always."

She put her discarded cloak away in the cupboard. "Dinner is served at six, which seems quite early. Iris intimated that we should not be late."

"My father doesn't appreciate tardiness."

"Neither do I." She came over and took his hand. "Are you all right?"

"Not particularly."

"There is nothing he can do to break our marriage contract. If I continue to behave myself, I'm sure he'll accept defeat."

"He never has before." Charles moved restlessly away from her.

"I doubt he'll murder me in cold blood."

"I wouldn't place a wager on it."

Ruby sighed. "I begin to understand why you don't come here very often. You are being remarkably negative."

He opened his mouth to reply and then reconsidered his answer. Ruby was the one who needed protecting, not him, and he was behaving in a most ungrateful manner.

"Perhaps being back in my old bedroom brings out the worst in me."

"This was your room?" She looked around the muted interior. "I cannot imagine you here at all."

"It's been redecorated to erase my obnoxious presence," Charles said. "I wonder what happened to my possessions?"

"Perhaps your mother will know." Ruby sat down to take off her boots.

"I doubt it. She never concerned herself much with mundane household matters."

"How nice for her." Ruby wiggled her toes. "I suppose we should dress for dinner?"

"If we wish to make the right impression, yes."

She looked up at him, her expression quizzical. "Is it important to you that we are accepted here? I thought you hated the place."

"I do hate it, but I have... obligations." She continued to stare at him and he continued. "To my mother."

"Not to the title and your father?"

He shuddered. "Never."

She consulted the dainty watch broach Caroline had given her for Christmas and stood up. "It isn't that late. Do you think I have time for a nap before dinner?"

"How can you be tired after all those hours confined in the carriage?" Charles asked.

She unbuttoned the top buttons of her high-collared blouse and yawned. "I don't know. I just am."

"Let me help you." He went to her side and continued the pleasurable task of unbuttoning her. "Do you intend to leave your corset on?"

"You can just loosen the strings for me."

He reached behind her and drew her close, bringing her against his chest as he searched for the bow of her corset. He dropped a kiss on her bared shoulder. "Are you sure you want to nap?"

"I thought you wanted us to be respectable?"

"Arriving at my father's dining table after thoroughly bedding you has its appeal."

She eased back, and he was relieved to see she was smiling.

"I could just relax you a little if that would help?" He undid the bow and kept his hands around her waist, his thumbs caressing her flesh.

"You are a devil," she murmured, her voice low. "I think I am rather too nervous to indulge in anything of a physical nature."

"That's a pity." He kissed the top of her head and stepped away. "Perhaps I'll take the opportunity to check in at the stables and make sure Caroline's coachman is being treated half as well as the horses."

"Excellent." Ruby climbed onto the bed and heaved a sigh. "Please wake me up at least an hour before we are due to go down. I do want to look my best for you."

AT FIVE MINUTES to six they descended the stairs. Ruby wore her best plum-colored silk gown with a paisley shawl draped over her shoulders. Caroline had insisted on lending her a set of garnet jewelry to wear with the dress and, after seeing the grandeur of the place, Ruby was glad she had accepted the offer. Charles wore full dining attire that had appeared magically pressed and laid out on the bed after he'd taken his bath. He looked very handsome, but his smile was absent, and his grip on her hand was almost painful.

She paused at the bottom of the stairs to look up at him and straighten his cravat. "It will be fine. I promise I'll behave."

"It's not you I'm worried about," he muttered. "My father and I can barely manage five minutes of conversation before one of us loses their temper."

She reached up to cup his freshly shaven cheek. "There is no reason for you to be angry, my dear. You are a happily married man coming home to show off his bride to his parents, and that's all there is to it."

He surprised her by smiling. "I appreciate you, my love."

"Good, because remember we are on the same side."

She placed her gloved hand on his sleeve and they went into the drawing room as the clock struck six. There was a small group gathered around the fireplace with Charles's father in the center.

"Good evening," Charles was all smiles as he turned to the first couple on his left. "May I present Mrs. Nash to you, vicar and Mrs. Theydon?"

"A pleasure, I'm sure." A woman who was slightly older than Ruby and much younger than her husband curtsied and offered Ruby her hand. "Congratulations on your marriage."

"Thank you." Ruby smiled warmly in return.

"I have only been married to my dearest Ernest for three years, so I still feel like a bride myself." She laughed and patted her husband's arm. "At least that's how Ernest makes me feel."

"How lovely," Ruby replied as the vicar smiled and nodded.

Charles drew her away and took her to meet an older woman seated by the fire. "This is my Great Aunt Isabel."

"Nice to see you married at last, young man, and ready to do your duty to your family and your title."

"Hardly that, aunt," Charles murmured.

His aunt frowned. "What's that you said?"

He increased his volume. "Nothing of import, dear one."

Great Aunt Isabel looked Ruby up and down. "She looks healthy and has good, wide hips."

"That's exactly what I thought when I saw her." Charles nodded. Ruby tried not to look at him in case she smiled.

"Where are you from, girl? What's your family?"

"My family name is Delisle, ma'am. I believe we can trace our ancestry back to the Norman conquest."

"Good stock." Great Aunt Isabel nodded. "And she speaks nicely." She turned to Charles. "She'll do much better than that child Augustus wished to foist on you, and I'll tell him so myself."

"I'd appreciate it if you did," Charles bent to kiss her cheek.

"Where's your mother?"

"I expect she'll be here in a moment," Charles said.

"She's always late." Great Aunt Isabel snorted. "Always with her head in the clouds,"

Ruby followed Charles over to where the earl was standing with a short man with large whiskers and a pugnacious expression.

"Good evening, sir. Lambton." Charles inclined his head before turning to Ruby. "Mr. Lambton is father's secretary and land agent."

"Pleasure to meet you. Mrs. Nash, and many felicitations on your recent marriage." Mr. Lambton bowed to Ruby.

"Thank you," Ruby said. "I consider myself a very lucky woman."

"Good evening, Mrs. Nash." The earl looked her over without favor.

"My lord." She curtsied.

He returned his attention to his son. "I would appreciate a word with you both in my study after dinner."

"Of course, sir."

The butler appeared at the door. "Dinner is served."

An older couple Ruby hadn't yet met—whom she assumed were some kind of family connection—went in ahead of them.

Charles paused at the door, looked back over his shoulder, and murmured, "Where is my mother?"

A figure appeared in the hall beyond the drawing room and waved at Charles. After a brief hesitation, they continued into the dining room and Charles pulled out a chair for Ruby.

"Who was that?" she asked as he placed her napkin on her lap.

"Miss Evans, my mother's companion. I assume she'll be bringing my mother in with her shortly."

After a few moments, the door opened again, and two women came through, the first rather plain and the other... was probably the most beautiful woman Ruby had ever seen in the flesh. She hardly looked old enough to be Charles's mother.

"I'm so sorry I'm late." The countess smiled as she took her place at the foot of the table in a flutter of floating draperies. "Time always gets away from me."

She glanced down the table at her husband who looked unamused and her smile faltered. "I really do apologize."

Charles, who was seated on her right, took her hand and patted it, his voice surprisingly gentle. "We'd barely sat down, Mama. There is nothing to worry about."

She grabbed his hand and squeezed it. "Martha said you had returned. How wonderful! I hear you have taken a bride."

Charles nodded. "May I present you to my mother, Ruby? She has always been my staunchest defender."

She turned to Ruby and considered her, a smile in her sapphire-blue eyes. "It is such a pleasure to meet you, my dear. If Charles chose you, I know you must be very special indeed."

"Thank you for welcoming me to your house," Ruby replied.

"It scarcely feels like my house," the countess said lightly.

"I've never felt quite at home here, but I believe Paul is very proud of it."

The footmen served the first course and corresponding wine, and then stepped back to line the wall as if awaiting the slightest command. Ruby had thought Caroline's dining arrangements formal, but they were nothing compared to the earl's. There appeared to be at least ten sets of cutlery to navigate, and as each end started with a spoon, she wasn't quite sure where to start. She glanced across the table at Charles who was conversing softly with his mother.

Beside her, Miss Evans cleared her throat and picked up the spoon at the outer edge of the array. "I do hope you had a good journey north, Mrs. Nash."

"Yes, it went very well." Ruby grabbed her own outer spoon and set it in her soup.

"Lady Lavinia was thrilled to hear of the viscount's marriage."

"Viscount?" Ruby asked.

Miss Evans looked amused. "I believe that is the designated title for the oldest son of an earl—not that Dr. Nash would ever use it, but I didn't want to presume."

"That makes me a viscountess." Ruby forgot about her soup and stared in horror at Miss Evans.

"It's only an honorary title until your husband inherits the earldom." Miss Evans looked across the table at Charles. "Did he not mention it to you?"

Ruby shook her head and started on her soup, which was delicious. By the time she'd regained her composure, two more courses had come and gone, and it was her turn to converse with the countess. Even she knew that talking across the table at her husband would be impolite, and considering what she wanted to say to him, probably ill-advised. He did catch her eye occasionally and offered her an encouraging smile, but she wasn't fully prepared to forgive him.

"I am sorry I was unable to attend your wedding," Lady Lavinia said. "My ill health means that traveling very far is impossible for me."

Up close, it was obvious that the countess's beauty was of a fragile nature and her claims of illness would account for the focus of care she was receiving from those around her.

"We had a very small wedding, my lady, but I know that Charles would've wished you to be there."

"He's a good boy." Lady Lavinia glanced fondly at her son. "Despite what his father says. I'm sure you will make him very happy."

"I intend to do my best, my lady."

"That is all I require." She patted Ruby's hand and sat back. "Martha? I am quite fatigued. Will you tell one of the footmen to inform the earl that I intend to go back to bed?"

Miss Evans failed to conceal her start of surprise or her apprehension at her employer's request. "With all due respect, my lady, I don't think the earl would take it kindly if you left during dinner. Would it be possible for you to wait until the ladies withdraw? We should be done quite soon."

"But I'm tired," Her voice rose slightly, drawing Charles's attention away from his conversation with Mrs. Theydon.

"Is everything all right?" Charles looked at Miss Evans and then at his mother.

"I want to be done with this," Lady Lavinia said in an urgent tone. "Martha doesn't want to help me escape."

"I'd be very sad if you left me now, Mama. I'm enjoying your company so much," Charles spoke quietly but compellingly. "Can you bear it a little longer just for me?"

She sighed, her lips quivering, her glance anywhere but at the head of the table where the earl was now staring at her with gathering disapproval.

"Will he be very displeased if I leave?"

"You know he will, Mama," Charles said softly. "Please stay."

"As you wish." She swallowed, her eyes bright with tears. "He'll still be angry with me whatever I do, but I don't want to draw his attention to you."

"I'm too big for him to beat now, Mama," Charles said.

She looked at him. "There are many ways to break someone's spirit, my dear, not all of them physical."

"I am aware of that." His smile had gone. "But remember this, if you ever decide you cannot bear it, you can always come to me."

Ruby decided to risk adding her voice to what was a very intimate conversation between mother and son, and softly said, "Charles is correct, my lady. You will always be welcome in our home."

Even as she made the offer, she was mentally attempting to rearrange her rooms to accommodate a woman used to a house full of servants and a constant companion. But if Charles wanted his mother with them, she wouldn't stand in his way. From what she had observed on her first evening at Nash Hall, the earl was a cold, unpleasant man who openly found his beautiful wife distasteful. Was it any wonder that the countess was like a plant starved of light and air?

The countess merely picked at her food and smiled, but she made no more mention of leaving, which meant that Ruby had more time to observe her fellow guests and absorb the grandness of her setting. How must it have been for Charles growing up in such a place? She already had a sense that he found the whole idea of inheriting the earldom distasteful, but was it even avoidable? She wasn't sure.

She was glad when the countess rose from her seat and smiled at the ladies. "Shall we adjourn to the drawing room?"

Ruby stood and followed her out with the others. They traversed several corridors before the countess went into another very grand room with a piano in one corner and three large windows overlooking the gardens. The walls were hung with green silk that depicted small birds and climbing plants in immense detail. There were silver and gold threads within the fabric that caught the gaslight and shimmered.

"It's like being outside, isn't it?" Miss Evans, who seemed to have made herself Ruby's helpmate, murmured. "I confess it is my favorite room."

"I've never seen anything like it," Ruby said. "My sister Caroline lives in a grand house, but it is nothing compared to this."

"The earl is very proud of his heritage."

"I can see why." Ruby paused. "I should imagine that can be hard to live up to for those around him."

Miss Evans's gaze went to the countess, who had taken her seat by the fireplace behind the tea trays. She hadn't poured any tea and was staring at the door as if wishing she could escape.

"I'd better go and help her distribute the tea," Miss Evans said.

"May I assist you?"

"Perhaps you might sit with the countess and engage her in conversation." Miss Evans hesitated. "If we can persuade her to remain at least until the gentlemen come in, I think the earl would be satisfied."

HAVING RECEIVED permission from the earl to absent herself, the countess blew a kiss to Charles and left the room. Charles barely had time to drink a cup of tea before the butler was at his side asking him to attend his father. He found Ruby, took her hand in his, made their excuses, and followed the butler to his study.

There were no gaslights burning, just a branch of candles reflecting in the mirror above the fireplace. They illuminated everything in the room except the man behind the desk. The earl had a glass of brandy at his side and a series of papers open in front of him.

"Please sit down."

They complied. Charles kept hold of Ruby's hand.

"I have decided to accept your marriage as valid."

Charles wanted to make some sarcastic remark, but reminded himself he had Ruby to think of now and that his father accepting the marriage was essential.

"I still believe Miss Barton would have been a superior choice." He paused to look at Ruby. "Did he mention Miss Barton to you, Mrs. Nash? I suspect he didn't. My son isn't known for his honesty."

"Charles did mention you had chosen a bride for him, yes," Ruby said. "But as we'd already acknowledged our feelings for each other, I was fairly certain whom he would choose." She smiled up at Charles and squeezed his hand. He desperately wanted to kiss her. "In truth, being forced to make a choice about his bride helped to make the decision to marry me easier."

"Indeed." The earl glanced down at the papers on his desk. "From what I have discovered, your family are hardly what I would consider 'suitable' to marry into my family, but needs must."

"I can assure you that we are quite respectable," Ruby said. "The Delisle family came over with William the Conqueror. My older sister is married to a viscount and my younger sister to a baronet."

Charles hastened to intervene as his father's expression hardened. "As you have agreed that the marriage is valid, surely such discussions are moot. We are quite content as we are and ask for nothing from you."

"Do you want children, Mrs. Nash?"

"If God wills it." Ruby held his gaze. "Of course."

"Good." The earl turned to Charles. "And how do you intend to support your family?"

"I earn enough to do that, sir."

"Any medical man who isn't pandering to the aristocracy in London makes a pittance. You probably earn less than a lower-ranked civil servant on one hundred and fifty pounds a year."

"There is an increasing demand for all kinds of medical services by the new middle classes."

"A demand you intend to fulfill?"

"Why not?" Charles smiled.

"I suppose that's what I should expect. You've always had a taste for low life." The earl's lip curled. "And what do you call yourself? A surgeon? An apothecary? A charlatan?"

"I trained in Edinburgh, sir, which as you well know is the best medical college in the country, if not the world. I consider myself a man who offers help with all branches of medicine within my general practice." Charles smiled again, which he knew would annoy his father, but he refused to be cowed about his choice of profession.

"If you didn't have a private income, you would not survive," the earl snapped.

"Then it's lucky I do, isn't it?" Charles held his father's gaze. "I also have a house to live in, enough food to eat, and the pleasure of my wife's company." He turned to look at Ruby who was listening intently. "What more could a man want?"

The earl sat back, his fingers tapping the desk. "You're still my heir."

"I am aware of that."

"If you do have children, they will know me and be aware of their lineage."

"I'm hardly going to keep my children from their grandmother, sir," Charles said lightly. "Now, is there anything else or shall we return to your guests? I'm sure they'll be wondering where you are."

"You may both leave, and you can make my excuses. I've had enough of company for one day."

Charles stood and offered his arm to Ruby. "My dear?"

She smiled and placed her hand on his sleeve before curtsying to his father. "Good evening, my lord. It was a pleasure to speak with you."

They were almost at the door before the earl spoke again. "There is one more matter I wish to discuss, Charles, but it can wait until tomorrow."

"As you wish." Charles nodded. He knew his father had barely toyed with him yet, but he'd take his victories when he could. "Good night, sir."

"That went rather well," Charles said as they made their way up to bed.

Ruby glanced up at him to see if he was joking, but for once he appeared to be sincere. "If you say so."

He opened the bedroom door and stood back to let her enter ahead of him. "Normally, I'd have left in a rage by now."

"Your father wasn't exactly welcoming, but he seemed resigned to our marriage," Ruby said cautiously. "And your mother was delightful."

"She can be quite charming when she puts her mind to it."

There was a knock on the door and a manservant entered and bowed. Charles waved him away. "Thank you but I can manage by myself."

"If you're sure, Mr. Charles."

"Yes. And tell the maid she does not need to come up, either."

"As you wish, sir."

Ruby raised her eyebrows when he left. "I might have wanted the maid. I have no idea how to get my hair out of this complicated shape she put it up in. There are pins everywhere."

"I'll help you. It's hardly difficult."

"Easy for you to say." Ruby presented Charles with her back. "You'd better get on undoing all these buttons, then."

He leaned in and kissed her neck. "You were wonderful, by the way."

"I hardly did a thing."

"You were kind to my mother and so pleasant to my father that he didn't know how to treat you." He started on the buttons. "He'll find a way to unnerve you at some point, because he can't bear to be bested. But you made an excellent first impression."

Her gown, which had a wide neckline and large stuffed sleeves, started to slip down her shoulders as Charles undid the buttons.

"Shall I do your corset while I'm here? Then you can step out of everything."

"Yes, please."

She sighed as he released the strings and let all her garments fall to the floor, leaving her just in her shift, stockings, and pantaloons. His arm came around her hips, bringing her tightly against him.

"Look in the mirror."

She angled her head to see their reflection and almost smiled. He was still fully dressed while she was almost naked.

"I look like your mistress."

"You look beautiful." His hands separated at her waist, one moving up to cup her breast while the other settled between her legs. "Mmm..."

She set one foot on the stool in front of her dressing table opening herself up to his caresses while they both watched the mirror.

"This is quite arousing," Ruby said. "Watching your hands move on me, your fingers—" She gasped as he slipped his fingers through the gap of her pantaloons and found her already needy flesh. His thumb settled over her bud and roughly pressed it in time to his thrusting fingers. She came, his gaze locked with hers as he pleasured her.

"I want more, and I want it now," Charles said.

He set a chair in front of the mirror and sat down, one arm wrapped around her waist and holding her still as he stripped her naked.

"You're still dressed." She had just enough breath to point it out before he started kissing her again.

"I'll manage." He undid his trousers. "Sit on my cock."

"Charles!" She was moving to obey him before she even realized it, her heart thumping, her whole body so eager for him—for this—that she forgot to complain about his orders.

"Perhaps next time we dine at Grafton Hall, I'll tell you to take off those pantaloons and be naked for me under those big skirts of yours," he murmured into her ear as she settled herself over him. "Then I can have you like this whenever I want."

He touched her between the legs, his fingers widening her as he introduced the broad head of his cock inside her.

"I should be shocked," Ruby said, gasping as she settled over his throbbing heat. "But—"

She climaxed before he was even fully inside her, and he held her still, one hand rigid on her hip. "Don't move."

"I'm doing my best."

"You're—" He groaned and thrust upward, bringing her down on him at the same time. It didn't take long for them both to climax, and he barely managed to pull out as they clung onto each other for dear life.

"I didn't realize you were so wicked," Ruby murmured against his neck.

"I suspect being in my father's house brings out the worst in me." He stood up, still holding her, and walked over to the bed where he set her down against the sheets. "I'd better get undressed."

"Yes, please." Ruby watched his lean body emerge with

primal satisfaction. The thought that he was hers was incredibly arousing.

His smile was surprisingly intimate as he climbed into bed and positioned himself over her, one hand on his still-stiff cock.

"Your admiration inspires me to do better."

She placed her hands on his shoulders. "They why don't you go ahead and prove it?"

CHAPTER ELEVEN

*I*t was odd to be woken by a maid and not to have to deal with the thousand tasks she usually managed every morning at home. Even as Ruby sipped her fragrant tea, her mind flew to how Nora was faring in Caroline's nursery. Bridget had accompanied her charge to Grafton Hall, and although Ruby knew that Nora was in good hands, she still worried. It was the longest she'd been away from her daughter since her birth, and they weren't planning on leaving until tomorrow.

"I'll take your evening gown down to the laundry, ma'am and give it a press." The maid scooped up her dress from the floor where Ruby had stepped out of it and into Charles's arms. "The silk's crumpled."

"Thank you."

Ruby's cheeks heated as the maid placed the dress over her arm. She wasn't normally so careless with her possessions and had to stifle an urge to apologize for creating unnecessary work. There was no sign of Charles or of his dinner garments, which indicated he'd either tidied them up himself when he'd left the bed, or someone had come in and done if for him.

"Breakfast is served until nine, ma'am," the maid said. "I'll come and help you with your hair after I've taken this down. The footman has drawn you a bath in the dressing room."

"There's no need to come back," Ruby said. "I can dress myself if you need to get on."

"Are you sure, ma'am?" The maid paused at the door, her expression doubtful. "I'm more than happy to help, and I'm sure you want to look your best."

Ruby didn't miss the subtle hint that the rumpled appearance of a Millcastle physician's wife wasn't quite up to scratch in an earl's house.

"Then please return when I've taken my bath."

"Yes, ma'am."

WHEN SHE REACHED the breakfast room, which was in a separate wing to the dining room, there was no one there except the butler, two footmen, and an array of lidded silver serving dishes on a long sideboard.

"Good morning, Mrs. Nash." The butler came toward her. "Would you prefer tea or coffee with your meal?"

"Tea, please."

A footman was instantly dispatched to the kitchen while the butler walked her along the line of chafing dishes, explaining the contents and adding whatever she asked for onto her plate. By the time she reached the end, her plate was rather full, and she was grateful the butler was carrying it.

"Would you care for some porridge, ma'am?"

"I think this is sufficient," Ruby said as he placed a large linen napkin on her knees and set out her cutlery in precise lines on the mahogany table. "Do you happen to know where Dr. Nash is?"

"I believe he is visiting the countess, ma'am. Do you wish me to inquire?"

"No, thank you. I'll join him when I've finished my breakfast."

The butler bowed. "As you wish, ma'am."

The food was delicious. She was tempted to help herself to more but didn't want to cause any gossip below stairs about her indelicate appetite. She dabbed at her face with her napkin and was just about to rise when the earl appeared in the doorway.

"Ah, Mrs. Nash. Will you be so good as to accompany me on a stroll around the long gallery?"

Charles had suggested his father hadn't finished with her, and it appeared he was right.

"I'd be delighted, my lord." Ruby offered the earl a pleasant smile, placed her napkin on the table, thanked the staff, and went to join him.

He didn't bother with polite chitchat as she walked beside him through a maze of dark corridors, up two flights of stairs, and into what appeared to be the oldest part of the house. He paused to unlock an arch-shaped oak door.

"We believe this wing was the original medieval hall of the house. One of my ancestors put in another floor to make the upper level usable and created a long gallery so that his family could walk during inclement weather."

"How practical," Ruby said as he stood aside to allow her to enter first. He wasn't as tall as Charles and barely topped Ruby, which made it hard to avoid his eyes.

The long gallery had a wide-planked oak floor with a carpet down the center, paneled walls, and an intricate beamed ceiling that immediately took Ruby's gaze upward.

"It is wonderful."

The earl didn't answer her, his gaze directed toward the pictures on the left-hand wall.

"Normally, I would ask my steward or housekeeper to show

you around, but what I have to say to you is best said in private."
The earl pointed at a portrait of a miserable-faced man in a lace
ruff. "This is believed to be the first earl of Nash—although the
title was longer back then and French."

Ruby strolled over to study the portrait. "I see where Charles
gets his nose from."

The earl came to stand beside her. "Are you not concerned
about what I have to say to you?"

"I am merely expressing my interest in your ancestors, my
lord—mine now, too, I suppose. I wouldn't wish to remain in
ignorance of such a grand family history."

She continued along the gallery, stopping to comment on
any of the portraits that caught her attention, the earl unwill-
ingly supplying the barest hints of information, his impatience
visibly growing because she refused to show any fear. They
reached the far wall where a group portrait took up the entire
space.

"Royalists, I assume?" Ruby peered closely at the numerous
dogs dotted about the composition.

"Not all. One son fought for parliament, the other for the
king."

"Clever." Ruby nodded.

"My family are survivors, which is why I expect Charles to
provide me with an heir to continue my line."

Ruby turned to face him. "Then you should be pleased that
he is married."

"Pleased is hardly the word I would use."

"Why not? Surely any woman who can bear children will
provide an heir?"

Ruby was aware she might be walking into a trap, but she
wasn't inclined to humor the earl's worst impulses.

"One has to wonder whether my son chose you to avoid that
certainty."

"If you are suggesting we don't intend to consummate our marriage, I can assure you that you're wrong."

"So I understand from my servants."

She refused to feel any embarrassment and held his gaze until he moved to the next portrait. "If there is something you wish to say, my lord, please go ahead. I'd like to visit the viscountess this morning."

"Did my son mention why he had to marry?"

"Because you require an heir and had picked out a young woman Charles didn't consider a good match."

"How well do you know my son, Mrs. Nash?"

Ruby shrugged. "Well enough to marry him, sir."

"Have you never wondered why a gentleman of his lineage ended up in a mill town working for a railway construction company?"

"I assumed he wished to make his own way in the world, and I applauded him for that."

"Perhaps you should ask him why he had to leave London."

Ruby kept her expression calm as the earl studied her. "We've all done things in our pasts that we aren't particularly proud of, my lord."

"I'm not concerned about the past but about the harm Charles might do in the future." The earl paused. "Harm to you and your future family."

"Are you warning me off my own husband?"

"I'm suggesting you keep a close eye on his temperament. He is more like his mother than you might assume and can become... addicted to things."

"Such as?"

He smiled. "This is merely a friendly warning that Charles is not quite the hero you imagine and that you would do well to be on your guard. Recently, I had to purchase all the gaming debts he left behind when he fled London, which was at considerable expense, and I'll get no thanks for it, I can tell you that."

The earl continued walking until he stood in front of a more recent portrait. Ruby reluctantly joined him, her thoughts in a whirl. She didn't for one moment believe the earl had anyone's best interests at heart other than his own. Was he attempting to drive a wedge between her and Charles when their marriage had barely begun?

"Here is my family in happier times when my oldest son was alive and my wife wasn't prostrated with grief."

Ruby stared at the portrait, his gaze drawn to the smiling face of a young Charles as he sat at his mother's feet cuddling a dog. The contrast between him, his father, and brother was stark. Their stiff posture spoke of heritage, duty, and pride, things Charles would now have to take on whether he wished to or not. Ruby's heart ached for the little boy. Was it any wonder he'd done everything he could to run away from such a fate?

The earl cleared his throat. "If you wish to attend the countess, her suite is at the other end of this corridor."

"Thank you." Ruby started for the door, leaving the earl behind.

She followed his directions and tentatively knocked on the suite's door. It opened and Miss Evans smiled at her.

"Good morning, Mrs. Nash. Have you come to see the countess? She is in excellent form today."

The sound of laughter filtered from another room and Ruby smiled despite herself. If the earl was all darkness, the countess was the light, and she knew which she preferred. Miss Evans showed her into a sunny sitting room decorated in shades of rose and cream looking out over the formal gardens at the rear of the house.

Charles stood up as she entered. "I was wondering where you were, my dear. Did Benson not give you my message?"

"I was somewhat delayed," Ruby said, unsure whether to bring up the earl in such pleasant company. "Good morning, my lady." She curtsied to the countess.

"No need for such formality, my dear." The countess gestured for Ruby to sit. "You may call me Lavinia, or Mother-in-law, or whatever takes your fancy."

"And you may call me Ruby." She smiled.

The countess wore a frothy cream confection of lace that seemed too grand to be described as a mere dressing gown. Her hair was down around her shoulders and her feet were tucked up under her on the couch. She looked barely old enough to have a child, let alone a grown son. Miss Evans came to sit beside Ruby and offered her some tea.

"Charles seems very happy, and I credit you for that," the countess said. "I've been telling him for years that he needed to settle down and take a bride."

"I consider myself very settled now, Mama," Charles assured her. "Ruby is a good influence on me."

"I'm glad to hear it." The countess paused. "Will you be staying for a while, Charles? It would be nice to have your company."

"Unfortunately, I have patients to attend to, and we'll have to leave this evening." Charles patted his mother's hand. "But I intend to bring Ruby to visit you more frequently."

"Or you could visit us," Ruby suggested. "We have space for you and Miss Evans."

The countess bit her lip. "I'm not allowed to leave Nash Hall."

Ruby looked at Charles. "Surely—"

"The earl would not allow me to visit you," the countess continued, her composure crumbling. "He prefers it if I stay here where he can keep an eye on me in case I embarrass him."

Ruby was about to reply when Charles caught her eye and slightly shook his head.

"Don't worry, Mama, we will enjoy coming to visit you here. Father really does have an excellent chef."

"I hate his food," the countess said.

Miss Evans smiled. "Yesterday you were singing his praises over those little strawberry cakes you love, my lady. I believe you ate the whole plateful and asked for more."

"I don't remember that at all." The countess's sunny mood disappeared as abruptly as a cloud passing over the sun. "All food tastes the same when you are a prisoner."

"Mama..."

The countess stood up. "I think I'll take a nap."

Charles rose to his feet. "Will you come down to dinner this evening before we leave?"

"I'll see." She cupped his cheek and kissed it. "Goodbye, my dear. Thank you for visiting me and bringing your sweet wife."

With an apologetic grimace, Miss Evans rushed over to the countess and gently supported her as she turned toward the inner room. The door shut behind them, leaving Ruby and Charles alone.

Ruby sighed. "I'm sorry."

"For what?" He wasn't looking at her, his gaze turned toward the closed door.

"Ruining everything?"

He finally turned. "You didn't ruin anything. My father does keep her confined here."

Ruby stared at him. He came over and took her hand. "Let's find somewhere more private and I can explain."

CHARLES TOOK Ruby through the walled kitchen garden and out onto the wide, tree-lined avenue beyond. There was some kind of folly or statue on the brow of the adjacent hill, and he headed toward it. He wasn't used to sitting around all day and was restless enough to kick his heels like an untried colt.

"Are you cold?" He looked down at Ruby. "I should have—"

"I'm fine. It's pleasant to be outside after all that grandeur."

"It is rather oppressive," he agreed. "My father has very high standards."

She shivered. "I can't imagine growing up here."

"It wasn't as bad as you might think. We had our own nursery floor. My father never came up there. If we transgressed, he sent for us, and we presented ourselves in his study to be punished."

He abruptly stopped speaking. Good Lord, he needed to be quiet. Now she was looking even more concerned.

"Your father waylaid me at the breakfast table."

Charles stopped walking. "He did what?"

"He invited me to join him for a stroll around the family portrait gallery."

"And what did he hope to gain from that?" His tone was icier than he intended and Ruby scowled at him.

"To intimidate me? Much as you are trying to do now?"

He let out a breath. "I apologize."

"Thank you." She watched his face for a moment before continuing. "I thought he had found out about Nora, but he said nothing about her."

"Then what did he base his threats on?"

"You."

"I don't understand."

Her smile was wry. "Out of the goodness of his heart he warned me not to trust you. He suggested you were as unstable as your mother."

"And what did you say to that?"

"I thanked him for his insights and asked for directions to the countess's suite."

He had a sense she wasn't telling him everything, but what she had shared was damning enough.

She glanced up at him. "I must confess I wasn't expecting him to try and set me against my own husband."

"He's always looking ahead. He's probably decided that if he can spread doubts about my fitness to be a father, you'll be more likely to do his bidding and return to Nash Hall to raise our children, preferably without me."

She nodded. "I suspected something of the sort. He must think me a fool."

"I wouldn't take it personally. He doesn't have a high opinion of any woman's intelligence." He gestured at the folly. "Can we continue our walk? I still feel too close to the house."

"As you wish."

She took his proffered hand, and they walked up the slope to the circular folly. It had a domed roof, stone walls, and round pillars that left it open to the elements. There was a bench just inside the entrance offering them an excellent view of the house and formal gardens below. Charles dusted the seat with his handkerchief, and Ruby sat down and looked up at him expectantly.

"What else did my father say?" Charles asked.

"I'm not sure it's worth repeating, as I didn't believe a word of it." She hesitated as if choosing her words carefully, which was enough to put him on his guard. "I think he was just trying to plant doubt in my mind as to your stability."

"Just," Charles said bitterly. "I'm his only surviving son and he's still trying to paint me as an unstable madman." He turned his back on her and took a few hasty strides before swinging around. "Did he say anything specific about my past conduct?"

For the first time she avoided his gaze.

"We promised to be honest with each other, remember?" Charles said.

Sighing, she met his gaze again, her hands clasped together on her lap. "He said you fled London to escape your gambling debts."

Ice settled in the pit of his stomach. Good Lord, his father wasn't playing around. "That's not quite true."

"Which part? That you fled, or that you gambled to excess?"

He winced. He'd forgotten she could be as direct as he was. "I left London with a patient who was recovering from a long illness. Her family trusted me to care for her on the journey north, and I stayed with them for several months until she recovered her strength." He hesitated, considering how much to reveal. "I realized that being away from London and all its temptations was good for me and I decided to stay away."

"I see."

"The gambling debts I incurred were during my younger, wilder days," he added when she didn't say anything else. "I borrowed foolishly and unwisely and ended up owing five times as much as my original loans. I started paying the interest back after I qualified, but I might as well have been pissing into a sieve."

Ruby gave a choked laugh which she quickly smothered. "I'm glad you told me," she said simply. "In truth, your father's warnings couldn't affect my regard for you, but no one likes to be ambushed."

"You're right."

"And if we do wish to stand together, I need to be better informed." She held his gaze, a challenge in her brown eyes.

"He bought up all my debts." Charles forced himself to speak. "He intended to use them to force me to marry Miss Barton."

"Ah." She nodded. "Now it makes much more sense."

He sat beside her and took her hand. Surely, he'd said enough to satisfy her and didn't need to mention his father's threats against his mother.

His faint hope died as his forthright wife asked her next question. "Why won't your father allow your mother to leave this estate?"

"She's not been well."

"Ever since he married her?" Ruby's eyebrows rose.

"He married her because she was beautiful, much younger

than him, and from a large family," Charles said flatly. "He expected her to provide him with a large family of his own."

"But—"

"Her health declined after my birth and worsened considerably after my brother's untimely death. She is a gentle soul whose spirit has been crushed by a man who could never understand her."

Ruby didn't reply for some time, her expression thoughtful. "You love her very much, don't you?"

"Yes."

"I am sorry that I upset her with my invitation to visit us."

"The fault lies with my father, not you." He brought her cold hand to his mouth and kissed her knuckles. "You must be bored to tears hearing all my family scandal. Shall we speak of something else?"

"If you wish." She eased her hand free of his and looked away. "Perhaps we should go back before we are missed."

CHAPTER TWELVE

t wasn't until they'd returned to Millcastle and shared a joyful reunion with Nora that Ruby had time to think more deeply about Charles's family. She'd asked him to be honest but still had a sense that he wasn't telling her everything. He'd been visibly agitated talking about his mother, and she hadn't wanted to force him into sharing things that might be deeply hurtful for him.

But even from her limited acquaintance with the countess, Ruby knew she wasn't just suffering from physical ill health. Her emotions ran close to the surface, and she plummeted from highs to lows with the agility of a kite buffeted by an uncertain wind. Ruby had felt similarly after Nora's birth, but the feelings had gradually diminished as time went on. The countess reminded her far more of Ivy and her fragile state of mind.

The earl's distaste for emotion was plain to see. Ruby couldn't imagine him tolerating a wife who couldn't be relied upon to perform her duties as his countess. He hadn't bothered to hide his polite contempt for her even from his dinner guests. If he treated her like that in public, how much worse might he be in private?

Ruby had met plenty of abusive husbands living in the slums of Leeds. Those men tended to settle arguments with their fists; whereas, the earl used subtler methods to undermine those he should love and support. And that included Charles...

Ruby set the kettle to boil on the range and set out the teacups and pot. Bridget had shown her an ingenious way to grill bread and cheese on a metal plate warmed over the range, and she intended to try out her new accomplishment when Charles came in at midday.

The back door opened, and Charles came in, his expression thunderous.

Ruby paused to stare at him. "Whatever is the matter?"

"That girl? The one who came here and stole the plate?" He took off his coat and hat and set his bag on the floor with a decided thump. "She's dead."

"Did you visit her at the brothel?"

"Of course not. She told me I wasn't worth her time or her money."

"I remember now." Ruby poured the boiling water into the pot and stirred the tea leaves before putting the lid back on. "I assume she found someone else to assist her."

"She bled to death and was left outside the brothel in the dead of night like refuse." He sat down and shoved his hands through his hair. "I warned her not to go to some back-alley practitioner."

"Then you did everything in your power to offer your assistance, and you should not blame yourself," Ruby said firmly as she poured the tea. "How did you find out she was dead?"

"I just had a police constable turn up in my consulting room."

"What?" Tea slopped onto the table as Ruby stared at him. "Why on earth were they talking to you?" She rushed to mop up the spill.

"Because several people saw her in my yard waiting to be

seen by the doctor and then heard her claim I was a charlatan as she left." He grimaced. "They asked me several very pointed questions as to my whereabouts over the past few days. For the first time in my life, I was glad to be able to tell them I'd been out of town visiting my father, the Earl of Nash. That sent them scurrying off in a hurry."

"That poor girl," Ruby said as she set the milk out on the table. "How desperately alone she must have felt."

"One thing I've learned in this business is that sometimes you can't force people to do the best thing for their health. It's incredibly frustrating." He drank some tea. "If I ever find out who did it, I'll have a few choice words for them and no compunction in informing the police."

Ruby couldn't help remembering the fierceness of the young girl who'd brazenly helped herself to not only the plate, but Charles's tea cakes and Ruby's handkerchief, too.

"I hope the police won't return," Ruby said.

"I doubt they'll want to question my alibi, my dear," Charles said dryly. He set a pile of letters on the table. "I brought in the post."

"Thank you."

Ruby sorted the mail while Charles drank two cups of tea and ate the grilled bread and cheese she prepared for him. Most of the letters concerned his medical practice but there was one from her mother and one from Miss Evans addressed to her. She set Charles's correspondence at his elbow and opened the letter from her mother. She had time to read while Nora was napping upstairs.

"Oh."

Charles looked over at her. "What now?"

"My mother is complaining that I don't visit her enough."

"You saw her two weeks ago."

"Indeed, and I have explained to her on several occasions that I don't have my own carriage, and I can't just visit her when the fancy takes me." Ruby kept reading. "She could always ask Ivy if her coachman could come and collect me, but I suspect she prefers to complain and do nothing." She stopped talking and reread the last paragraph. "Ivy is expecting again."

Charles had been sorting through his letters at a rapid pace and discarding most of them onto the floor. "I'm somewhat surprised at that," He said cautiously.

"It's too soon." Ruby held his gaze. "Perhaps I should visit her after all."

Charles nodded. "I'm sure the nurse can care for Nora if you wish to go today."

"I'll hire a gig at the coaching inn," Ruby said. "It's too far to walk."

He frowned. "I'll hire a suitable carriage. I'm coming with you."

"Do you have time?" she asked as he rose to his feet. "I don't wish to inconvenience you."

He kissed the top of her head and gathered up his post. "I always have time for you, my sweet."

She raised her eyebrows at that, and he smiled. "My dear girl, don't look so skeptical. You accompanied me to Nash Hall. The least I can do is visit with your sister."

As he turned to leave, a small square of paper floated down to the floor. He bent to pick it up and held it out to Ruby. "I think this might be yours. It must have been caught up in my medical bills."

"Thank you." Ruby took the letter, went still for a moment, and then shoved it hastily into her apron's pocket.

"I'll be ready to leave at two," Charles said before he left, apparently unaware of her panicked state. "Bridget should be back from her morning off by then."

Ruby concentrated on her breathing and carefully folded her mother's note, her fingers shaking. She should read Miss Evans's letter first, but she knew she wouldn't be able to concentrate until she'd dealt with the other missive. She took out the much folded and grubby square of paper. The original direction to Grafton Hall had been crossed out and her new address written on the other side of the note.

She unfolded it to reveal more of Sidney's distinctive handwriting.

Ruby, I went to Leeds. They told me you'd left and returned to your sister. I hope you are enjoying the luxury provided off the backs of the working class. I would like to see my daughter. Please reply to the above address and your letter will get to me eventually.

Sidney.

"No..." Ruby whispered. "You said you'd set us free. Do you want to destroy all the comfort I've gained for myself and Nora?" She reread the note, her indignation rising with every word. "And how dare you sneer at the people who took us in when you left us with nothing!"

She crumpled the paper in her fist, went over to the fire, and dropped the letter on top of the burning coals. She prodded it vigorously with the poker until it became nothing more than ash.

"That's what I think of you, Sidney Fellows!" she addressed the fire. "Leave us in peace."

She returned to the table and poured herself another cup of tea, shuddering at the bitterness of the brew. It was unlikely that Sidney would ever have the opportunity or the funds to present himself at Grafton Hall, but she would warn Caroline just in case. He had no right to interfere with the life she'd painstakingly built from the ruins of their relationship.

It struck her then that she'd stopped loving him well before Nora's birth and that she might have been the one to leave if he hadn't left first. She swallowed hard and reached for her handkerchief, her composure close to breaking. Perhaps she should read Miss Evans's letter and distract herself.

Dear Mrs. Nash,

I apologize for the familiarity in writing to you when we are barely acquainted, but I thought you should know that the earl has hired a private investigator to discover details of your past. I happened to be in the entrance hall when this man and his lordship were passing through and I overheard their discussion. As the earl is always very thorough in the pursuit of his goals, I urge you to be on your guard.

Yours sincerely,

Martha Evans.

Ruby stared out of the kitchen window at the brick wall beyond. Had Charles mentioned anything to his mother about Nora—or the less-than-honorable circumstances of their first meeting—that the countess might have then revealed to the earl? Would she have given him such information without realizing the danger? From what Ruby had seen she did have a tendency to blurt out her truth.

Surely Charles wouldn't have willingly handed his father ammunition against his own wife… But he was very fond of his mother and might have thought the notion that she already had a step-granddaughter would cheer her up.

Ruby took a sheet of paper and her inkwell from the drawer in the dresser and considered what to say to Miss Evans in reply. She couldn't be too obvious. It was possible the earl insisted on reading all his staffs' correspondence.

Dear Miss Evans,

She tried to frame her first sentence and had no idea how to continue. With a sigh, she set the paper and pen back on the dresser and went outside to take in the washing. Charles didn't like her doing the maid's job, but it was starting to rain, and she didn't want damp sheets spread out to dry all over the house. The rain in Millcastle wasn't clean, being full of soot and debris from the factories, and it made washing white items particularly hard.

She gathered in the sheets, enjoying the faint hint of warmth and sunshine still concealed in their depths, and hurried back inside just as the rain worsened. With both Eliza the maid and Bridget being out, it took her a while to fold everything to her satisfaction. Eliza would use the flat irons when she returned and copious amounts of starch to make the sheets crisp and ready for use again.

The back door opened, and Bridget came in, the fake bird on her best bonnet as bedraggled as its owner.

"Got caught by the rain right at the top of the street, ma'am." Bridget took off her bonnet and shook it vigorously. "I'll go upstairs and change and bring Nora down for her midday meal."

"Thank you, Bridget."

Bridget paused at the inner door. "Are you all right, ma'am? You look a bit upset."

"I'm quite well." Ruby gestured at the letters on the table. "I'm just ruminating on the news I received."

"I wish I had someone to write letters to who could read them proper," Bridget said. "With me mam gone, my brothers aren't bothering to keep up with their book learning."

"That's a shame," Ruby said.

"It is, indeed, ma'am." Bridget went into the hallway, and moments later, Ruby heard her booted feet stomping up the first staircase.

Ruby got up and started preparing Nora's food. If she could keep herself busy for the next few hours, perhaps the shock of the correspondence she'd received would lessen, and Charles would see nothing but her usual competent self.

CHAPTER THIRTEEN

When they arrived at Ivy's house, Charles turned to Ruby. "Do you wish me to offer my medical services to your sister, or should I wait to be asked?"

Ruby had been unusually silent on the journey, her expression turned inward, which was surprisingly unsettling. It was alarming how much he'd come to crave her good approval in such a short time.

She looked at him as he helped her down from the gig. "I'd rather you wait. She might not wish everyone to know about her condition yet."

Charles snorted. "Pregnancy is a natural occurrence."

"Yes, but it's still not discussed in polite company. As you well know, many things can go wrong along the way."

"I am aware of that. I attended pregnant ladies in London who refused to remove an item of clothing or allow me to touch them even if half the household, including the husband, was present. How did they expect me to offer a medical opinion under those circumstances?"

"How indeed?" Ruby said. "Perhaps we should wait and see what Ivy wants before we get ahead of ourselves."

"As you wish." He knocked on the front door.

The manor house was a charming building settled deeply into its surrounding environment. There was a large conservatory to one side where Ivy's husband, Ian, a noted botanist and plant collector, promulgated and grew new species. Charles found the subject interesting and was more than happy to be taken off by Sir Ian to view his latest experiments if the ladies didn't require their presence.

"Charles?" Ruby suddenly spoke. "Did you mention Nora to your mother?"

Surprised by the question, he paused before answering. "No, I didn't. Why would you ask?"

"I know that you are very close to her, and I simply wondered…"

Her voice trailed off, leaving him feeling confused. It was unlike his plain-speaking wife to be at a loss for words.

"I wouldn't tell her without your permission, and even then, I'd be wary. My mother sometimes forgets to be careful when she's upset."

"You mean she might reveal the truth to your father."

"Exactly. And he would be delighted to hear of anything to our detriment so he can use it against us."

Ruby bit her lip. "What if he finds out anyway?"

He focused all his attention on her. "Has something happened I should know about?"

"Miss Evans wrote to me. She believes your father has hired a private investigator to look into my background."

Charles cupped her chin so that she had to look up at him. "I don't care what the old bastard does. We're married and that's the end of it."

She searched his face, her gaze never wavering. "Thank you. I must admit I was feeling quite vulnerable."

"Don't." He bent his head to kiss her. "We'll beat him together."

Further discussion was interrupted by the polite cough of the butler, who'd opened the door to admit them.

"Good afternoon, Dr. Nash, Mrs. Nash. Please do come in. I'll go and inquire if her ladyship has come downstairs."

"Thank you."

"I meant to tell you," Charles murmured as they were ushered into the hall. "An old friend of mine from medical school, Malcolm Fraser, will be coming to have dinner with us tomorrow night."

"Will he." Ruby took off her bonnet and set it on the hall table. "And what are you proposing to feed him when we have nothing but a few scraps of lamb left?"

"Send the cook out to buy something."

"With what?"

He frowned. "Money, I assume."

"I've already spent this week's food budget, because I wasn't expecting guests."

He dug into his pocket and brought out a handful of coins. "Help yourself. Mrs. Mainwaring paid her bill this morning, so we're in funds."

"I'll set it against her account." She counted the coins and put them in her purse. He was glad to see her restored to her usual calm self. "Thank you."

"Mrs. Nash, Dr. Nash?" The butler had returned. "Her ladyship is in the morning room if you wish to follow me."

Charles followed Ruby into the large, light-filled, oak-beamed room and discovered the entire Delisle family were already there. The sisters made a formidable trio, all so different, but united by their scarred past and their desire to succeed.

"Mrs. Delisle, Lady Caroline, my lady." He bowed. "How very pleasant to see you all."

Ivy came over to grasp his hand and offered him a kiss on the cheek. She looked rather fragile, which worried him. It was surprisingly hard not to inquire as to the state of her health.

"Ian said to tell you he is in the conservatory if you wish to join him. He'll bring you back in time for some refreshment."

"Thank you," He looked over at Ruby, who nodded. "Then I'll leave you ladies to chat."

DESPITE RUBY'S best efforts she'd been unable to get Ivy to speak frankly about her pregnancy or her feelings about it. Every time she tried to reintroduce the subject her younger sister told her not to worry, and that everything was fine. Despite Ivy's words, Ruby wasn't convinced. When she suggested Ivy should speak to Charles she was met with a firm no and a plea not to interfere that put an end to the conversation.

To her surprise Charles hadn't been worried by Ivy's rejection of Ruby's offers of help. He'd reminded her that a pregnancy was of a long duration, and that Ivy might change her mind, and decide to consult him after all. Despite her worries, Ruby had to concede he was right and was determined not to interfere. Her sister had grown in strength over the past years and had the right to determine her own desires.

AFTER YET ANOTHER crisis at the navvy camp, Ruby didn't get the opportunity to speak properly again to her husband until they were dressing for dinner for following evening. Dr. Fraser was expected at six and Bridget had already taken charge of Nora and would remain upstairs with her. Mrs. Jenkins had done all the cooking, leaving Ruby with the luxury of time to change. Charles had insisted that they didn't need to dress up for his old friend, but Ruby was determined to at least make an effort.

As they moved around their small bedroom, she was aware

of their current ease with each other—the way he helped with her corset and she straightened his cravat. She smiled up at him, and his hands closed on her hips.

"What?"

"Look at us behaving like an old married couple."

He raised his eyebrows. "Not that old. Although after today, I've decided not to put myself in the middle of two injured men still wanting to fight."

"Later, I'll rub some of that liniment you love to prescribe on you."

He mock frowned at her. "That liniment makes us a lot of money, and unlike many others, it actually works."

She kissed him and he kissed her back, drawing the moment out until she was breathless and had one hand buried in his thick hair. He cupped her bottom and drew her tightly against him.

"Now look what you've done. I can hardly greet our guest looking like this, can I?" She undulated her hips and he groaned. "Mrs. Nash..."

"Yes?" She shivered as he pressed his mouth against her throat and bit her neck.

"You are the devil." He glanced over at the bed. "Do we have time to...?"

"Absolutely not." She eased away from him and sank down onto her knees, her fingers busy on the fastenings of his trousers. "But I think I can accomplish *something* in the time we have."

"Ruby, you don't have to— Oh God, that's good. Don't stop."

She would've laughed, but her mouth was busy with other tasks, drawing his stiff length deep while she concentrated on pleasuring him. It didn't take long to accomplish her goals as he came fast, her name harsh on his lips as he gripped her shoulders.

She rose to her feet and patted her hair. "We really should get on. Can you help me with the fastenings of my dress?"

RUBY WAS STILL SMILING when she went downstairs to greet her husband's guest. They'd decided to eat in their formal dining room, which, like the parlor, faced the street at the front of the house. On most days, they all ate together in the kitchen, which was always a warm and welcoming place.

Eliza had stayed late with Mrs. Jenkins to help serve the meal, which meant the kitchen was busy, and Ruby's presence was not required. Someone knocked on the front door. Ruby went to answer it, only to be firmly set aside by Eliza.

"I'll get that, ma'am. We want to do things nice and proper, don't we?"

"Of course." Ruby went meekly into the parlor where a fire had been lit. There was the sound of voices and then Charles came in with their guest.

"Ruby, this is my friend, Dr. Malcolm Fraser."

He shook her hand like she was a colleague, his grey eyes pleasant in his unremarkable face.

"A pleasure, Mrs. Nash." He spoke with a soft Scottish burr. "Thank you for inviting me into your home."

"You are most welcome, Dr. Fraser." Ruby smiled at him. "Would you care for a drink before dinner?"

"I have a decent whisky, Fraser," Charles said. "I borrowed it from my father's cellar last time we visited, and I've been looking forward to tasting it."

"You're inviting me to join you in imbibing stolen goods?" Dr. Fraser asked. Charles showed him the bottle and his eyebrows went up. "Ah, then in that case, I can't say no."

"Would you like a glass, Ruby?" Charles asked as he poured the whisky.

"No, thank you."

"May I get you something else?" He surveyed the silver tray which had been a wedding gift from Ruby's mother. "There's probably some sherry or port."

"I'm fine. I'll just go and check on dinner." She left the two men to chat and went into the kitchen where Mrs. Jenkins was carefully pouring soup into a tureen Ruby hadn't seen before.

"Where did you get that?"

"We borrowed a few things from Mrs. Hepworth, ma'am." The cook finished pouring and set the lid on top of the dish. "Eliza and I wanted to make sure your first dinner party was a success."

It was on the tip of Ruby's tongue to say that having one old friend around to dinner hardly constituted a grand occasion, but their thoughtfulness was such a pleasant surprise that she smiled instead. "Thank you."

"Now you go and take your place as the lady of the house," Mrs. Jenkins said. "I'll send Eliza in to let you know when dinner will be served."

The soup was excellent and was followed by a succulent joint of beef, spiced rice pudding, and coffee served in a silver pot that definitely didn't belong to them. Not having to cook meant that Ruby enjoyed the dinner and could take part in the lively conversation around the table. Dr. Fraser might sound mild, but he had decided opinions about the health of the working class and the lack of resources available to make things better. Ruby found herself nodding in agreement with him far more than Charles, who had a very cynical opinion on life in general.

"This is all very well, Ian, but who will pay for it?" Charles asked. "The mill owners?"

"Don't they want their workforce to be fit and healthy?"

"Labor is cheap. There are thousands of people flooding into the cities desperate for work. They can easily replace those who are no longer fit for it."

Dr. Fraser shook his head. "You're a hard man, Charles."

"I just have very little faith left in humanity," Charles said. "They'd never admit it, but factory owners are no better than the aristocrats who run this country. They're both out to make as much money as possible from those beneath them and be damned to the consequences."

Dr. Fraser winked at Ruby. "At least he's just as critical of his own kind as he is of the industrialists."

"He is something of a cynic," Ruby agreed.

"And you two might be considered starry-eyed idealists," Charles countered. "Nothing will improve until the laws of this country change, and as no one in power wants anything to change, things will stay the same."

"But what of the mill owners and industrial giants who want the power of the vote? And the industrial towns with no representation in parliament?" Ruby asked. "Or the working men who will strike to force change?"

Charles sighed. "I'm not saying I don't have sympathy with the idea of expanding the vote, but I doubt we'll see much progress in our lifetimes."

"That's a very negative viewpoint, Charles," Dr. Fraser said. "If we all work together—"

Charles spoke over him. "Then we'll end up on a transport to Australia for treason against the crown."

"Protest doesn't have to be violent," Ruby pointed out. "Sidney always said—" She smiled. "Not that it matters now. Does anyone want some more coffee?"

It wasn't until Dr. Fraser had left and they were getting ready for bed that Charles surprised her by returning to their previous conversation.

"Sidney believed in writing petitions to parliament and protesting peacefully, did he?"

"He believed in many causes," Ruby said.

"I always assumed he was a man of action, not an idealist."

"A man can be both of those things." Ruby met his gaze calmly. "His strength was in persuading others to join the cause of universal suffrage. He was much in demand as a speaker at rallies."

"A true hero of the working class."

"Hardly that. He was just a man who believed he could change things and was willing to put his beliefs into action."

"You make him sound quite admirable."

"In many ways he was," she said simply. "I certainly admired him."

"Even when he abandoned you?"

Ruby raised her chin. "Why are you behaving like this?"

"Like what?" Charles ripped his shirt over his head and threw it on the chair. "I'm merely asking myself how you can bear to live with a man like me who is so unlike the heroic Sidney."

"That is unfair." Ruby said.

He sat down on the side of the bed to take off his trousers and stockings. Ruby picked up his shirt and smoothed it out before hanging it back in the cupboard. She turned around and bumped straight into Charles's chest.

His arms came around her. "I'm sorry."

She stayed rigid in his arms.

"I think I might be jealous of Sidney."

Startled, she looked up at him. "What on earth for?"

"God knows." His smile was wry. "I've never thought of myself as a jealous type, but here we are."

She cupped his chin. "I chose to marry *you*."

"We both know that was for practical reasons that suited us both, which means I have no right to be jealous at all."

"Or any need," Ruby reminded him. "I don't regret anything, do you?"

He studied her closely and she held her breath. "No, nothing at all."

"Then come to bed," Ruby said. "And let's not speak of this again."

CHARLES ROLLED onto his back and studied the ceiling. He'd made love to Ruby with his usual thoroughness and a hint of something else—some desperate need to convince her that he was better, that she would never find anyone like him. Which was absurd because they were married, and unless one of them died, they were bound together for life.

He'd never thought of Sidney as competition before but hearing Ruby talk about him at dinner had given him an unpleasant jolt. The fact that she admired Sidney was even worse. How could she admire a man who'd abandoned her? He resisted the urge to snort which might wake her up. Because she was an idealist and Sidney apparently was a hero of the revolution…

Sidney was also a fool who had left Ruby and his child behind in his quest to bring the working man the vote. If Charles ever had the misfortune to meet him, he might have something to say about that. Malcolm laughed at him being a hard man, but he'd never abandon someone he professed to love.

He went still, his mind registering the distant rattle of a train pulling into the station nearby. The only explanation for his behavior was that he was in love with his wife. And what the bloody hell was he supposed to do about that?

CHAPTER FOURTEEN

*R*uby sat at the kitchen table, staring into space, her cup of tea growing colder by the minute. She'd instinctively known Charles wouldn't appreciate Sidney writing to her, which was why she hadn't told him about the letter. His confession of jealousy made matters worse. If she mentioned Sidney's note now, Charles would want to know when she'd received it, and she'd either have to lie, which never sat well with her, or get into just the kind of argument she'd been hoping to avoid in the first place.

She looked up as the back door opened, and Bridget came in carrying Nora.

"Lady Caroline's outside in her carriage, ma'am. She wants to know if we'd like to go up to the hall with her and have tea."

"Yes." Eager to escape her own thoughts Ruby got up. "That would be lovely. I'll just put my bonnet on."

ONCE NORA and her nurse were settled in the nursery, Caroline took Ruby down to her private sitting room at the rear of the house.

"I'm glad you could come," Caroline said as they both sat down. "Francis says I'm worrying about nothing, but he doesn't know Ivy as well as we do."

"What's wrong?" Ruby was more than willing to discuss someone else's problems rather than dwelling on her own.

"It's that physician Ian has found for her. He's insisting Ivy should stay in bed, eat the blandest of diets, and be regularly bled. I don't think that any of that is good for her."

"I agree. It will give her far too much time to worry herself into a state over her condition." Ruby frowned. "I'm surprised at Ian encouraging it."

"He's terrified she's going to lose her mind," Caroline said bluntly. "I can't blame him for worrying, because she did act very strangely after the birth of her first child, but that's no reason to confine her to bed and insist on a regime fit for an invalid."

"Do you think she would allow Charles to visit her?" Ruby asked.

Caroline smiled. "I was hoping you'd suggest that. Will you ask him?"

"Yes, but I know he'll insist on having the consent of both Ivy and Ian before he interferes in any professional capacity."

"I'll speak to them both." Caroline looked slightly less worried. "I'm fairly sure Charles wouldn't suggest such measures. When I was pregnant, he told me to continue with my daily activities, to eat well, and to rest when my body required it."

"He is somewhat straightforward in his advice," Ruby agreed. "Some of his female patients don't appreciate him at all."

"I'm sure they don't." Caroline rang for tea and sat back down again. "Are you content in your marriage, sister? You appear to be thriving."

"I am surprisingly content," Ruby admitted. "From the most difficult of beginnings, we have begun to create a good life together."

Caroline's expression softened. "I am so pleased, and to think Charles is the heir of an earl! Francis will be most displeased if he has to give precedence to a mere doctor."

"Francis won't give a hoot," Ruby said. "He is the least peer-like peer I have ever met."

"I believe he secretly prefers being known as the terrifying Captain Grafton," Caroline agreed.

"Charles wants nothing to do with the estate or the title. The only person he cares for at Nash Hall is his mother. I have no idea what he will do when the current earl dies."

"Hopefully that won't happen for many years," Caroline said. "You said the earl was hale and hearty."

"Yes, and extremely displeased with me and his heir."

"He'll soon change his mind when he sees what a success the marriage will be."

"As to that…" Ruby took a quick breath. "Sidney wrote to me."

Caroline went still. "Dear Lord, what did he want?"

"To see me and his daughter at his convenience." Ruby paused. "The letter was addressed to me here at the hall. Did you not see it and send it on?"

"No." Caroline frowned. "Francis usually deals with the post and leaves mine on the breakfast table when he's finished sorting it." She rose to her feet. "Come on, let's ask him before he leaves for town."

"There's no need to—" Ruby realized she was speaking to herself as Caroline had already left. She followed her sister down the corridor, across the entrance hall, and into Francis's study where a lively conversation had already started.

Francis was staring down his nose at his wife, his expression calm as she questioned him about the letter.

"I did see something addressed to your sister. I merely wrote the new address on it and sent it on." He glanced over at Ruby as she came farther into the room. "I had no idea the letter was from Sidney. I would have opened it if I'd known."

"You can't open other people's letters!" Caroline said.

"I can if I believe they might cause harm to people I care about." Francis gestured at the chairs in front of his desk. "Will you please sit down, and I'll explain?"

Caroline scowled at him and sat with something of a flounce. Ruby sat too, her apprehensive gaze on Francis, who looked slightly irritated at being called out by his wife.

"As it was posted in Leeds, I assumed the letter was from an acquaintance of yours, Ruby, and simply decided to forward it on to you."

"Sidney said in the letter that when he visited Leeds, he was told I'd gone to live with my sister." Ruby paused. "I don't recall giving him your address, but it's possible he worked it out from what he did know of my family."

"I gave him my address," Francis said.

Ruby stared at him. "Why?"

"If you recall, when I came to Leeds to reclaim Ivy, I met Sidney."

"And?" Caroline prompted him. "What on earth did you two have to say to each other?"

"I wanted him to know that the Delisle family were under my protection." There was a hint of steel in Francis's voice. "I wished him to carefully consider how he dealt with you after I left, Ruby."

"You threatened him," Ruby said baldly.

Francis raised an eyebrow. "I merely put the suggestion in his head that he would answer to me if any harm befell you."

"It wasn't your place to do that."

He shrugged. "I offered to support his endeavors if he continued to support you."

"Financially?" Ruby shook her head. "Sidney would never agree to that."

Francis looked down at his joined hands, and a coldness settled in Ruby's stomach.

"He didn't... accept a bribe?"

"Let's just say that he didn't repudiate my offer immediately, shall we?" Francis met her gaze. "And, as you returned to us, the measures I set in place are no longer of any importance."

"Except that he wrote to me," Ruby said slowly. "And he wants to see his daughter."

"And what does Charles think of that?"

Ruby grimaced. "I haven't discussed it with him yet."

"I doubt he'll be surprised," Francis said. "I mentioned my interaction with Sidney to him on your wedding day. We even had a wager about it."

"Then I'll make sure to tell him what Sidney has done now," Ruby said.

The idea that Charles had been privy to Francis's schemes to "protect" her was somewhat infuriating, but she had no intention of sharing her annoyance with Francis, who was far too adept at using other people's misfortunes against them.

Despite her efforts, Francis smiled, which meant he'd already guessed there was some disharmony. "Why don't you stay for dinner, and I'll ask Charles to join us? Perhaps we can all put our heads together and find a solution to this problem."

CHARLES HAD BARELY alighted from his gig at the front door of Grafton Hall when Ruby appeared and took his hand.

"May I speak to you privately? Caroline and Francis have gone upstairs to the nursery to see their children before dinner."

"What's wrong?" he asked as she drew him around the side

of the house and away from prying eyes. He'd had a difficult day, and he wasn't in the best of moods.

She let go of his hand, walked on a few paces, and then turned to face him. "Francis said you knew he had warned Sidney off."

Charles blinked at her. Of all the things he'd been expecting her to say, this wasn't one of them. "I vaguely remember him mentioning something on our wedding night when he caught me skulking in his study, but it didn't seem particularly important."

"You obviously thought it important enough to wager on it."

"Did I?" Charles raised his eyebrows. "In truth, you seem remarkably better informed about this matter than I am, and I'm still at a loss to discover why you're cross with me about it."

"You didn't think I deserved to know Francis had shared private information about Sidney with you?"

"Why in God's name would I think that? Sidney abandoned you. Neither Francis nor I wished him to encroach on your life again. Francis simply attempted to ensure that Sidney understood that." He paused. "And why has this come up now? Six months after our wedding?"

A flash of something that looked remarkably like guilt crossed her face before she replied. "That's hardly important. I just want to make sure that we are on the same side before we go into dinner with that shark, Francis Grafton!"

"He's your brother-in-law," Charles pointed out. "He's on our side."

"Francis only cares about protecting Caroline's reputation. The rest of us and our petty lives annoy him immensely."

"But Caroline would never forgive him if Sidney harmed you again, so in this instance, I believe you can trust him to do the right thing." Charles shivered as the wind caught the tails of his coat. "May we go in now? I've had a very long day."

"Yes, of course," Ruby said stiffly. "I apologize for bothering you with my petty concerns."

"Oh, for God's sake, don't be a martyr. I promise I'll do my best to support whatever it is you want."

Ruby set off for the house without him, and he followed, aware of a headache throbbing at his temple. For a moment, he wished the entire Delisle family in Hades, so he could go straight to bed.

Francis barely waited until the servants had withdrawn from the dining room before mentioning the dreaded Sidney's name. "I'm glad you could come to dinner, Charles. Caroline and I are wondering how we might assist you with the potential reappearance of Sidney."

Charles set down his soup spoon. "Reappearance? Don't tell me he's turned up here?" He looked over at Ruby to find her avoiding his gaze. "You didn't mention that, my dear."

"I doubt he has the time or the funds to be chasing across the country to find Ruby," Francis continued. "But his letter indicates—"

"What letter?" Charles directed his question at his wife.

She sighed. "I was going to tell you, but Francis—"

"Don't blame me, sister-in-law. I merely and unknowingly redirected the letter to you." Francis turned to Charles. "If I'd known who it was from, I would have burned it on the fire."

"I assume Sidney wishes to see you," Charles said to Ruby.

"He wishes to see Nora."

"The daughter he willingly abandoned."

"There's no need to snap at me." Ruby sat up straighter. "I have no intention of allowing him to do so, or of giving him our new address."

"I'm glad to hear it." He held her gaze, his voice pleasant. "Perhaps Francis might write to him on your behalf and decline."

"I'm happy to do that," Francis said. "And if he does turn up here, and he might, as I understand there are some strikes planned in the summer, I will ensure that no one in my family or my employ will assist him in finding you."

Charles had no doubt that, just like his father, Francis's word was law in his own kingdom, which extended well into the murkier side of Millcastle. No one would dare to offend Viscount Grafton-Wesley, alias, Captain Francis Grafton, because the consequences would be swift and brutal.

"Ruby and I will discuss this, Francis, and give you our answer tomorrow," Charles said. "If my wife agrees?"

"Yes, of course." Ruby fussed with her napkin.

"Perhaps you should stay the night?" Francis suggested. "Nora is well-settled in the nursery."

Caroline, who had remained quiet during the conversation set her hand on her husband's arm. "I assume Dr. Nash needs to be home in case he is called upon by a patient in need. Why don't we keep Nora and Bridget here for the night, and let Ruby and Charles leave so they can have the conversation in private?"

Ruby nodded. "Thank you, I believe that would be for the best."

His wife had probably realized she'd roused his temper. If their past disagreements were anything to go by, she was relishing the argument ahead as much as he was.

Caroline ensured that the rest of the meal passed without further controversy and made no complaint when Charles decided not to stay at the table to drink port, claiming he needed his wits about him if he was called out. Their gig was retrieved from the stables and they went home mainly in silence, which was unusual in itself.

When they arrived home, most of the house was in darkness, apart from a lantern in the horse's stable and a light in the hallway.

"Go on in while I deal with the horse," Charles said and handed Ruby the backdoor key. With a variety of potent medicines stored within the house, he was always careful to keep them locked away from those who would abuse them.

As he stabled the horse and turned back to the house, the kitchen window lit up showing Ruby's presence within. He realized he was more annoyed with Francis, and the way he'd handled this affair, than he was with his wife. With a last pat for the horse, he made sure to lock the stable door and went into the house.

Ruby had put the kettle on and was setting out cups for tea. Charles sat down at the table and waited for her to join him, which she did with some reluctance. She took her time fussing over the pouring of the tea.

Only when there was nothing left to do did she look at him, her brown gaze steady. "I'm sorry."

Having expected her wrath, Charles studied her, surprised by the frankness of her apology.

"I should have told you about the letter, but it caught me unawares. I was so angry I put the note on the fire and burned it." She paused. "Sidney made some derogatory comments about Caroline and Francis, so I'm glad Francis didn't read the letter."

"He wouldn't have taken that well," Charles agreed.

"I have no desire to see Sidney," Ruby continued. "But he is Nora's father."

"Surely he gave up his right to see her when he left you both to survive on your own?" Charles suggested.

"It's not that simple, is it?" Ruby sighed. "He could take her away from me, and no court in this land would stop him."

"Give me leave to doubt that," Charles objected. "You weren't married to him, and I believe the poor law states that you alone are responsible for your child's support until at least the age of seven." He drank some tea. "And how would Sidney find the funds to take you to court? He has no rights here, Ruby. I am convinced you have nothing to worry about."

"If that is true, why did he bother to write in the first place?"

"I assume that finding you gone on his return to Leeds might have stirred his conscience."

Ruby nodded. "That's possible. Sidney always likes to do the right thing."

Charles kept his thoughts about that to himself and finished his tea. "I wouldn't worry too much. If Sidney does turn up, Francis will deal with him."

"And who will win your wager?" Ruby asked.

"Ah, that." Charles made a face. "Francis believes Sidney will want money to stay away from you. I don't."

Ruby looked horrified. "Did Francis already give him money?"

"I think he intimated that it would be in Sidney's best interests to stay well away from the Delisle family and that if Sidney needed funds for his 'cause', Francis might be willing to accommodate him." Charles framed his response with caution, unwilling to reveal anything he'd promised Francis to keep secret.

Ruby sat back. "As if Francis would support universal suffrage. It's simply a bribe."

"Yes," Charles agreed. Ruby deserved to hear the truth.

"I don't like any of it," Ruby said, his voice surprisingly unsteady. "I hate the thought that Sidney could simply turn up and ruin my life."

Charles reached across the table and took her shaking hand. "I won't let that happen. I promise you."

He was appalled to see the sheen of tears in her eyes and couldn't stand the sight of his brave and beautiful wife in distress. If Sidney was standing in front of them right now, Charles wouldn't be responsible for his actions...

"Don't look like that." Ruby squeezed his fingers.

"Like what?"

"Coldly furious. As if you are imagining disemboweling something."

"I can't help how I feel." He held her gaze. "Shall we forget about Sidney and go to bed? We have the house to ourselves."

"I am not running around this house naked with you in pursuit."

Admiring the tremendous effort of her teasing response, he stood up and took her into his arms. "I just want to hold you like this. Will that do?"

She looked up at him, her expression so vulnerable it made his heart hurt. "Yes, that would be absolutely delightful."

"Then let's go to bed."

CHAPTER FIFTEEN

*R*uby helped Eliza peg out the washing in the stable yard. It was a windy day, perfect for doing the laundry. All the household except Charles and Nora were involved in the exercise, which required boiling gallons of water in the outhouse and vigorous agitation to release the dirt from the clothes and bedding. It was exhausting work, but Eliza and Mrs. Jenkins made little of it despite knowing they'd have to go home and do it all again for their own families.

Charles was finishing up in his consulting room and was due to go up to the navvy camp for his regular afternoon clinic. Nora was taking a nap upstairs while the rest of them battled with the sheets.

A horse and rider dressed in an unfamiliar livery came through the gate into the yard and dismounted in front of Ruby. "You." The rider pointed at her. "Fetch your master."

Eliza stepped in front of Ruby and wagged her finger in the man's face. "You speak to my mistress with respect, or I'll send you on your way with a flea in your ear!"

"I apologize, ma'am." The man bowed and offered Ruby a

sealed letter. "I have an urgent message from the Earl of Nash for the doctor."

"I'll see that he gets it at once," Ruby said. "Would you care to step inside for a cup of tea while we care for your horse?"

"No thank you, ma'am. I've already secured accommodation at the Station Hotel stables. I'll wait there until I hear from Dr. Nash."

He turned, remounted his horse, and clattered off, ducking his head to avoid the low brick arch over the exit.

Ruby watched him leave and then turned to Eliza. "I'll just take this into Dr. Nash. I won't be a moment."

She went inside and through the internal door that led to Charles's consulting room. She paused until she heard him say goodbye to his patient then knocked and went in.

"What is it?" he asked.

"There's a message from your father." She held out the letter.

He took it, broke the seal, and read rapidly. "My mother is unwell. My father requests our presence."

Ruby touched his shoulder. "Both of us?"

"Yes. Can you make arrangements for Nora to be cared for?" There was no hint of emotion on his face. "There is a hired carriage awaiting us at the Station Hotel to take us to Nash Hall."

"I'll speak to Bridget," Ruby said. "And then I'll pack some essentials."

Despite Ruby's concerns, they were on their way north within an hour. Mrs. Jenkins, Eliza, and Bridget had assured her they could look after Nora and keep the house running for as long as Ruby needed. She'd taken a moment to scribble a note to Caroline, and the stable boy had taken it to Grafton Hall.

Charles had said very little, his expression hard to read, but she knew him well enough now to see his fear for his mother.

She risked a question. "Charles? Has your mother been ill like this before?"

He started as if she'd roused him from a deep sleep. "She... is somewhat prone to the symptoms of nervous collapse."

"What does that mean?" Ruby asked.

"Sometimes she becomes too tired and low to leave her bed for days, and on other occasions she is full of energy, and cannot sleep at all."

"Is there a reason for her illness?"

"Apart from being married to my father? I'm not sure. She can be fine for months and then suddenly relapse with no warning." He looked out of the window and said under his breath, "I just hope to God that she is all right."

"I'm sure she will be." Ruby sought his hand and found it clenched into a fist.

"My father wouldn't insist on my presence if things weren't dire." He swallowed hard. "In the past, he's threatened to confine her more closely."

"That's horrible," Ruby said. "We must find a way to help her."

He didn't reply, his gaze fixed on the approaching gatehouse. The gatekeeper had already come out, and the carriage went swiftly up the drive to Nash Hall. Ruby almost wished for less haste as she dreaded what they might find when they arrived.

There was no sign of the earl as the butler welcomed them into the house, but Miss Evans appeared promptly, her expression extremely agitated as she ran down the stairs, almost stumbling in her haste.

"Dr. Nash, thank God you're here. I don't know what to do."

Charles went over and took her hands in his. "How is my mother?"

"I don't know!" She glanced wildly up at him. "She's gone!"

It took Charles a second to recover from the shock and to hear Ruby's gasp of dismay behind him.

He gripped Miss Evans's hands and made her look at him. "Tell me what happened."

The butler cleared his throat. "If I might suggest you withdraw to the morning parlor, sir? There is a fire made up, and I've already sent for some refreshments."

Charles abruptly turned to blast the man's offer to oblivion, only to have Ruby step in front of him. "That's an excellent idea. Come along, Charles." She took Charles's arm. "There's no need to discuss such matters in the hall."

Miss Evans followed Ruby and Charles along the corridor, and the butler showed them into the charming room and discreetly withdrew.

"Now, tell me everything that has happened," Charles said, trying to pretend he was dealing with any patient but his mother.

Miss Evans gripped her hands together at her chest. She was very pale. "Yesterday morning the earl came to speak to Lady Lavinia in private. After he left, she was very agitated. I asked her repeatedly what was wrong, but she refused to confide in me. Eventually, she asked me to make her a sleeping potion and went to bed." Her voice cracked. "I put her bed, but when I went to check on her later, she wasn't there, and the sleeping potion hadn't been touched. I immediately searched the house and then the gardens but I could find no trace of her."

"Did you inform my father?" Charles asked.

"Not at that point. It's not the first time she has gone for a walk in the grounds and either lost her way or forgotten the time."

Charles nodded. He was well aware of his mother's propensity to wander. Miss Evans was being kind about why his mother might not have returned to the house.

"There are certain staff members whom I trust to search for

Lady Lavinia with the utmost discretion. When I failed to find her, I sent them out but with no success." Miss Evans grimaced. "I felt obliged to inform your father when her ladyship hadn't been found by dinner time."

"And how did he take the news?" Charles asked.

"He…" Miss Evans struggled to speak and her eyes filled with tears. "He said that it would do her good if no one searched for her until the morning. I begged him to change his mind but he refused."

"Damn him to hell," Charles said softly as Ruby came to stand beside him.

"Early this morning the vicar came to see the earl and said his wife had discovered Lady Lavinia down by the stream when she'd taken her dogs for a walk. She was soaked to the skin and unconscious." Miss Evans visibly gathered herself. "The vicar arranged for Lady Lavinia to be taken to the vicarage as it was the closest house and next door to the village doctor."

"Then we should go there," Charles said, turning to the door.

But Miss Evans carried on speaking. "I walked down at lunchtime, Dr. Nash, thinking I would bring some of her home comforts and… She wasn't there anymore, and no one would tell me what had been done with her."

Miss Evans began to cry. Ruby offered her a handkerchief and a supporting arm around her shoulders.

"I am so sorry, Dr. Nash. I feel as if I have failed both you and your mother."

"No fault lies with you, Miss Evans," Charles said. "Your care for my mother has been exemplary."

The butler came in with a tray of refreshments and set them on the table.

"Is my father in, Benson?" Charles asked.

"I believe he has just returned, Dr. Nash. Shall I inquire if he wishes to see you?"

"No, tell him I'll speak to him in ten minutes in his study."

CHAPTER SIXTEEN

"$\mathcal{I}$'m coming with you," Ruby said as Charles finished his tea.

He strode toward the door, his expression cold. "There's no need."

"There is every need." Ruby went toward him. "You are angry about what has happened to your mother. If you immediately lose your temper, your father might not be very forthcoming about where your mother is."

"Then come if you insist, but allow me to deal with my father in my own way."

Inwardly, Ruby sighed. "As you wish."

She followed him down to the earl's study. Charles went in without knocking. Ruby was surprised to see that the earl awaited them.

"Ah, Charles. You arrived in excellent time. I thought it was difficult for you to get away?"

"If you didn't require my immediate presence, why did you write to me?" Charles asked, his tone as arctic as his father's. "Where is my mother?"

The earl sat down behind his desk. "She's in a safe place."

"Where?"

"That is hardly your concern."

"As her only surviving son and a practicing physician, it is very much my concern, sir. Please give me her direction, and I will visit her immediately."

The earl looked down at his desk and moved some papers around. "I don't think that would be wise. She was quite... manic. She had to be heavily sedated to prevent her from harming herself."

"She was found unconscious by a stream last night after you refused to search for her," Charles said. "She could hardly be considered dangerous."

"She became agitated when she woke up at the vicarage. Mrs. Theydon was frightened when she started raving." The earl's small smile made Ruby want to slap him. "She was quite relieved when I took Lavinia away and even thanked me."

"Why didn't you bring her here?" Charles demanded.

The earl sighed. "Because it is obvious that Miss Evans is no longer able to contain your mother's excesses." He paused to write a note. "That reminds me. I must dismiss her without a reference immediately."

Ruby stepped as close to Charles as she dared and took his hand. His fingers were shaking, but no sign of his agitation reached his voice.

"Please give me the address of the establishment where my mother has been taken," Charles said.

"I regret I cannot do that."

"Why not?"

"Because you, like Miss Evans, are not conducive to Lavinia's continuing health. She has been agitated since you left."

"I understand that she only became agitated after you visited her in her chambers, sir," Charles snapped. "Perhaps you might care to explain what you did to cause her such distress?"

"I had to share some devastating personal news with her

about your wife." The earl turned to look at Ruby. "Perhaps you might care to leave the room while I discuss a somewhat delicate matter with my son?"

"I'm not leaving my husband, sir." Ruby met his gaze head on.

"Anything you wish to say to me can be said in front of Ruby," Charles agreed.

"I thought to spare you distress, Mrs. Nash, but so be it." The earl turned back to Charles. "I have some information about your wife that you might find distasteful to hear."

"I doubt it."

"It is one of the reasons why I fear I cannot allow you both to see your mother."

Ruby and Charles exchanged a cautious glance as the earl set his pen back in its inkwell.

"I thought, perhaps, that if I shared this shocking information with you alone, Charles, you could decide what you wanted to do about it, and whether you wished your wife to be allowed to see your mother."

"I must confess to be all at sea, sir," Charles said slowly. "Are you suggesting that you will give me my mother's location as long as I don't tell my wife or bring her to visit my mother?"

The earl inclined his head. "Exactly."

"That's... absurd."

Silence fell as the earl continued to stare at Charles. "You might feel differently when you know of her perfidy."

Charles squeezed Ruby's hand. "How about you tell me the address and then share your concerns about my wife, and I will decide what I intend to do next."

"I'm not stupid, my boy. The moment I give you that address, you'll be off with no thoughts as to the consequences to your name and the reputation of your family."

Ruby cleared her throat. "I am more than happy to withdraw if you wish your father to give you the address, Charles." She didn't care what the earl said about her, if Charles was able to gain access to his mother.

"I'd prefer you stay here." Charles stared at the earl. "Tell me what my wife has done then, sir."

"She has deceived you mightily." The earl produced a sheaf of notes and slid them across the desk to Charles. He made no effort to pick them up. "Until a year ago, she was living with a man who wasn't her husband." The earl waited but Charles said nothing. "Does that not disgust you?"

"Not particularly. Please go on."

"She had a bastard child." The earl looked at Ruby. "Can you deny that, ma'am?"

"No, I cannot."

"She obviously saw you as an easy mark, Charles." The earl sighed. "She abandoned her lover, and God knows what she did with her child in order to end up in Millcastle where she entrapped you into marriage."

Charles turned to Ruby. "Do you think he's talking about our Nora?"

"I believe he is." Ruby smiled up at him.

The earl sat back in his chair, his expression thunderstruck. "You *know* about this child?"

"Know about her? I tuck her into bed most nights and read her a story, sir. She's almost one now and such a delight. Now have you finished with your pathetic threats? We need to find out where you've put my mother."

The earl visibly gathered his composure. "Not from me."

"That was obvious from the moment we began this conversation," Charles said. "You staged this whole drama simply to get me up here to make me abandon my wife." He paused. "The fact that you used my mother's fragility to further your cause makes me sick to my stomach."

He turned toward the door and Ruby followed him, her head held high. It wasn't until they were in their bedroom that

Charles spoke. "The absolute *bastard*." He sank into a chair and put his head in his hands.

Ruby knelt at his feet and put her hand on his knee. "We will find her. He can't keep her hidden away forever. People will talk."

He swallowed hard, displaying a vulnerability she hadn't seen in him before. "He is so determined to punish me for being his heir that he's willing to hurt everyone I care about just to crush my spirit and bring me to heel."

Ruby had come to the same conclusion but kept her thoughts to herself so she could concentrate on helping Charles. "We should go and speak to Mrs. Theydon," Ruby suggested.

"I hardly think she'll help us if she was frightened out of her wits."

"I suspect your father claimed that was the case simply to justify his actions to take your mother from her care." She rose to her feet and put one hand on his shoulder. "We also need to speak to Miss Evans. If your father has dismissed her without a reference, she'll need somewhere to go."

"Miss Evans can come back with us," Charles said and rose to his feet. "Why don't you go and find her while I arrange our transport to the vicarage."

A GRATEFUL MISS EVANS was dispatched to pack her belongings while Ruby and Charles took a gig down to the vicarage. A rather flustered Mrs. Theydon admitted them and offered tea. Charles hurried off to speak to the vicar in his study while Ruby went to sit with Mrs. Theydon. The unheated drawing room contained little except the necessary furniture and had large windows that rattled when the wind blew. Having grown up in households used to economizing, Ruby recognized the signs of an income pushed to its limits.

After a few minutes of polite conversation while they awaited the appearance of the tea tray, Ruby turned to the matter at hand. "We are so grateful for your care of the viscountess, ma'am. Charles was beside himself with worry when he was informed his mother was missing."

Mrs. Theydon pressed her hand to her bosom. "I almost shrieked when I discovered her on the river path, her hand trailing in the water, her dress soaked through from the rain." She shivered. "I thought she might be dead. I confess that a thousand thoughts crowded through my mind, making it almost impossible to act! It wasn't until one of the dogs licked her face and she made a small sound that I was able to go toward her and offer my assistance."

"Was she conscious at that point?"

"Not really, but I was simply relieved she was alive. I ran back to the vicarage as quickly as I could and got help to bring her up to the house."

"That was very well done of you." Ruby paused as the maid delivered the tray, and the vicar's wife poured them both a cup of strong tea.

"Lady Lavinia has always been very kind to me, Mrs. Nash. It was the least I could do when she was in such a terrible state."

"She is a very sweet lady," Ruby agreed. "It is a shame that on some occasions her nerves get the better of her. Miss Evans told me the countess went out for a walk yesterday afternoon. She must have got lost when it started to rain, mistook her way home, and ended up by the river. I know the staff at the hall were searching for her for hours." Ruby sipped her tea and studied Mrs. Theydon over the rim of her cup. "I understand that the countess behaved badly to you when she regained her wits."

"Anyone waking up in a strange bed would be confused and frightened." Mrs. Theydon pressed her lips together. "I took no offense."

"The earl described her as manic."

Mrs. Theydon looked anywhere but at Ruby. Eventually, after a glance at the closed door, she returned her attention to her guest. "I would not have described her in such a manner, ma'am."

Ruby held her gaze. "I suspect she only became agitated when the earl appeared."

Silence fell between them, until Mrs. Theydon cleared her throat. "My husband owes his living to the Earl of Nash."

"I can assure you that anything you tell me will not reach his ears," Ruby said. "We are simply trying to ascertain where the earl took the countess so that we can assure ourselves that she is in good hands."

Mrs. Theydon worried at her lip.

Ruby set her cup down and leaned forward. "Did anyone in your household hear where the earl planned to take her?"

"One of our stable hands carried the countess down the stairs into the earl's carriage. He was ordered to accompany the earl to provide assistance."

"Has he returned yet?"

"Yes, Michael came back early this morning."

"May I speak to him?" Ruby asked. "I can ask for him in the stables, and you need not be involved any further."

Mrs. Theydon made a face. "I'll probably be in trouble for saying anything at all if my husband finds out, but I cannot bear to see the countess treated so harshly." She paused. "She was so afraid of him it broke my heart."

Ruby rose to her feet. "Thank you. I hope we meet again in more pleasant circumstances. If the earl does accuse you of anything, just pretend you know nothing about it and that it was all my own idea to speak to your staff."

"I hate to lie, but in this instance, I think I will take your advice." Mrs. Theydon remained seated. "I will stay here and finish my tea and remain in blissful ignorance of where my guests are and to whom they are speaking."

"Bless you." Ruby smiled at Mrs. Theydon and left the room.

She found her way to the kitchen where a cook was stirring something on the range and the maid was busy washing up.

"Can I help you, ma'am?" the cook asked.

"I think I left one of my gloves in the gig. I'm just going to make sure it is there."

"Stables are across the courtyard, ma'am. I'm sure someone will be able to help you."

"Thank you." Ruby smiled at the two women. "If Dr. Nash inquires as to my whereabout, please tell him I'll be back very shortly."

"Mary was just about to take a pot of coffee into the vicar's study. She can mention it to Dr. Nash while she's in there."

"Thank you." Ruby went through the scullery into the courtyard beyond. The rain had stopped, and she took a few deep breaths before going into the hay-scented stable. There was a boy tending to their gig and she went over to him.

"Is Michael here?"

"Yes, miss." He gazed at her expectantly.

"May I speak to him?"

"Yes, miss." He ran toward the interior of the stable and yelled at the top of his voice, "Lady here wants to see you, Mr. Stones!"

There was a disturbance in the loft above and the sound of grumbling as someone came down the stairs, brushing hay off his shoulders. "I've been up all night, lad, I was just having a kip. Why are you shouting me bloody ear off?" He saw Ruby and came to a sudden stop. "Sorry, miss."

"Are you Michael?" Ruby went toward him. "I'm sorry for disturbing your rest, but there is something very particular I'd like to ask you."

CHARLES SPENT quarter of an hour with the vicar and learned nothing except that the vicar was too afraid of the earl to comment about anything, which wasn't exactly a surprise. When the maid came in and mentioned Ruby had popped out to the stables and that he wasn't to worry himself, he wondered what on earth he was supposed to do. Was there some hidden meaning in her message? Should he immediately join her? His dilemma was increased when the vicar suggested they take their coffee in the drawing room with the ladies.

He acquiesced and was somewhat relieved when Ruby joined them shortly afterward, her expression as composed as ever.

After another twenty minutes of polite conversation, he caught her eye and rose to his feet. "We should be getting back, my dear. We are due to leave this evening and we must say our goodbyes to my father."

"Of course." Ruby stood, too. "We just wanted to thank you for helping Lady Lavinia. It was such a relief for us to know she had been found and cared for."

"It was the least we could do," the vicar said. "I will pray for the countess with special intent tonight."

"Thank you." Ruby curtsied to the vicar and then to Mrs. Theydon.

Charles took her hand and they left the parlor. It wasn't until they were in the gig and driving back to the hall that Ruby spoke again. "I know where your mother is."

Charles almost dropped the reins. "What on earth?"

She smiled at him. "One of the stable hands at the vicarage had to help carry your mother into the earl's carriage. He ended up accompanying her all the way to the end of her journey."

"You have the address?"

"Yes. Now all we have to do is collect Miss Evans, avoid the earl, and get away from Nash Hall as quickly as possible."

CHAPTER SEVENTEEN

"It isn't much of a plan," Charles grumbled as they set forth from Nash Hall. Miss Evans was seated beside Ruby, and she looked as if she might cry.

"If you have another suggestion, I'm more than willing to hear it," Ruby said somewhat tartly. "At the moment, we know little about this place except that it is a big old house in the middle of a park. Michael only carried your mother in through the front door and went no further."

"How about I just walk in there, demand to see her, and carry her out myself?" Charles said.

"That is certainly an option, but one might assume that your father has told them to keep her there until he says otherwise."

"He'll leave her there to rot," Charles growled. "He might not have succeeded in alienating me from you, but he has gotten rid of my mother."

"And we will endeavor to correct that as soon as we have gathered the necessary information."

Charles didn't appreciate her calmness and let it show. "What if she's chained up in a prison cell?"

"Then you have my permission to get her out immediately."

"Thank you." He glared at her. "Not that I need your permission."

She had the audacity to smile at him with far too much understanding and sympathy. "We're far more likely to be successful if we work together, Charles. You know that."

"I agree with Mrs. Nash, Doctor," Miss Evans spoke for the first time. "If you can convince them to allow you to see her, we will know how she fairs and can make our plans to free her."

"I'll do my best," Charles said. "But my behavior depends very much on the circumstances I find her in."

Ruby patted his hand. "Absolutely."

They completed the rest of the journey in silence. Eventually, they arrived at the house Michael had given them direction to. There was a large gate, beyond which was a sweeping drive lined with elm trees. The gatekeeper greeted them and allowed them entry after Charles gave his name and profession. When the carriage stopped outside the house's main door, Charles got out and left the ladies behind.

He knocked on the door and was admitted by a very large man who looked like he belonged in a boxing ring.

"I am Dr. Charles Nash." He gave the giant his card. "I've been sent to assess the condition of Viscountess Nash."

"I'll see if anyone can attend to you. It's late. Stay here, sir." The man turned to leave.

Charles wandered around the entrance hall which looked remarkably like every other country house he'd ever visited. The scent of roast beef came from behind one of the closed doors and the occasional maid rushed past with a tray, acknowledging him with a swift nod of the head. There were no blood-curdling screams or "patients" visible. By the time the man returned, Charles had completed his tour and had a decent understanding of the layout of the ground floor.

"Follow me."

Charles went up the shallow stairs and was directed into the first room at the top of the landing.

There was a man sitting behind an ornate desk who rose to greet him. "Dr. Nash?"

"I do apologize for disturbing you at such a late hour. When my father contacted me about what had happened to my poor mother and begged me to offer my professional opinion on her state, I could not refuse him."

"Quite understandable. I am Dr. French, and I am in charge of this establishment." He gestured for Charles to take a seat.

"I was unable to reach my mother before she was brought here." Charles paused. "If I had been present, I probably wouldn't have advised taking her away from the comfort of her home, but I suspect my father panicked."

"The earl was certainly concerned about his wife's state of health. We corresponded a few months ago about finding a suitable placement for her, but her arrival was something of a surprise."

"From what I understand, this... behavior came as a shock to everyone around her," Charles said. "I can only hope that it was an aberration and not a sign of things to come."

God, he hated sounding like he agreed with his father, but it was the only way to get Dr. French to believe they were all on the same side.

"Time will tell." Dr. French smiled. "I believe she is sleeping at the moment." He paused. "We haven't done a full assessment of her mental state yet. We gave her some laudanum to calm her down."

"Very wise." Charles nodded. "After coming all this way, I would appreciate seeing her. I promise I won't wake her up. I just want to be able to reassure my father that she has settled in well and is no longer a danger to herself or anyone else."

"I think we can arrange that." Dr. French stood up. "If you care to follow me."

Charles noticed the bunch of keys that hung from Dr. French's waistcoat chain when he came around the desk.

"I suspect that after a few weeks of peace and quiet, her ladyship will be ready to return home," Dr. French remarked as he led the way along the corridor. Each room had a number on it and a peephole. It reminded Charles of a luxurious prison. "From what I understand, she has never been violent or needed severe treatment. I don't allow such practices here anyway. I truly believe that nature is the best healer."

There was a note of sincerity in Dr. French's voice that surprised Charles. He would expect him to use such language talking to a prospective patient's family, not a fellow professional, but maybe because Charles was both he was being cautious.

"Here we are. It is one of our best rooms and overlooks the gardens." Dr. French unlocked the door of number twenty-four and ushered Charles inside. It was a pleasant room that reminded Charles of his mother's own suite at Nash Hall.

There was a nurse sitting by the bed who rose as they came in and put her finger to her lips before walking over toward them.

"Lady Lavinia is fast asleep," she whispered.

"Thank you, Nurse Sugden," Dr. French said. "This is Dr. Nash. He is not only a physician but the countess's son."

"She's been no trouble, Doctor," the nurse addressed Charles. "Just a little weepy and very tired."

"You may approach the bed, Dr. Nash. I don't think she will wake up."

"Thank you."

Charles went over to the bed, sat in the chair, and stared carefully at his mother's beautiful face. She had a slight bruise on her forehead—likely from her fall by the river—but otherwise seemed in perfect health. Some part of him wished she had been in dire straits, because then at least he could've vented some of the anger burning inside him on her captors...

He took out his pocket watch, held her wrist, and checked her pulse, which was slow but regular. The action helped calm him and consider what to do next. He didn't want to leave her, but from what he could tell she was in no danger at present. Eventually, he stood up, kissed her gently on the forehead and went back to Dr. French who had remained discreetly with the nurse by the door.

"Thank you. I must confess I am greatly relieved to see her being so well taken care of."

Dr. French smiled. "In our profession one hears such horror stories of patients being imprisoned in appalling conditions. I quite understand your desire to see her and confirm that all is as well as he could be."

"My father made an excellent choice." After one last look at his mother, Charles stepped away from the bed. The nurse resumed her seat, and Dr. French followed him out into the corridor.

"We will monitor her closely over the next few days." Dr. French paused. "I understand that she has a tendency to wander."

"So, it seems." Charles kept his tone as neutral as Dr. French's.

"When she does feel ready to venture outside, we will take care of her, I promise."

They continued on past the office and back down the stairs to the well-guarded front door. Charles turned to shake Dr. French's hand.

"Thank you for letting me see her."

"You are most welcome. The earl seemed disinclined to visit, but if you wish to do so I'd leave it a few days until she settles in and come next weekend? I believe we'll have her in a good state by then."

"I'll write to you if I am able to visit," Charles said. He picked up his hat and cloak from the hall table. "Goodnight, Dr. French, and thank you for your time."

The doctor unlocked the front door and let him through. Charles heard the door lock behind him. He was relieved that the carriage still stood where he'd left it. After giving the coachman some instructions, he got back in to find Ruby and Miss Evans regarding him anxiously.

As they pulled away, he took Ruby's hand. "It isn't as bad there as I feared. I've asked the coachman to stop at the first decent inn. We'll have something to eat and I can tell you everything I found out."

RUBY FINISHED the last of her roast pork and sat back. "That was excellent. I'm so glad you suggested that we stop for a while, Charles. I've hardly eaten anything today."

Miss Evans, who had asked Ruby to call her Martha, continued to eat her dinner. Her composure under such stressful circumstances was admirable. From Martha's account, the earl hadn't even bothered to inform her of her dismissal in person and had sent his land agent to tell her to pack her bags and leave immediately without her quarterly payment or a reference.

Charles finished his wine and glanced at the door. "I'll go and get the maid to clear the plates. We don't want to linger here for too long."

Like Martha, Charles appeared far more in control than Ruby had expected, but she knew him well enough to see the signs of agitation he fought to conceal.

"Do ask if there is any pudding," Ruby said as he rose to his feet. "I'd quite enjoy something sweet."

"I'll inquire."

He left the room and returned shortly with the maid who took away the dirty plates and replaced them with a steamed jam pudding, custard, and a selection of cheese and port.

Once she'd left, Charles poured himself a glass of port and resumed his seat. "My mother didn't appear to be in any imminent danger."

Ruby helped herself to the steaming pudding. "That is good to hear."

"Dr. French, who runs the establishment, appears to be a good man."

"Even better."

"He thinks it would do her good to stay there for a few weeks to regain her strength and equilibrium."

"And what do you think about that?" Ruby asked.

Charles grimaced. "As things stand, I can't think of any reason why she shouldn't receive such care. The issue is whether my father intends to keep her there permanently."

"Did Dr. French suggest that he would?"

"He didn't. He seemed to think my father would be happy to have her back." Charles drank more port. "I'm not convinced that is the case."

"Would it be possible for you to ask the earl what his intentions are?" Martha asked. "One might think that as he has dispensed with my services, he has no intention of allowing her to return."

Charles nodded. "I assume he might try to use her as a bargaining chip against me. It wouldn't be the first time he has compelled me to follow his orders in return for him not ruining my mother's life."

"That's... awful," Ruby said. "I had no idea."

He flashed a quick smile at her. "No need for both of us to worry about such things, my dear."

Momentarily forgetting Martha's presence, Ruby reached across the table and took his hand. "But I *want* to worry. You're my husband."

He brought her hand to his lips and kissed her knuckles while Martha kept her gaze firmly on her bowl of pudding.

"I suggest we wait until my father contacts me," Charles said. "If he wishes to use her against me, he'll let me know."

"I suppose Dr. French will tell him that you visited," Ruby said. "I do hope the earl doesn't try and move her again."

"That is my worst fear," Charles said quietly. "I will write to Dr. French and ensure that he keeps me informed as to her progress and whereabouts." He finished his glass of port and sat back. "My father holds all legal rights over my mother's existence, and there's nothing else I can do."

DESPITE THEIR ARRIVAL home well after midnight, Ruby still had to get up the next morning to see to Nora, and Charles was due at the navvy camp. Despite her tiredness, she hadn't slept well, her mind worrying about too many things she had little or no control over. At one point, she'd reached for Charles, and finding him awake, had kissed him with a purpose that led to lovemaking that was as tender and fierce as their current emotions. She didn't regret that closeness, even though she knew she'd be tired all day.

Nora was teething, her cheeks red, her temperature elevated, and neither Bridget nor Ruby could soothe her. She wanted to grizzle, drool, and constantly be held by her mother. After a few unsuccessful attempts to hand her over to Bridget so that she could get on with the monthly accounts, Ruby had given up, wrapped Nora in her shawl and tied it closely around herself like the mothers who worked in the mills.

Nora finally nodded off, and Ruby was able to get on—as long as she stood and swayed like a ship at anchor, which meant she did the accounts standing beside the dresser. It wasn't the most comfortable of positions, and Ruby's back soon began to ache.

Martha came down the stairs just before midday and seeing Ruby, immediately started apologizing about oversleeping, of not being of any help, and her desire to set forth and find employment that very day.

Ruby introduced her to Eliza and told her not to worry about her employment prospects for at least a few days until they were all in a fit state to discuss them.

Martha didn't seem convinced. "I cannot be a burden, Mrs. Nash. I do have some savings, but—"

Ruby patted her shoulder. "If you truly wish to be useful while you are here perhaps you can offer Dr. Nash your assistance. He desperately needs someone to organize his patients and his records."

"I think I could do that," Martha said. "Where is Dr. Nash?"

"He's out at the moment, but he'll be back for dinner. You can talk to him about it then." Ruby turned to Eliza. "Why don't you take Miss Evans out and show her around town?"

Eliza blinked at her. "What about my work?"

"I think you can be excused for an hour or two."

"You'll tell Mrs. Jenkins it weren't my idea?" Eliza asked suspiciously.

"Yes, I will." Ruby turned to Martha. "It's a pleasant day to see Millcastle. Perhaps you might ask Eliza to take you to the park and then our fine new railway station, which is almost on our doorstep."

After years caring for the mercurial countess, Martha was

well used to picking up on others' moods "How lovely. I'll go and get my cloak and bonnet."

Half an hour later, when Bridget had gone upstairs to tidy the nursery, Ruby finally sat down to eat. Nora slept on, her small hand pressed to her mother's heart, her cheeks as red as her mother's namesake. Ruby smoothed her daughter's sparse, fair hair and kissed the top of her head. It if hadn't been for the ache in her back, she would almost have forgotten Nora was there. It felt natural to have Nora so close, reminding her of the days after her birth when even Sidney had been entranced with them both.

There was a knock on the front door. Realizing she was the only person around to answer it, Ruby heaved herself out of the chair and went out into the hallway. There was a man silhouetted in the panes of the stained-glass panels. Ruby took her time unlocking the door and opened it just as the man removed his flat cap with a flourish and grinned at her.

"Ruby."

Her heart faltered and she took a step back, cradling Nora's head in one hand. It was a mistake because it enabled Sidney to get his foot in the door.

"Is that my daughter?" His face softened. "Good Lord, she's grown."

"Don't touch her."

He paused, his expression full of concern. "What's wrong? Is she ill?"

"She's teething." Ruby couldn't stop staring at the man who'd once been her everything. "You can't come in here, Sidney."

"Why not?" His smile was a delight. "I'm sure you've told your new husband all about me."

"I have told him, and that's why you're not welcome."

"I heard he was a gentleman. What will he do? Challenge me to a duel? Come on, Ruby. I have a right to see my own child."

"Not here," Ruby said. "Where are you staying?"

"Nowhere I'd want you to visit." Sidney's smiled disappeared.

Ruby gathered her senses. "I'll meet you tomorrow at the railway station at nine in the morning."

"With my child," Sidney said.

"That depends on how she is faring." Ruby met his gaze. "I'm not risking her health again, Sidney."

He had the grace to look away. "All right, then. Nine o'clock it is."

CHAPTER EIGHTEEN

*C*harles finished eating his dinner and got up to put the plate in the sink. Ruby had already made the tea and the pot was sitting on the table with a jug of milk ready to be poured.

"I wrote to Dr. French today and gave him this address. I claimed that the earl wished me to deal with any medical matters relating to my mother's care. If he checks with my father, there might be hell to pay, but he might not. I'm still waiting for him to show his hand."

Ruby didn't appear to have heard him. He cleared his throat.

"Did you hear what I said?"

"Yes, that's excellent news." She poured the tea.

"Hardly that." He paused, but she still wasn't attending to him. "One might almost think you weren't listening to me."

"I'm sorry. Nora's been teething all day and refused to have anyone care for her but me."

"Well, you are her mother."

"I am aware of that." Ruby glared at him. "I take my responsibilities very seriously, indeed."

He raised an eyebrow. "I wasn't suggesting otherwise. I

meant that of course she'd want to be with the person she loves the most."

She grimaced. "And now I need to apologize again."

"There's no need. I'm not exactly a pleasure to be with when I come home in a bad mood."

She tried to smile, but he sensed it was forced. He was trying hard to be conciliatory but it still didn't come easily to him.

"If you want to go to bed early, I'll do the dishes and stoke the fires," he offered.

She took a deep breath. "Sidney came to the house this morning."

He went cold. "He came *here*? How did he get the address?"

She shrugged. "I have no idea."

"What did he want?"

The question came out more harshly than he'd intended, but he was desperately trying to read her face and work out if she was pleased by this unexpected development or as horrified as he was.

"He wanted to see Nora."

"And did you allow that? Did you welcome him into our house?"

"Of *course*, I didn't." She raised her chin. "I asked him to leave."

"I assume he didn't like that." Charles paused. "Did he threaten you?"

"That's not Sidney's way. He usually gets what he wants using his charm." Ruby sighed. "I offered to meet him tomorrow at nine at the railway station."

He wanted to ask why she needed to see him at all, but he wasn't stupid. Sidney was Nora's father and that complicated matters.

"If he just wants to see Nora, I could take her for you," he offered.

"You'd do that?"

"Yes, of course." He frowned.

"It's very good of you, but I need to see him myself. If I don't, I fear he'll keep coming back, and I couldn't bear it."

"We could both go."

She reached across the table and took his hand in hers. "I think I have to do this alone, Charles."

He eased his hand free. "No. You're choosing to do it alone."

"If I need your help, I promise I will ask for it."

He studied her face, the strength in it, the purpose in her eyes, and sighed. Loving someone was far more complicated than he'd anticipated, and this was one of those times when his instincts went against his logic.

He tried for honesty. "I'm... worried about you seeing him alone."

"I'll be in a very public place. If he attempts anything under-handed, I'm fairly certain someone would stop him."

"What if he tries to take Nora?"

She sat up straight. "I will fight to the death rather than allow that to happen." He smiled and she frowned. "What is so amusing?"

"You are my warrior queen wife. I'd wager you'd win if he tried anything."

"Thank you." She smiled back at him. "I appreciate your confidence in me. I haven't even decided if I will take Nora with me. She isn't well."

"You can make that decision in the morning," Charles said. "Now, why don't you go to bed. I'll check that Nora is well and lock up."

Ruby rose to her feet and came to stand next to him, her fingers curving around the back of his neck. "Thank you," she said simply.

"For what?"

"Trying so hard to be good about all this." She leaned in and gently kissed him on the forehead. "When all your instincts tell you to take charge and make things right for me."

"You already know me too well." He grimaced.

"Which is why I am appreciating your restraint." She kissed him again, this time on his mouth. "Don't take too long coming to bed, will you?"

"I'll be as quick as I can," he promised with some alacrity.

She patted his cheek, went out into the hall, and climbed the stairs. He knew she'd check on Nora herself, but he'd also take a look just to make sure that Bridget had everything necessary for a teething baby.

A curious sense of peace came over him as he continued to sit at the table. All his senses were telling him that Ruby had no intention of leaving with Sidney, which was surprisingly gratifying. He couldn't imagine life without her now. She not only understood him but supported him without question. And she trusted him...

He finished his tea and stood up. The least he could do was trust her in return.

RUBY DRESSED in her most severe gown and braided her hair tightly to her head. She didn't want Sidney suggesting she had become too comfortable in her life and had forgotten the struggles of the working class. Nora had woken up in a far better mood, and Ruby decided she would take her to see Sidney after all. Her fingers shook as she attempted to button up the back of Nora's dress.

Bridget tried to help her. "Where are we off to this morning, ma'am?"

"I have to take Nora to meet someone at the railway station." Ruby smiled at the nursemaid. "You don't need to accompany me."

"Then I'll get on with sorting Nora's clothes out. She's outgrown some of them, so I can set them aside for when she becomes a big sister." Bridget winked at Ruby.

Ruby smiled and glanced at the nursery clock. She had quarter of an hour before she was due to meet Sidney, and the walk to the station would barely take five minutes. She hadn't seen Charles at breakfast. He'd gone out at dawn to visit one of his patients and hadn't yet returned.

Nora cooed and patted her cheek, and Ruby smiled at her daughter. Nora looked nothing like the thin, sick wraith who'd arrived at Caroline's. She was now "blonde and bonny" as Bridget often said.

"I'll help you get the perambulator into the yard, ma'am," Bridget said. "It's hard work for one."

"Thank you." Ruby set a new knitted cap on Nora's head and lifted her child into her arms. She'd already donned her outdoor things and was ready to leave.

She now had ten minutes before she was due to meet Sidney. Her hope of Charles appearing had become minimal. She'd told him she didn't need his help, and it appeared he had taken her at her word. Suddenly, she wished he was here to send her off with some strong words of advice and was cross with herself for being so contrary. His good opinion had become far too important to her to ignore.

She carried Nora carefully down two flights of stairs and out into the stable yard, which was mercifully free of patients as word had gone out that the doctor wasn't there. Bridget was rearranging the pillows and drew back the blankets so Nora could be placed in a cocoon of warmth.

"Be a good girl for your mam, Nora, no crying now!" Bridget blew the baby a kiss, grinned at Ruby. "I'll see you later, ma'am."

"Thank you, Bridget. I have my key, so please remember to lock the door behind you."

"Yes, Mrs. Nash." Bridget turned back to the kitchen door.

Ruby spent an unnecessary few minutes fussing with the blankets and retying the ribbons under Nora's chin before putting on her gloves and heading out onto the street. The pavement had recently been finished, for which she was grateful. It led directly to the imposing frontage of the Millcastle railway station, which Mr. Hepworth had built with his navvies. There was a hackney cab rank out the front, a very smart hotel on the left, and the parish church where she'd been married took up the right-hand corner with the graveyard hard up against the new lines of the track.

As it was a weekday, the majority of the town were still at work, and the station was relatively quiet. Ruby went into the ticket office where a line had formed at the window. She saw Sidney sitting on one of the benches looking at his pocket watch. He glanced up and rose to his feet with a quick smile.

"Punctual as ever. Good morning, Ruby." He smiled at Nora who was regarding him with great suspicion. "Good Lord, she's grown."

Ruby wheeled the perambulator into the farthest corner from the door, and Sidney followed her over.

"There's a waiting room," he said. "Would that be quieter?"

"I think this is fine." She fussed with Nora's blankets. "It will calm down once everyone has bought a ticket for the train and gone through the gate."

"Have you been on the train?" Sidney asked as he sat on the bench beside the pram.

"Not yet."

"I have. It's quite terrifying, especially in the tunnels. I prefer the mail coach." He looked directly at Ruby. "May I hold my daughter?"

"Yes, of course," Ruby said. "But don't be surprised if she is a little shy with you."

Sidney grimaced. "I'm aware that I am a stranger to her. Is your husband good with her?"

"He treats her as he would his own child," Ruby said as she carefully handed Nora over to her father.

"That's... good." Sidney contemplated his daughter. "She looks like me."

"Yes."

"Except for her eyes, which are brown like yours." He offered Nora his finger. She grabbed hold of it with alacrity and brought it to her mouth, making Sidney wince.

"She's teething," Ruby said.

"So, I see." He made no effort to stop her gnawing on his knuckle. "I probably deserve to be savaged."

"Where are you headed after Millcastle?" Ruby asked rather pointedly, having no time for guile or any need for it.

"Liverpool, I think. I've been asked to speak at the shipyards." He kept his attention on Nora.

"This is hardly on your way," Ruby said.

"I know."

"Then what made you come?"

He sighed. "When I returned to Leeds and heard you'd left, and in such bad circumstances, I felt... guilty."

"How did you expect me to survive with no wage coming into the home?" Ruby asked.

"I suppose I took you at your word when you assured me that you would be all right."

"You were very keen to leave us, Sidney. I merely gave you the opportunity to do so without a fight."

"Mayhap you should have fought with me."

"I was exhausted. I had nothing left to give," Ruby said simply. "When Nora became ill, I had to bury my pride and find someone to help me. I had just enough money to get close to Millcastle, and I knew that Caroline would take us in."

"She can well afford to do so." Sidney sneered. "Living as she does off the notorious Captain Grafton."

"They saved our lives, Sidney." Ruby made him hold her gaze. "You should be grateful."

"Grateful to a man who tried to bribe me to leave you alone?" Sidney demanded. "He said he would always take care of you, and that if I ever as much as damaged a hair on your head, he'd come after me."

Ruby looked at him for a long moment as several things suddenly became clear.

"What?" Sidney raised his eyebrows.

"That's why you left, isn't it? Because you knew that whatever happened Francis would take us in. And now you have the gall to castigate him for doing so." Ruby shook her head "Did you take his money as well, Sidney? Is that how you are able to travel so freely around the country?"

"I did not take his filthy money," Sidney said. "I am funded by working men." He set his jaw. "I did not come here to rake over the past. I wanted to see if you and my daughter were all right."

"And you have seen that we are both thriving," Ruby said. "Who gave you my address?"

Sidney grimaced. "That's the other reason why I'm here."

"Did you seek out Francis first to ask for money? Or did someone up at Grafton Hall mistakenly give you my address? I know my sister and her husband would not do so."

Sidney handed Nora back to Ruby, and she resettled her into the perambulator.

"For the last time, I have taken no bribes from Francis Grafton for myself or my cause, and I never will," Sidney said. "I was contacted by another individual on behalf of a gentleman of means."

"Who?" Ruby asked.

"A gentleman who offered to fund my cause if I was willing to make things difficult for you."

A horrible suspicion entered Ruby's head and would not be

shaken. She remained silent and waited to see what Sidney would say next.

"Are you acquainted with the Earl of Nash, Ruby?"

Ruby straightened and turned toward the station exit. "Come with me. You need to speak to my husband."

CHARLES ATE his fish-paste sandwich and looked around the unusually quiet kitchen. Bridget was upstairs in the nursery, Eliza had the morning off, and Mrs. Jenkins had gone shopping. He had a private patient to visit at three in the afternoon, but until then, his time was his own. He glanced at the clock on the mantelpiece. It was almost nine thirty, and Ruby hadn't returned from her meeting with Sidney.

He stopped chewing and set down his sandwich. Should he go and look for her? It had taken every ounce of self-control he possessed to leave the house at dawn and let Ruby deal with Sidney alone. Had he made a terrible mistake? Had Ruby realized she still loved Sidney and left with him, or had Sidney done something unspeakable?

He rose to his feet and was just about to head for the door when he heard voices in the stable yard. Leaving the remains of his meal on the table, he went to open the backdoor and found Ruby with the perambulator and an unfamiliar man.

"Charles," Ruby said. "You have to speak to Sidney."

"Why would I want to do that?" Charles asked, his gaze on the other man. He looked vaguely familiar. "Unless you wish me to tell him to leave you alone, or else."

The man had the audacity to smile. "Ruby is quite capable of telling me that herself, Dr. Nash. There is another matter she insisted I speak to you about."

"Then I suppose you'd better come in."

Charles helped Ruby bring the perambulator inside and

parked it in the hall. She immediately took Nora in her arms and started up the stairs.

"I'll be down in a moment. Why don't you make us all some tea, Charles?"

Charles eyed Sidney and gestured toward the kitchen. "Come along, then."

"Thank you, Dr. Nash."

Charles filled the kettle and set it on the range to boil before turning back to Sidney, who had remained standing just inside the door, his leisurely gaze taking in the kitchen. He wore the rough clothes of a navvy, a handkerchief knotted carelessly at his throat, and a flat cap.

"Sit down."

Sidney took off his cap to reveal hair the same blonde as Nora's and sat at the table. Charles spooned tea into the pot and set out three cups along with the pitcher of milk.

"You're not working class," Charles said. "You've done an excellent job trying to conceal your accent, but I can still hear it. In fact, I feel as if I've met you before."

"If you're the Earl of Nash's son, we might have met at school," Sidney said.

Charles paused in his task to stare intently at Sidney's face. "Yes, Harrow or Eton. What's your last name?"

"Fellows."

"Knew your older brother, George," Charles said. "He was a fine cricket player."

"I would assume he still is."

"Don't you see your family?" Charles asked as the kettle came to the boil. After warming the pot and rinsing it he set the tea to brew. "I should imagine your choice of career was considered even more radical than my own."

Sidney shrugged. "I'm the fourth son of an impoverished baronet. I only attended Eton because my godmother paid my fees."

"Does Ruby know?"

"About what?"

"Your privileged roots."

"I can't say it ever came up."

"I bet it didn't. How can you appeal to the common man when your father's a member of the aristocracy?"

"Only a minor member. I have no expectations of inheriting the title from him.

"Still. I'll wager your ardent followers don't know that either. Do you work hard to conceal your upper-class drawl when you orate?" Sidney's smile had gone. "Bit of a shocker, eh?"

"Do your employers and patients know that you are the son of an earl?" Sidney countered.

"Some of them do." Charles sat back at the table, facing Sidney. "I've got nothing to hide."

"Your father thinks otherwise."

"What in God's name do you have to do with my father?" Charles asked.

Ruby came into the kitchen and obviously heard his last question. "That's why I brought him to speak to you, Charles. I fear your father is attempting to interfere in our affairs again." She took a seat at the end of the table between the two men. "Sidney said he was contacted by a man who had been investigating me for your father."

"The man Miss Evans mentioned seeing at the hall," Charles said. "Go on."

Ruby turned to Sidney. "Yes, please elaborate."

"I was speaking at a rally in Leeds, and I was approached by a Mr. Simms. He had a lot of questions about you, Ruby. At first, I did my best to avoid answering them, but Mr. Simms was persistent. He tried to bribe me, and when that didn't work, he threatened that his employer would have me put in prison."

"That does sound like something my father would do,"

Charles said as he poured out the tea. He only realized he'd taken Ruby's hand when she squeezed his fingers. "What did he want to know?"

"Whether Ruby and I were married." Sidney looked from Charles to Ruby. "I told him we had never married, because we considered it an outmoded concept that denied women their rights as independent individuals."

Charles barely managed not to roll his eyes as Sidney continued. "Mr. Simms suggested that if I swore on oath that we *had* been married, his employer would provide all the necessary documentation to back up my claim."

"And what did he offer you in return for doing him such a service?" Charles asked.

"Five thousand pounds."

Charles whistled. "A small fortune. Did you take it?"

"I told Mr. Simms I needed time to think about it and that I wanted the name of his employer. He was reluctant to reveal it, but after a few drinks one night, he blurted out everything I needed to know, including your address, Ruby."

"Why did you say you'd think about his offer if you were insulted by it?" Charles asked. "Why didn't you immediately send him away?"

"Because at the time, I didn't know exactly what was going on. As far as I knew, Ruby was still in Leeds and had nothing to do with the Earl of Nash."

"That's why you went to find me and wrote that letter," Ruby said.

"Yes. Then I knew you'd left Leeds, and I had to assume you'd gone to your sister."

"And what made you decide to turn up here?" Charles asked.

Sidney grimaced. "Because Mr. Simms came to find me, wanting an answer."

"Five thousand pounds is a lot of money." Charles sipped his tea. "I should imagine you could do a great deal to aid your cause with such a sum."

"I have no intention of taking it, Dr. Nash." Sidney glared at him. "I simply wished to understand why the offer was made in the first place."

"How very worthy of you." Charles didn't bother to try and hide the skepticism on his face.

"I am aware of the reasons why you might not like me, Dr. Nash, but I can assure you that I would never betray Ruby or my child."

"Surely you betrayed her by leaving her to fend for herself in Leeds?"

"Charles..." Ruby tried to intervene.

"Or did it not occur to you that with no wage coming in and no ability to earn one, Ruby and Nora would starve to death?"

"I offered her a *choice*, Dr. Nash. She chose to stay behind," Sidney said calmly. "She is an independent being, capable of making her own decisions."

"She had just had your child. How in God's name did you expect her to survive? On air? On your elevated and totally useless *ideology*?"

Sidney said nothing.

"You believed Ruby should follow you adoringly around the country with a newborn at her breast, enduring whatever conditions were thrown at her?" Charles raised his eyebrows.

"Other women do so," Sidney said. "Women work twelve-hour shifts at the mill with their babies strapped to their chests."

"I know what women are capable of. I see it every day in my work," Charles snapped. "But implying in your 'holier than thou' way that Ruby somehow failed you by not being willing to follow you is ridiculous." He turned to Ruby. "He offered you no choice, my dear."

She raised her chin. "Can we get back to the matter in hand?

What can we do about this blackmailing scheme orchestrated by your father?"

There was a lot more Charles wanted to say about the matter, but he'd prefer to say it when Sidney wasn't present.

He took a deep breath, took a slug of tea, and turned back to Sidney. "How long do you have before Mr. Simms demands a final answer?"

"Two days."

"Do you have somewhere to stay in Millcastle?"

Charles didn't miss the swift glance Sidney gave Ruby before he replied. "I can find lodgings if necessary."

"If Ruby doesn't mind, you can stay in our spare room." He looked at his wife and she nodded, if a little stiffly. "I'd like you close at hand."

"Do you have a plan?" Sidney asked.

"The glimmerings of one." Charles rose to his feet. "I need to go and speak to Francis. I promise I'll be back in time for dinner, my dear."

CHAPTER NINETEEN

*A*fter Charles returned from his visit to Francis, they had sat down for a somewhat awkward dinner with Martha and Sidney. Ruby wasn't sure which of the men annoyed her the most with their ability to talk about her without asking her opinion. At one point, she considered leaving them to it, but she was eager to know what Charles intended to do to thwart his father, and so she sat through the meal mainly in silence, only speaking to Martha when necessary.

At Charles's direction, Sidney wrote a note to Mr. Simms asking to meet at the George and Dragon, a disreputable coaching inn still owned by Francis in the worst area of Millcastle. Francis would be thereabouts when Mr. Simms offered his terms to Sidney. If everything went to plan, Francis, in his capacity as the local magistrate, had the legal authority to charge Mr. Simms with attempted blackmail. What happened after that was still a subject of much discussion.

Ruby left Charles to make sure Sidney had everything he needed in the second spare bedroom, and after checking on

Nora, she went into their bedroom. Charles arrived when she was already in her nightgown and brushing out her hair.

He took one look at her and held up his hand. "I'm sorry I invited Sidney to stay here. I didn't want him disappearing off on his white horse."

"There's no need to be so contemptuous of his cause," Ruby said. "It is a righteous one."

"Righteous." Charles sat down to take off his stocking and trousers. "People like Sidney make me sick."

"Because they are brave?" Ruby spun around to face him, her hairbrush in her hand.

"No, because their romantic idealism destroys people."

"There are always martyrs to a cause."

"And did you wish to be one of them?" Charles paused in his undressing to glare at her. "Is that why you let him leave you?"

"Perhaps."

He raised an eyebrow and she shot to her feet.

"Or perhaps I was a coward. Did you ever think of that, Charles?" Her voice cracked. "Perhaps I was too afraid to go with him. Too afraid to believe he would find a way to care for us as he promised."

"You think *you* let *him* down?"

Ruby nodded, her throat tight with unshed tears.

"That's absolutely bloody ridiculous!" Charles snapped. "How *dare* he make you feel as if you failed him when it was all his fault?"

"He has a cause he believes in. In the end I was too weak, too feeble, and too scared to—"

He stood, took hold of her shoulders, and gently shook her. "Don't ever say that again," he growled. "If you'd gone with him, he wouldn't have cared what became of you, because he's a bloody fanatic!"

"I couldn't go. Not with Nora in the state she was in. I—"

He kissed her "You're a pragmatist, and there's nothing

wrong with that. Nora's alive because you came to Millcastle. Don't ever forget it."

Ruby gazed into his eyes and saw the blazing conviction within them.

"But I failed—"

He kissed her again, this time more roughly. "You survived, and you didn't fail your daughter or yourself. No one can live up to Sidney's lofty standards, not even him." He paused to draw her more closely against his body. "I bet he has a private income from his family."

Her brows creased. "We never discussed money. Sidney believed it was vulgar to do so."

"Did you know that Francis sent him money for your keep?"

"No." Ruby looked up at him. "He never said anything about it." She paused. "I could've used that money to feed Nora."

"Yes." Charles steered her toward the bed. "Now start to direct your anger at the person responsible, rather than at yourself."

"Not at you?" She sighed. "I fear I am quite angry about everything tonight."

He smiled as he lowered her onto the bed. "As long as no one can see where you bite and scratch me, I'll be happy to assist you in any way you wish, my dear."

She nipped his ear, and his whole body came to life. His kisses became bolder and went lower and soon she didn't care if Sidney heard her screaming her pleasure to the whole world.

BY TWO O'CLOCK THE next day, all was in place. Mr. Simms had agreed to meet Sidney, Francis was at the inn, and all that was left was for Charles and Sidney to make their way to the meeting point. Charles would take Sidney as far as the old town square and show him the inn. It had miraculously survived the building of the railway station—mainly because Francis was one of the major shareholders.

"I think I'll have to come back to Millcastle soon," Sidney said, his gaze on the old tenement buildings that housed most of the mill workers. "This place needs me."

"To disrupt the workforce and make them strike? And they'll starve while you waltz off to your next appointment flogging rebellion? You'd be better leaving them alone."

"To this?" Sidney swung around and gestured at the broken windows, the refuse running down the center of the road, and the stick-thin children playing in the filth. "I suppose you only treat private clients and can turn a blind eye to such misery."

"I treat everyone, including the navvies in the camps," Charles said evenly. "I am well aware of what this town needs."

"Then you should be on my side."

"If there is a side, I'm on the one where I'm doing my damndest to make things better for people one patient at a time. I don't have time for the politics or the grandstanding."

"You should. As a physician and the son of a peer you'd be listened to. If you wish for some information as to how to start, I could—"

"No, thank you. If I have my way, we'll cross paths as little as possible. I don't like you upsetting my wife."

They walked in silence for a moment, avoiding the worst of the potholes that pitted the rough road.

"Ruby seems content with you," Sidney commented.

"Why wouldn't she be? I'm unlikely to disappear off into the night, leaving her to starve."

"As you're now the heir to a thriving earldom, I doubt she will starve. It's interesting that she chose to live with another man with an aristocratic past. It's almost as if, despite her supposed convictions, she really can't shed her need to be with her own class."

Charles turned, grabbed Sidney by the throat, and slammed

him against the wall of a nearby building. "You will never speak of my wife in such disparaging terms again, or I will find you, and you won't like the consequences."

Sidney turned red in the face as he struggled against Charles's grip. "I didn't... mean."

"Yes, you did, you pious, self-serving little hypocrite. You took the allowance meant for her and spent it on yourself, leaving her and your child with nothing." Charles let go of Sidney with a final shake. "You aren't worthy to kiss the hem of her gown."

Sidney took great heaving breaths. "You're insane."

"No, I'm simply protective of what is mine." Charles glared at him. "And don't give me that balderdash about her being an independent woman capable of deciding her fate for herself—I bloody well know that. She needed your support, and you failed her because your cause is more important to you than your family."

"Fine!" Sidney looked at him. "Maybe you've got a point, but I swear she willingly stayed behind. I would've taken her."

"And chastised her when she couldn't keep up? Or when she had no strength left for anything but the child you shared? You claim to want equal opportunities for all, but you're incapable of understanding the real struggle that every woman who has a child goes through."

"I meant her no harm," Sidney said. "I took her at her word that she considered herself my equal in our struggle."

"Because it suited you to see her as another version of you, and not the person she was," Charles said flatly. "Any fool knows that carrying a child is life-changing. A woman cannot be as selfish as a man when she has a child."

Sidney took a deep breath. "That is all behind us now. Ruby has made her choice, and I accept that."

"How gracious of you." Charles started walking again. "I'm

glad we've sorted that out. Just make sure you tell Ruby that you have no further claim on her."

He waited at the corner while Sidney, looking somewhat shaken, walked across the dilapidated square to the George and Dragon, a low timber-framed building that had probably looked its best a hundred years previously when it was a thriving coaching inn.

Charles checked his pocket watch, careful not to let it be seen too visibly, considering the present company. After a quarter of an hour, he was to go into the hostelry to see what had occurred.

It seemed to take forever for the fifteen minutes to be up, but eventually he strode into the inn, bending his head to avoid the low, curving beams. The landlord saw him coming and pointed down one of the corridors.

"His lordship's in there. He said to tell you to join him."

"Thank you."

When he entered the room, he was immediately aware that things must have progressed nicely, because Mr. Simms looked like a man who knew he was in a very precarious position indeed.

"Good afternoon, Dr. Nash." Francis looked up from his perusal of a set of documents on the table.

"Viscount Grafton-Wesley." Charles bowed. "How may I assist you?"

"I need you as a witness to this case." He indicated Mr. Simms. "This man, acting on behalf of the Earl of Nash, attempted to blackmail Mr. Fellows and cause him to perjure himself by swearing to have married a woman who is not, in fact, his wife."

"I just did what his lordship asked me to, sir, I—" Mr. Simms was obviously rattled. "I had no idea—"

"That's a lie." Sidney, who was leaning against the wall, arms folded over his chest, spoke up. "Mr. Simms specifically told me that he knew people who could forge all the necessary documents if I just went along with the earl's plan."

Francis readied a pen and a clean piece of paper and looked up at Mr. Simms. "I will ask the landlord to restrain you in the cellars until I have spoken to the Earl of Nash."

"You can't do that!" Mr. Simms protested.

"I'm the local magistrate, Mr. Simms. I can do anything I bloody well like." Francis wrote quickly, the pen scratching on the paper. "If you don't want to stay here, I can easily arrange transport to take you to Leeds to wait for your trial in the county gaol."

"No! I'll stay here." Mr. Simms was sweating profusely. "I'd die in that place."

"I concur," Francis said. "Dr. Nash, will you call the landlord? Once you've had time to consider your options, Mr. Simms, perhaps you'd be willing to write your confession?"

"It was all the Earl of Nash's idea, sir."

"Then make sure to put that in your confession, won't you? It will certainly help the judge look kindlier upon you. Smith will provide you with writing implements if you want to get started right away."

The landlord came in, and after a short consultation with Francis, took Mr. Simms away with him.

After the door shut behind them, Sidney came forward and sat at the table. "And now what?"

Francis looked at Charles. "That's rather up to Dr. Nash. You do know it's almost impossible to get a conviction for such a thing against a peer of the realm?"

Charles read through the charges Francis had started to draw up. "I agree that it would not end in a conviction, but as a lever to force my father's hand..." Charles paused. "It might do very well, indeed."

"Then tell me exactly how you wish me to word the documents, and I'll have a copy made for you—and of Mr. Simms' confession—by tomorrow."

"Thank you." Charles detailed his requirements to Francis and then looked over at Sidney. "And thank you, too."

"It's the least I could do." Sidney pressed his hand to his heart. "Despite what you think of me, Dr. Nash, I am a man of honor."

"You've certainly helped," Charles said, still unwilling to concede more than the most basic praise. "May I suggest you take your leave of my wife and your daughter with all speed, and depart? A yearly visit to see Nora would be acceptable if you insist."

"You're a hard man, Dr. Nash," Sidney said as he rose to his feet.

"I'm glad you think so." Charles shook Francis's hand and stood up. "Now, why don't I escort you to my home where you can collect your belongings and leave?"

RUBY HAD SENT Nora out with Martha and Bridget and awaited the return of Charles and Sidney in the kitchen. She'd thought about preparing lunch, but in her present agitated state, the idea of eating didn't sit well with her. Eventually, she heard voices outside, and tried to look calm as Sidney and her husband came in through the back door.

Charles immediately came over and kissed her cheek. "It went very well."

"I'm glad to hear it. Shall I make some tea?" Ruby was quite proud of the evenness of her voice.

"I have to leave," Sidney said. "There is a train in half an hour going to Leeds and Dr. Nash has very kindly bought me a ticket for it. I need to be there for a meeting this evening."

Charles looked over at Ruby. "Perhaps you might want to

help Sidney pack while I make the tea? I'm sure you have plenty to talk about."

"Yes, of course." Ruby rose to her feet.

She went up the stairs to the spare bedroom. Sidney had already made the bed and crammed all his belongings into a small pack he carried on his back. Ruby knew all his worldly possessions were contained in that bag and that he needed nothing more to survive except the goodwill of his supporters.

She turned as he came into the room. "I see that you are all packed. There is nothing I can do for you."

He took possession of her hand and looked down at her, his vivid blue gaze as mesmerizing as ever. "I wish you nothing but the best, Ruby. That is all I have ever wanted, and if Dr. Nash makes you happy, then I am glad for you."

"He's a good man," Ruby said. "He will treat Nora as his own child."

"May I come and visit her occasionally?" For the first time in his life Sidney sounded unsure of himself. "I know I don't deserve—"

"You may come, but we will decide together when she is older how we tell her exactly who you are."

"Yes, of course." He nodded. "Dr. Nash did make me think about the plight of women in society and the additional burdens of motherhood. It was something I had not fully considered until now." He picked up his pack. "I will have to discuss it with my committee."

"If you write to me, I'll write back," Ruby offered.

"You know I'm a terrible correspondent, but I'll do my best." He smiled and shouldered his bag. "I'll stop in the park on my way to the station and say goodbye to Nora."

"That's an excellent idea."

Ruby followed Sidney down the stairs into the kitchen where Charles had made tea for her and was standing ready to open the backdoor to hasten Sidney's exit.

"Goodbye, Dr. Nash." Sidney shook Charles's hand. "I hope your plans to outwit your father succeed."

"So do I." Charles returned the handshake. "I'll walk you to the station."

Ruby watched them leave and sank down into the nearest chair. She had no tears left for Sidney. His departure was a relief, as was the fact that they'd parted on good terms. He'd always be Nora's father, but he no longer held any allure for her. She could see him for what he was—a man with lofty ideals who sometimes forgot to look down and see the chaos he caused in his own life.

She poured herself some tea and considered what they had left to eat for dinner that had not already been consumed by their unexpected guests.

Eventually, Charles returned and joined her at the table. "Sidney stopped in the park to say goodbye to Nora. She cried when he tried to hold her. He is now safely on the train to Leeds."

"One might think you made sure he was leaving."

"There's no doubt about it. I'd had quite enough of him." He drank his tea in one gulp. "I've never felt entirely comfortable around these so-called leaders of men."

Ruby reached out and covered his hand with her own, her sense of pleasure and joy in his tempestuous company overwhelming her. "Thank you."

"For what?"

"Tolerating him."

He snorted. "Barely."

"He said you made him think about the plight of women."

"About time someone did," Charles said, very carefully not looking at her. "Did he apologize?"

"In his own way," Ruby said. "I must confess to being glad to see him leave."

"Truly?"

"I don't regret any of the decisions I've made, Dr. Nash."

"Good. Neither do I." Charles cleared his throat and sat back. "Now all we have to do is ruin my father's plans for my mother."

Ruby smiled.

"What?" he asked.

"The house is quite empty for the next hour or so."

"And?"

Ruby stared at him until he suddenly stood up and reached for her hand. "Then come along. We don't have much time."

CHAPTER TWENTY

*C*harles had considered long and hard how he wanted to approach his father about his plans for his mother. He was very aware that he'd only have one chance to influence his father's thinking and that if he got it wrong, he might never see his mother again.

To his surprise, Ruby had agreed to stay home in Millcastle with Nora. She'd assured him she had faith in his ability to deal with his father—an unexpected vote of confidence that had filled him with optimism. Now, awaiting the earl in his study at Nash Hall, Charles wasn't quite so sure.

He turned as his father came in and instinctively braced himself. Nothing good ever happened to him in this place, but he couldn't allow past hurts to destroy his chances before he even began.

"Good afternoon, sir." Charles inclined his head. "Thank you for seeing me."

He waited as the earl made a great production of settling himself behind his desk, finding his spectacles, checking his pocket watch, and opening his dreaded copy book where he noted all his daily transactions in minute detail.

"For a man who always insists he is gainfully employed and cannot leave his patients whenever I require his presence, you seem remarkably adept at making time for your own desires," the earl commented.

"I believe this matter was important enough to see you in person, sir." Charles paused. "I didn't want to put it in writing."

"I've already told you to keep your nose out of your mother's business. I had a letter from Dr. French the other day saying you had visited her."

"I was concerned about her health."

"But I did not give you leave to attend her."

"I'm a physician. I'm required to offer my assistance when it is merited."

"I will not have you interfering in her care." The earl glared at him. "If you attempt to influence Dr. French or any member of his staff, I will remove your mother and put her somewhere else—possibly abroad—so think on that before you try anything stupid."

"I have no intention of removing her from Dr. French's care." Charles paused. "From what I could see, she is in excellent hands."

The earl frowned. "Then why are you here if not to bully me into doing your will?"

"I'm trying to protect our family name."

"When have you ever tried to do that?"

Charles shrugged. "Perhaps now that I have a wife and child, I've become more... sensitive about my reputation."

"That child is a bastard," the earl said flatly. "She will never inherit a penny of Nash money."

"She's still my child to raise," Charles said.

The earl looked at his pocket watch. "If you could get to the point. I have an engagement at two with my land agent."

"Not with Mr. Simms?" Charles sat down, uninvited.

"I am not familiar with that name."

"Oh, I think you are." Charles smiled. "I'm certain Benson could confirm he's been here on more than one occasion. Miss Evans saw him as well."

"If I have met with him, I cannot precisely recall when it was or what trifling matter we discussed." The earl fiddled with his pen and inkwell, avoiding Charles's gaze.

"Balderdash. You hired him to investigate my wife."

There was a long silence before the earl looked up. "And what if I did? I have a right to know what kind of blood is being brought into my lineage."

"Then I'm sure you were reassured that my wife's family are truly unremarkable."

"I told you what I thought about her suitability on the last occasion we met. I haven't changed my mind. She is a woman of loose morals who had a bastard child."

"I'm glad to hear you say that you consider the child to be a bastard," Charles said. "Because Mr. Simms told me otherwise."

The earl set down his pen with some force. "If you have something to say, Charles, get on with it. I don't have time for your insinuations."

"I thought you should know that Mr. Simms is currently under arrest."

"What's that got to do with me?"

"Quite a lot, actually, which is why I came all this way to see you." Charles tried for a sympathetic smile. "Apparently Mr. Simms was caught attempting blackmail." The earl looked bored, and Charles continued. "He attempted to make a man perjure himself and swear on oath that he had been married. When the man protested, Mr. Simms told him not to worry, that his employer had the means to forge any documentation necessary to meet a court's threshold."

Charles reached into his coat pocket, brought out the documents, and laid them on his father's desk. "I have a copy of the charges and Mr. Simms' full confession."

His father made no effort to reach for the documents or read them.

"I'm obliged to inform you that you are named in these documents as Mr. Simms' employer and thus a party to the accusation of blackmail. The magistrate who signed the papers is very keen to see that justice is served equally and that the man who gave the orders is considered equally liable for the crime."

"No one would convict a peer on such flimsy evidence."

"I'm aware of that. But imagine the dent to your reputation when Mr. Simms comes to trial at the county assizes, and your name is read out as his employer. Such a matter would be of great interest to the local press, and who knows how wide the story might spread if other publications picked it up?"

Charles continued when the earl said nothing. "As the event happened in Millcastle and intimately involves my family, I might be asked to comment myself. Such a sordid tale, too, of a man attempting to blackmail an innocent hero of the working class into destroying a happy marriage. I've never been a good liar, sir, which is why I decided to bring the matter to you before it becomes public. God knows what I might say if given a national stage by the newspapers."

The silence lengthened, but for once Charles found it easy to bear.

Eventually, the earl picked up his pen. "What do you want? Money?"

"Hardly, sir. Blackmail appears to be your weapon of choice, not mine. All I require is a guarantee of my mother's future safety and a written assurance that she and Miss Evans will be restored to this household as soon as Dr. French recommends such a course of action."

"Why would you think such an assurance from me would be carried out?"

Charles shrugged. "One might hope that your word is your bond—that's what you've always told me. If that is no longer the case, then I'll simply sit back and watch your reputation be destroyed in the courts."

The earl was the first to drop his gaze. "I don't know what happened to Miss Evans after I sent her packing."

"Don't worry. I know exactly where she is." Charles smiled. "I'm sure she'll be delighted to resume her position when my mother returns."

"I haven't agreed to your terms, yet."

Charles rose to his feet. "I understand that you will need time to consider this matter." He reclaimed the papers. "If I don't hear from you by the end of the week, I'll assume you are happy for Mr. Simms to be sent for trial."

"What is the name of the local magistrate on those documents?"

"Oh, you won't want to bother him, sir," Charles said lightly. "Despite your rank, Viscount Grafton-Wesley will have no qualms in issuing charges against you if you dare to interfere." He paused. "He is also very willing to allow the matter to drop as a favor to me if certain terms are complied with."

The earl sat back. "Grafton-Wesley."

"Yes. He's my friend and not a man to be trifled with." Charles smiled. "Aren't you proud of me for cultivating the acquaintance of gentlemen who can be useful? It is a skill I acquired from you, sir." He put the documents carefully in his pocket and turned to the door. "I won't stay the night. I do have to get back for my patients, and my wife is expecting me."

The earl said nothing more and Charles walked out into the hall and finally let out his breath. It was an unusual feeling to have bested his father. He was fairly confident that the earl's dislike of scandal would stop him from allowing the case to go forward.

If it didn't, then Charles would use every means possible to ensure that his mother was safe with him and that she never had to worry again. He'd already talked through several plans with

Francis and was paying Nurse Sugden a weekly fee to write to him about his mother's condition. If anything changed, he'd know about it quickly and would act to recover her from Dr. French's care.

He went to find Benson to let him know he was leaving. A year ago, he would've raged against his father but ultimately done little to change his fate. He'd almost come to believe that he was as worthless as the earl insisted. But he did have standards, and when people he loved were in danger, he'd found his strength to defend them, and it felt very satisfying.

He stepped into the kitchen, noticing how little activity was going on when the earl was the only person in the house. He found Benson polishing the silverware in his pantry.

"Mr. Charles!"

"I have to get home, Benson. While I go and alert the stables to bring my gig out, would you do me a favor? I need you to write me a list of all the times a Mr. Simms visited this house. It appears that he might be in some trouble. I want to make sure that the earl isn't implicated in any manner."

"I can go to the stables *and* write that letter for you, sir." Benson took off his polishing gloves.

"There's no need. I'll talk to the groom. The quicker I can get away, the better." Charles smiled. "If the earl asks if I have spoken to you about this matter, please assure him that I have taken all the relevant details and will take them to the magistrate involved."

It was only when he was on the Great Northern Road that Charles remembered he'd have to get a statement from Miss Evans as well. The more evidence he could produce that the earl had knowingly engaged in a campaign to destroy his own son's marriage, the better.

～

Ruby sat in the kitchen watching the clock on the mantelpiece tick through the long hours of waiting for Charles to return. Martha had kept her company after Nora and Bridget had gone upstairs. Ruby had told Martha everything about Sidney, the blackmail attempt, and how Charles intended to use it to his advantage in his dealings with the earl. At first, Martha was skeptical that anything could damage the Earl of Nash, but after some consideration, she agreed that blackening his reputation would be unacceptable to him, and that he might accept Charles's terms.

Martha had offered to stay up until Charles returned, but Ruby was determined to wait on her own. With her whole future in doubt, she needed to hear the news by herself and knew Charles would be honest with her.

As time passed, her mind did conjure some fears where it was Charles who capitulated to the earl. In her soul—at the very core of who she was and who she believed Charles to be—she couldn't believe it would happen.

She'd almost fallen asleep when she heard his key in the backdoor, and she hastened to her feet.

He came in, his hat in his hand and stared at her, his blue gaze unbearably serious. "I think it's going to be all right."

With a strangled cry, she ran straight into his arms. He dropped his bag and gathered her to him, his cheek pressed to the top of her head, his hand curving around her neck as she sobbed.

Eventually, she managed to look up at him. "I never cry."

"I am well aware of that." He handed her his handkerchief. "But perhaps such a momentous occasion merits it."

He took her hand and settled her back into her chair. "Is the kettle hot? I'd love a cup of tea."

"I'll make it." She attempted to rise, but he shook his head.

"I've been sitting for hours. I need to stand for a while."

"Are you hungry?" Ruby asked, her voice husky from the

unexpected weeping. "There's bread and cheese in the pantry and an apple pie Martha made."

"I'll find something. You stay put."

He stripped off his heavy driving coat and went to hang it in the hall with his hat. He removed his boots, set them in the scullery to clean, and washed his hands before returning to the kitchen where the kettle was coming to the boil.

It took all Ruby's remaining energy to hold her tongue while he brewed the tea, cut himself a slice of bread and cheese, and finally sat opposite her.

"I gave him a week to decide what he wanted to do," Charles said between sips of tea. "I'm sure he'll try to think of a way to wiggle out of it, but I don't see him succeeding."

He looked exhausted, a faint hint of stubble on his chin and purple shadows beneath his eyes. Knowing the earl, it couldn't have been easy to face him down.

"I'm very proud of you," Ruby said.

"Why? For finally having the balls to stand up to a bully?"

"He's still your father," Ruby pointed out. "He's always had immense power over you."

"And my mother." He frowned. "I almost think she'd be happier at Dr. French's, but I fear that if she doesn't go home, my father will find some way to make her life worse by moving her to another less salubrious facility."

"You know he would," Ruby agreed. "At least if she is back at the hall, Martha can keep us informed as to her wellbeing."

He nodded, his attention turning to the consumption of his bread and cheese and another cup of tea. As she watched him eat, Ruby's heartrate returned to normal, and a curious sense of wellbeing consumed her.

"I suppose that before I embarked on this crusade to right wrongs and pay off old scores, I should have asked you whether you wished me to." He chased some crumbs around his plate with his finger and didn't look at her. "You might have welcomed the opportunity to dissolve our marriage and run off with Sidney to campaign for votes for women."

"Yes." Ruby nodded slowly as if considering the idea. "It does have some appeal."

He reached across the table, and wrapped his long fingers around her wrist, easily encircling it. "I'm afraid that my appreciation of universal suffrage doesn't extend to you, my dear. You're my wife, I love you, and I cannot imagine letting you go."

She looked up from their joined hands to find his gaze waiting for her. Despite his bold words, there was still a hint of need in his eyes that spoke to her heart.

"Then perhaps we are destined to universally suffer together?" she suggested. "Because I find that I cannot do without you, Dr. Nash."

"And?" He raised his eyebrows.

"Isn't that enough?" Ruby asked.

"That you need me? Not really." His thumb caressed the soft skin of her wrist. "I'd like to hear the words."

In reply, she rose to her feet and made her way upstairs, pausing on the landing to make sure that all was quiet around her before entering the bedroom and lighting a single candle by the side of the bed. By the time Charles joined her, she had taken down her hair and removed all her clothing except her shift. He halted by the door and then closed it behind him.

"You left without finishing our conversation."

She walked toward him and reached up to cup his stubbled chin. "Sometimes actions are better than words."

She eased his coat from his shoulders. The wool was slightly damp and smelled of smoke and coal dust. She began unbuttoning his waistcoat. "I love you, Charles Nash. I didn't mean to. I didn't think I had the capacity to love anyone again, but you proved me wrong." She undid the last button, set his waistcoat aside, and eased his shirt free of his trousers.

His skin slowly emerged from his clothing, and she kissed

every exposed inch with loving devotion, aware of his harried breathing and his barely concealed desire to throw her onto the bed and have his way with her.

When he was naked, she took off her shift and pressed herself against him, the hardness of his shaft trapped between their bellies. She wrapped her hands behind his neck until he lowered his head enough to kiss her.

"I know our marriage began as one of convenience, but I would not have found a better man if I'd looked for years."

"I'm not a good man." It amused her immensely that he was trying not to scowl at her. "I'm too honest, I have a tendency to argue, and my father has consistently tried to erase you from my life. Why in God's name are you willing to put up with all that?"

"Because you love me," Ruby said simply. "And I know that you will continue to love me and let me be myself until the end of our days together."

"That's hardly cheerful," Charles objected. "It's true that you have your irritating points, but I'll put up with them, because the thought of not having you in my life is unbearable."

"Then it seems as if we are stuck with each other," Ruby said and kissed him.

"Thank God for that." Charles picked her up, swung her around, and settled her on the side of the bed. He stood between her thighs and leaned over her, his expression intent. "Now can I touch you?"

"Yes, please."

He kissed his way down her throat to her breasts, and she sighed as his teeth grazed her nipple.

He briefly looked up. "I must warn you that I am feeling rather possessive tonight."

"I'm glad to hear it." Ruby scratched her fingernails down his back, making him shudder. "Will you come inside me tonight?"

He went still, his breathing ragged. "Ruby…"

"I've done the calculations you suggested, and I believe the risk of a pregnancy is very low," Ruby said. "I only finished my monthly bleed yesterday."

His hand tightened on her hip. "Would you like me to check your arithmetic?"

It was Ruby's turn to glare at him. "Not right now, thank you."

"Thank God." He cupped her mound, seeking her wetness, pressed three fingers deep, and exhaled. "I hope you're ready for me because I fear I can wait no longer nor promise to be gentle."

In reply, she drew him closer, watching as he pressed his cock home, and then there was nothing but the sensation of him filling her completely and immediately thrusting deep. She came almost instantly, and he groaned, sliding one hand underneath her to cup her buttock and open her even wider. He rolled his hips, bringing his body against hers in such pleasing ways that she gasped his name and climaxed again.

He growled and drew her up onto the bed completely, hooking her heels on his shoulders and pounding into her like a man possessed. Ruby didn't want the sense of being at one with him to stop, but the force of his passion soon had him struggling to hold back the inevitable.

"Come for me. Come inside me." Ruby pressed on his chest. His heart was beating so fast, she could feel it vibrating against her palm. "Please, I want you."

He nodded, his teeth set in a grimace, pushed forward once more, and climaxed in long pulsing waves with a heartrending roar. He collapsed over Ruby, only catching himself with one hand before he crushed her. He buried his face in the pillow beside her and closed his eyes. Ruby turned her head so that she could observe him more closely.

He opened his eyes and stared at her. "That's it. You're mine, now. For good."

She smiled and reached out to touch his aristocratic nose. "And you're mine."

"I've been yours since the day I met you, and you wouldn't stop being disagreeable." His voice was sleepy as he drew her closely against his side.

"I was barely conscious," Ruby countered.

"Still disagreeable, though." He yawned and kissed the top of her head. "Would you mind continuing this conversation tomorrow? I've had a very long day."

Satisfied that they would be arguing the point for years to come, Ruby graciously let him fall asleep. She lay awake for a while, her mind circling through recent events. Sidney's arrival, the earl's machinations—nothing had been completely resolved, but perhaps that was how life went. You simply made the best of it and carried on.

After her disastrous liaison with Sidney, she'd expected an existence dependent on the charity of others, but she'd found so much more. Charles's proposal had changed both of them for the better, and she would always be grateful to him for having the courage to ask. She hadn't expected to come to love him so quickly and to find that love returned.

The last train came behind the house and into Millcastle station, setting off a faint rattle in the windows and the strange humming of the iron tracks. Ruby kissed Charles's shoulder and he muttered something incomprehensible.

At some point they'd have to deal with the matter of the earldom and the implications for their future, but she'd learned not to court trouble. Despite everything, she truly wished the current Earl of Nash a very long life... Long *and* miserable.

CONTINUE THE SERIES WITH MR. TOTTON'S CHRISTMAS MIRACLE...

Chapter One

Mr. Thomas Totton bade his employer a cordial goodnight and left the office. It was only a ten-minute walk back to his house in Mare Street, but it was dark, the path icy, and the streetlights were not yet operational in his part of town. He passed the new railway station that his employer, Mr. Elijah Hepworth, had brought to Millcastle with the sheer strength of his will. It was currently deserted, the last train had left on the half hour, and the next wasn't expected until morning.

He knew far more about the workings of the railway station, and the hotel next to it than anyone in Millcastle, apart from Mr. Hepworth, and was quietly proud of what they'd achieved.

Goods from Millcastle could now travel to new destinations, opening up the factory markets and increasing profitability.

He turned left at the corner after the Station Hotel and walked down the cobbled pathway between the two rows of new red brick houses he'd helped design with Mr. Hepworth's architect. The detached houses were for the new rising middle class--mill managers, overseers, station masters, and the professional gentlemen of Millcastle. Each had three stories and a cellar, four large bedrooms, servants' quarters at the top, and an inside water closet. Thomas thought they were very fine and had been delighted when his employer had offered him the opportunity to buy one at a reduced rate.

Thomas paused to open the back gate and entered the neat garden at the rear of his property. The garden was laid to grass with wide flower borders on two sides. Having never owned a garden before, he hadn't had much time to think of what to do with it. He was considering consulting with the municipal authority who had recently laid out the town park. He'd never had much time for flowers in his life, but he was impressed by the colorful displays.

There was a light on in his kitchen window and he stopped to stare at the figure illuminated within.

He didn't need a live-in housekeeper.

He shouldn't have offered her the position, but he didn't regret it.

She'd come to him without references or experience, yet he'd allowed her to stay, and she'd proved her worth.

And yet... he knew nothing about her apart from the name she'd given him—Elinor Smith—and even that might not be real.

It was lucky he worked so hard and had no time for friends because he was fairly certain they would've warned him off hiring a woman like her. He wasn't even sure if she deserved to be called Mrs., because she'd never mentioned a spouse living or dead. At least the title gave her the veneer of respectability they both needed to maintain their relative positions in society and for her to manage his house.

Despite all her efforts to hide it, she was beautiful in a way that made men stop and stare. Her hair was the darkest chocolate brown and her eyes the color of violets. Not that he'd noticed these things when he'd first encountered her alone and desperate at the notorious George and Dragon coaching inn in the center of town.

He still wasn't sure what instinct had made him stop when she'd called out to him, but he had paused to listen to her tale of woe, and, incredibly, he'd believed every word of it.

She'd come to Millcastle to work as a governess only to find that the position was not as she'd imagined, and that the letter writer was an elderly man with no children simply wishing to entrap her within his house and use her as he wished. When he'd met her off the coach, instinct had told her he wasn't being truthful. She'd asked about his children and he'd become angry and defensive, seemingly unable to remember the names he'd fabricated in his letter. He'd tried to force her to get into his carriage, and she'd made a scene, racing toward the entrance of the inn where she'd run straight into—him.

Thomas shivered as the first faint hint of snow brushed his cheek. He looked up at the silent, falling flakes that would soon mask the scars of the growing industrial town he'd helped create. Not that he wasn't proud of what he'd achieved. He'd grown up with nothing and now had an excellent job, a fine house to live in, and—Mrs. Smith.

He shook off his foolish thoughts and marched up to the back door, wiped his feet on the mat and stepped inside. There was no sign of his housekeeper, but the fragrant smell of beef stew perfumed the air and the house was warm around him. These days he never had to think about rationing coal or light, which was a blessing.

He took off his boots and set them in the scullery along with his coat and hat. When he entered the kitchen, she was there with a warm towel in her hands and a welcoming smile.

"Good evening, Mr. Totton."

"Mrs. Smith." He inclined his head.

"Was it starting to snow?" she asked as she handed him the towel. "The butcher told me he could smell it in the air, but I didn't quite believe him."

"Yes, but it's not really settled yet." He washed his hands in the bowl of warm water she'd left for him in the sink and dried them with the towel. "But it looks like it will."

"A white Christmas," she said, her expression pensive. "When I was a child, I expected every Christmas to have snow and was rather annoyed when it didn't happen. I remember getting quite cross with my papa when he refused to take me ice skating because the lake wasn't properly frozen over."

Thomas imagined Mrs. Smith as a child and wondered how any parent could've denied her anything. On the very rare occasions when she shared anything about her childhood, he had the impression that it had been a happy one. What had happened to overset that? He'd never had the courage to ask.

He set the towel down. "I'll eat in the kitchen tonight, if that's acceptable to you, Mrs. Smith. There's no point wasting money to set a fire in the dining room just for me."

In truth, the house was far too large for a man without a family. He occupied the main bedroom, Mrs. Smith had a room on the floor above, and, as there was no other live-in help, the rest of the rooms remained unoccupied.

"As you wish, Mr. Totton." She turned toward the stove. "I just need to check my dumplings."

While she had her back to him, Thomas was able to study her at his leisure. Her dark hair was braided and secured at the nape of her neck in a neat bun. She wore one of the two day-dresses she owned in a serviceable brown and had a large work apron tied around her waist. When she served in the dining room on the rare occasion he had guests, she wore a white apron and added a lace collar to the round neck of her dress.

After stirring the pot, she laid the table and gestured for Thomas to sit down.

"Thank you." He took his usual seat. "It was a very busy day at work."

"Mr. Hepworth expects a lot of you." Mrs. Smith filled a jug of water from the pump and set it on the table along with two glasses. She also put the tea pot down and poured him a cup.

"He pays me well enough to demand the best," Thomas said as he stirred in some sugar and drank the strong brew down in one gulp. "Although, some days I do wonder how I manage to get everything done."

"Everyone speaks very highly of you, Mr. Totton," Mrs. Smith said.

"That is very kind of you to say so, ma'am, although I doubt all of them truly like me. I represent Mr. Hepworth, and he remains a divisive figure in this town. Not everyone appreciates the railway or the navvies who built it."

"Then they are fools because the railway brings prosperity." She refilled his cup and went over to the stove to get the cast iron pot containing the stew. "It also allows the common man to travel further than ever before. Who would not appreciate that?"

"Have you been on the train, Mrs. Smith?" Mr. Totton inquired.

"Not yet, but I intend to. I'd like to see the sea again." She took the lid off the pot and a cloud of steam rose over the rounded dumplings. "Shall I serve you your dinner, sir, or would you rather help yourself?"

"You may do it." He watched her ladle a hearty portion onto his plate. "But make sure you leave enough for yourself."

She fetched the bread, which he knew she made herself, and

a slab of golden butter from the local dairy. He waited until she had settled back at the table before he spoke again.

"If you wish to take leave over Christmas, Mrs. Smith, you are more than welcome to do so."

She looked directly at him. "You are planning on going away yourself?"

"No, but it just occurred to me that you haven't taken a single day off since you got here over a year ago, and that you are due a holiday." He paused. "Perhaps you could take that trip on the train to the coast."

"That is very kind of you, but I'd rather stay here." She looked down at her plate. "I have no one to go with or to visit."

"You have no family at all?" Thomas asked.

"None that would wish to acknowledge me." Her quick smile spoke of past tensions.

Thomas chewed a chunk of beef as he framed his next question. "You are estranged from your kin?"

"Yes."

"I find it hard to believe that anyone would be so cruel as to cast a woman such as yourself adrift, Mrs. Smith."

"But you don't know what I've done, Mr. Totton. I could have threatened to murder the lot of them."

He met her gaze. "I doubt it, ma'am."

"There are far worse things than murder," she said quietly. "Things that leave wounds that can never heal."

"I don't believe that Mrs. Smith. Time and distance have a way of healing all wounds."

"You never speak of your own family, sir."

He knew she was deliberately changing the subject, but it had been a long, trying day, he was tired, and suddenly all he wished to do was tell the truth.

"My wife and child died in a house fire in Leeds."

Mrs. Smith's sharply indrawn breath was audible. "How... terrible."

"It's one of the reasons why I was willing to follow Mr. Hepworth on his travels up and down the country to build new railways. I hated going home to the silence." He looked around the kitchen. "This is the first house I've ever owned."

He almost started as Mrs. Smith reached over and patted his hand. To his knowledge, it was the first time she'd touched him in public. She withdrew her fingers before he could move his own.

"There is no need for sympathy, ma'am, it was ten years ago, and, as I said, time is a great healer." He swallowed hard. "In truth, I can barely remember what my wife and bairn looked like anymore."

Her continued silence made him feel like an emotional fool. He poured himself more tea. "If neither of us have plans to leave Millcastle for yuletide perhaps you might care to accompany me to Mr. Hepworth's for Christmas day? Mrs. Hepworth invited us both and it would save you having to cook."

She was slow to reply. "I'm sure they invited you, sir, but me? I'm hardly of the right class."

"You're probably better bred than the lot of us," Thomas said bluntly. "You'll fit right in." He met her worried gaze. "In fact, I'd be glad if you did come with me. I always have to partner some dotty old aunt who doesn't know quite what to make of me."

"I'll come if you want me to," Mrs. Smith said.

"Good." He smiled at her and applied himself to his dinner. "Is there any pudding?"

Afterwards, they sat in companiable silence in the front parlor. Mr. Totton read the newspaper while Elinor darned his socks. She felt the first faint stirring of disquiet. Should she attend the festivities? She'd kept her head down for a year and no one had recognized her, which was a miracle in itself. She should have asked Mr. Totton for a list of exactly who was attending just in case anyone from her past life turned up and recognized her.

But how likely was it that the Hepworth's, who weren't from the nobility, would have friends who were? And what questions would Mr. Totton have if she demanded such a list?

She yearned to leave the house and simply enjoy Christmas with the man who had taken her in without question and had never asked her to explain herself. He'd helped her when she'd begun to believe there were no good men left in the world. At least, she'd known how to keep house—her stepmother had made sure of that when she'd decreed that Elinor's place was no longer with the family and that she needed to work for her keep.

What had astounded her then, and continued to do so, was that not a single person in her father's family had stood up for her. They'd all meekly allowed the new Lady Redmayne to do as she pleased to her husband's only daughter. Her Great Aunt Matilda had tried once—offering Elinor a home—but she hadn't been allowed to leave because that might have exposed her step-mother's plans to the wider world.

"Oh."

Mr. Totton looked up at Elinor's involuntary exclamation.

"Is something wrong, ma'am?"

"I don't have anything to wear."

His gaze went over her. "You seem perfectly adequately clothed to me."

"For the event at the Hepworth's."

"Ah, perhaps you should pop into your dressmaker and ask if she has anything you might purchase."

"I don't have a dressmaker and I'm not sure I wish to waste the money on a new gown I'd only wear once," Elinor explained.

"I appreciate your frugality, Mrs. Smith, but on this occa-sion, I think you should reconsider. My wife always used to say that one good dress would last a woman a lifetime."

Elinor tried to remember the days when she'd changed her clothes at least four times and left everything on the floor for someone else to pick up. Her father had loved to see her in a new dress...

"Madame Lisette's on the corner of the town square sometimes had second-hand dresses for sale," Mr. Totton wasn't finished. He was always a very thorough man, "I'd try there."

"Thank you for the suggestions," Elinor replied. "Perhaps it would be simpler if I didn't go."

He looked at her over the top of his newspaper. "I would be disappointed if you chose not to accompany me." He returned his gaze to the page, leaving her biting her lip.

He never asked anything of her and she owed him everything.

With a sigh, she mentally reviewed the contents of her savings account. "I'll do my best, sir, but I can't promise anything."

He nodded, his attention on whatever he was reading, and she returned to her darning until the clock on the mantelpiece chimed nine times. They were both early risers. She had to get breakfast started and he had to leave on time for his job with the demanding Mr. Hepworth.

"Time for bed," he murmured as he did every night. "I'll check the locks."

"And I'll make sure the kitchen fire is banked."

Elinor rose to her feet, put her mending away, and went into the kitchen where she hung her apron on a hook behind the door and stretched out her spine. She'd started her Christmas preparations months ago and Mr. Totton would still be getting his plum pudding and mince pies whether they went to the Hepworths or not.

She made sure all the gas lamps were off and mounted the stairs, a single candle in her hand. He was waiting for her at his bedroom door, his gaze serious as he raised an eyebrow in a question. She nodded and he drew her into his bedroom, closing the door behind her. She blew out the candle leaving them in total darkness, but it didn't matter. She knew how to undress him in the blackness, the hard lines of him, the curve of his buttock and the rough hair on his chest. He knew her just as well, his fingers sure and steady as he unbuttoned the back of her dress and the waistband of her petticoats so that she could step out of them.

She lay down on the bed and he joined her, his callused hands everywhere, exciting her as no other man had with the honesty of his touch and his gratitude for everything she gave him in return. She hadn't been a virgin when she'd come to him, and he'd never asked her about the whereabouts of Mr. Smith.

His breath caught as she ran her fingernails down his back, and he quickly parted her thighs finding her slick and ready for him. With a groan, he pushed inward, his shaft thick and hard enough to give her pleasure she'd never had before and the patience to teach her how to achieve it.

When she'd first come to his bedroom, he'd been shocked—horrified that she thought that had been his intention all along —that she somehow owed him her body for saving her. But that wasn't it. She'd simply sensed he'd be kind, and she'd needed that more than life itself. She'd been hurt, afraid, and desperate to find someone who could erase her fear without expecting an explanation. Mr. Totton had understood—giving her yet another reason to be grateful to him.

They never spoke of their nighttime liaisons, but they were frequent and intensely enjoyable. Elinor closed her eyes as she came, her hands in his hair, her heels locked on his hips holding him deep within her. She sensed his determination to pull out before he climaxed even as she foolishly tried to stop him. But he was stronger than her both physically and mentally and always spared her the horror of a pregnancy.

Afterward, she'd be grateful and embarrassed by her own instincts, but he never scolded her. Perhaps he understood her better than she realized. She repaid his kindness by never lingering or expecting soft words and embraces. She slipped from his bed without a word leaving him in the darkness as she'd found him, leaving the warmth of his bed for the cold reality of her own room and its narrow window and meager fire.

Elinor washed in cold water, shivering as the sponge scraped over her most private parts where he'd pleasured her with the relentless efficiency he brought to everything he did. She put on her nightgown and climbed between the sheets she'd starched and ironed the day before. It was quiet outside apart from the call of the foxes in the fields behind the railway station. She was more used to the sounds of the countryside than those of the town having been brought up by her ailing mother at the family's country house.

She pictured the rose garden behind the vast house, her mother pausing to smell the flowers, and snip off the best of them for the arrangements that filled their home. She'd been too busy running around to stay with her mother, something she bitterly regretted now. If she'd known her mother only had months to live, she would have stuck to her side like glue. She pictured her brother Robert waving at them from the house. Where was he now? When he'd returned from India, what story had they told him about her absence?

Elinor determinedly closed her eyes. There was no point dwelling on the past. She had an occupation, money in her savings account, and a good man to take care of. What more could any woman want than that?

End of Sample
To continue reading, be sure to pick up Mr. Totton's Christmas Miracle at your favorite retailer.

ALSO BY KATE PEARCE

FOR A FULL LIST PLEASE GO TO KATEPEARCE.COM/BOOKS

The Diable Delamere Series
Historical Romance
Completed Series

Regency dukes, disinherited aristocrats and a plot to assassinate the
Prince Regent create plenty of problems for all the heroes and heroines
as they struggle to trust each other in an ever-changing game of love,
deceit and treachery.

.

The Millcastle Series
Historical Romance

On the cusp of the industrial revolution in the northern town of
Millcastle the old and the new clash both in matters of business and of
the heart. Can love flourish among the rush to make a profit?

.

The Harcourt Twins Duology
Historical Erotic Romance
Completed Series

Identical twins Gideon and Gervase Harcourt share more than a
birthday and an insatiable interest in sex. They also believe in sharing
their sexual expertise with the women they lust after in whatever
combination is required. But when two very different women enter

their lives will they be able to reconcile their complicated needs with their desire to fall in love?

.

The House of Pleasure Series
Historical Erotic Romance
Completed Series

Enter a Regency house of pleasure where nothing is forbidden and every sexual desire you have ever imagined can come true...

.

The Sinners Club Series
Historical Erotic Romance
Completed Series

When intrigue collides with heated passion behind the closed doors of the Sinners Club there is nowhere left to hide.

.

The Morgan Ranch Series
Contemporary Western Romance
Completed Series

A Northern Californian ranching family torn apart by tragedy reluctantly return home to discover not everything was as they thought it was, and that love, and forgiveness can sometimes go hand in hand.

.

The Millers of Morgan Valley Series
Contemporary Western Romance
Completed Series

When the mother you haven't seen for twenty years asks to visit your family ranch and set the record straight, how will her ex and six adult children react? The loves and sometimes messy lives of a ranching family.

.

The Three Cowboys Series
Contemporary Western Romance

The Three Cowboys series centers on three retired Marines living on a ranch in Northern California coming to terms in their own different ways with their experience in combat. From grumpy Noah and an unexpected baby to unruffled Luke who hides things almost too well, and the prickly puzzle of Max, each man will find the perfect woman to bring them to their knees—but not without navigating a lot of bumps in the rocky road to true love along the way.

.

The Turner Brothers Series
Contemporary Erotic Western Romance
Completed Series

As the oldest sibling in a spectacularly dysfunctional family, Grayson Turner has made it his life's mission not only to distance himself from his famous father, but to connect with the half-siblings his father's multiple marriages scattered across the country. Getting to know his siblings and creating trust between them hasn't been easy, but Grayson is determined to succeed because he, Jay and Dakota all deserve a happy ending with the women they love.

.

The Obsidian Series
Sci-Fi Romance

Join a renegade band of telepaths roaming the galaxy to protect and rescue their race from the evil empire intent on destroying them.

The Planet Valhalla Series

Sci-Fi Erotic Romance

Completed Series

One human female crash lands on a planet full of men descended from the Vikings, one of whom is the King who claims her as his mate—what could possibly go wrong? A sexy romp through the stars with excessive sex, a touch of humor and some very satisfied women...

The Triad Series

Sci-Fi Erotic Romance

Completed Series

Welcome to an imaginary world where civilizations, clash against the new and unknown, where telepaths are revered and reviled, and where your destiny can be preordained by a living oracle. Add in a group of super-soldier telepaths rescued from Earth and forming sexual triads for life becomes even more complex and life changing.

The Kate Pearce Paranormal Romance Series

Paranormal Historical Romance

A collection of lighthearted historical paranormal holiday novellas centered in a mystical faerie-ridden village in Cornwall. If you enjoy love at first sight, mistaken identity, ghostly and mystical advice, and fated lovers then you're in for a treat!

The Kurland St. Mary Mysteries Series

Historical Mystery

Writing as Catherine Lloyd

Completed Series

Join wounded cavalry hero Major Sir Robert Kurland and Lucy Harrington the rector's eldest daughter as they solve crimes in their quiet little village and gradually learn to appreciate each other.

.

The Miss Morton Mystery Series

Historical Mystery

Writing as Catherine Lloyd

Miss Morton, the daughter of a disgraced peer, is forced to seek employment and navigate her way through a society that no longer wishes to acknowledge her existence. But with her no-nonsense employer at her side, Caroline discovers her rebellious nature and that family and friends can be found in the most unlikely of situations— even while investigating the occasional murder.

ABOUT KATE PEARCE

New York Times and *USA Today* bestselling author Kate Pearce was born in England in the middle of a large family of girls and quickly found that her imagination was far more interesting than real life. After acquiring a degree in history and barely escaping from the British Civil Service alive, she moved to California and then to Hawaii with her kids and her husband and set about reinventing herself as a romance writer.

She is known for both her unconventional heroes and her joy at subverting romance clichés. In her spare time she self publishes science fiction erotic romance, historical romance, and whatever else she can imagine. You can find Kate at katepearce.com.

- a amazon.com/author/katepearce
- g goodreads.com/katepearce
- BB bookbub.com/authors/kate-pearce
- f facebook.com/KatePearceAuthor
- X x.com/kate4queen